RADCLYFFE

THE Lonely HEARTS CLUB

What Reviewers Say About Radclyffe's Books

A Matter of Trust is a "...sexy, powerful love story filled with angst, discovery and passion that captures the uncertainty of first love and its discovery." – *Just About Write*

Shield of Justice is a "...well-plotted...lovely romance...I couldn't turn the pages fast enough!" – Ann Bannon, author of *The Beebo Brinker Chronicles*

"The author's brisk mix of political intrigue, fast-paced action, and frequent interludes of lesbian sex and love...in *Honor Reclaimed*...sure does make for great escapist reading." – *Q Syndicate*

Change of Pace is "...contemporary, yet timeless, not only about sex, but also about love, longing, lust, surprises, chance meetings, planned meetings, fulfilling wild fantasies, and trust." – *Midwest Book Review*

"Radclyffe has once again pulled together all the ingredients of a genuine page-turner, this time adding some new spices into the mix. *shadowland* is sure to please—in part because Radclyffe never loses sight of the fact that she is telling a love story, and a compelling one at that." – Cameron Abbott, author of *To The Edge* and *An Inexpressible State of Grace*

Lammy winner "...*Stolen Moments* is a collection of steamy stories about women who just couldn't wait. It's sex when desire overrides reason, and it's incredibly hot!" – *On Our Backs*

"With ample angst, realistic and exciting medical emergencies, winsome secondary characters, and a sprinkling of humor, *Fated Love* turns out to be a terrific romance. It's one of the best I have read in the last three years." – *Midwest Book Review*

"*Innocent Hearts*...illustrates that our struggles for acceptance of women loving women is as old as time—only the setting changes. The romance is sweet, sensual, and touching." – *Just About Write*

Lammy winner "...*Distant Shores, Silent Thunder* weaves an intricate tapestry about passion and commitment between lovers. The story explores the fragile nature of trust and the sanctuary provided by loving relationships." – *Sapphic Reader*

In *When Dreams Tremble* the "...focus on character development is meticulous and comprehensive, filled with angst, regret, and longing, building to the ultimate climax." – *Just About Write*

Visit us at www.boldstrokesbooks.com

THE
Lonely
HEARTS CLUB

by

RADCLY*ff*E

2008

THE LONELY HEARTS CLUB

ISBN10: 1-60282-005-8
ISBN13: 978-1-60282-005-0

THIS TRADE PAPERBACK IS PUBLISHED BY
BOLD STROKES BOOKS, INC.
NEW YORK, USA

FIRST EDITION, FEBRUARY, 2008

CREDITS
EDITORS: RUTH STERNGLANTZ AND J. B. GREYSTONE
PRODUCTION DESIGN: J. B. GREYSTONE
COVER GRAPHIC: SHERI (graphicartist2020@hotmail.com)

By the Author

Romances

Innocent Hearts	shadowland
Love's Melody Lost	Fated Love
Love's Tender Warriors	Turn Back Time
Tomorrow's Promise	Promising Hearts
Passion's Bright Fury	When Dreams Tremble
Love's Masquerade	

The Provincetown Tales

Safe Harbor

Beyond the Breakwater

Distant Shores, Silent Thunder

Storms of Change

Winds of Fortune

Honor Series / Justice Series

Honor Series	Justice Series
Above All, Honor	A Matter of Trust (prequel)
Honor Bound	Shield of Justice
Love & Honor	In Pursuit of Justice
Honor Guards	Justice in the Shadows
Honor Reclaimed	Justice Served
Honor Under Siege	

Erotic Interludes: *Change Of Pace*
(A Short Story Collection)

Erotic Interludes 2: *Stolen Moments*
Stacia Seaman and Radclyffe, eds.

Erotic Interludes 3: *Lessons in Love*
Stacia Seaman and Radclyffe, eds.

Erotic Interludes 4: *Extreme Passions*
Stacia Seaman and Radclyffe, eds.

Erotic Interludes 5: *Road Games*
Stacia Seaman and Radclyffe, eds.

Acknowledgments

I've walked these halls, driven these streets, and even played softball on these fields. It was a joy for me to revisit these places in the company of old and new characters. As always, it is my hope that you enjoy the journey, too.

My thanks go to my first readers Diane, Eva, Jane, Paula, and RB, as well as to my editors, Ruth Sternglantz and J.B. Greystone, and the generous proofreaders at Bold Strokes Books for making this a better book. All the credit goes to these dedicated individuals and the responsibility for any shortcomings to me.

Sheri was the soul of patience working on this cover, especially when I kept saying "could you just…" and the result, as always, far exceeds my limited vision.

To Lee, for her never-ending belief in me. *Amo te.*

DEDICATION

For Lee
Heart's Desire

CHAPTER ONE

"Congratulations, Liz, you're pregnant."

Liz Ramsey clutched the edge of the examination table, causing the ridiculous paper gown to pull open. Exposed, she felt vulnerable and somehow a little bit out of control. She was never out of control, not in the courtroom or the bedroom or anywhere else. Except, of course, right at that moment she felt as if she might cry or laugh hysterically, and there wasn't a damn thing she could do about it. So much for her iron-clad control.

"Liz?" Dr. Marta Thompson asked, a frown replacing her pleased grin. "Are you okay?"

"Yes," Liz said quickly, fashioning a smile that from years of practice she knew would appear genuine. When you spend your days in front of a jury needing to convey emotions you sometimes do not feel, you become adept at adjusting your facial expressions to almost any circumstance. And right now, she was in one of those free fall situations where the only thing she could do was put on a show of confidence and hope it was believable. "Of course. I'm…just surprised."

"It's not unusual for it to happen this way," Marta said reassuringly. "I know we tell everyone that it may take two or three tries, but a goodly proportion of our mothers get pregnant right away." Her smile returned and she clasped Liz's arm. "You just got lucky, honey."

"Lucky," Liz echoed, her own smile still firmly in place. "Yes, I really did, didn't I?"

❖

Fifteen minutes later, armored in her power suit and heels, and once more in charge of her life, Liz barreled down the stairwell in the Silverstein Pavilion, too keyed up to wait for an elevator. What she needed was to find her anger. Anger was a very fulfilling emotion, and she had relied on it frequently in the last two months to shut out her hurt and confusion. She hit the door on the first floor stairwell at a dead run, executed a sharp right turn as soon as she stepped into the lobby, and smacked into a brick wall. At least, for the first few seconds it *felt* like a brick wall—until she heard a muffled oath, and the impediment to her forward motion gave way. Stumbling, Liz skidded to a halt and stared, stupidly, she feared, at the woman lying on the floor in front of her.

"Oh hell, I'm sorry," Liz exclaimed, kneeling beside the prone figure. A glimpse of institutional green beneath the unbuttoned white lab coat spelled hospital employee. A quick glance to the left breast pocket revealed a plastic name tag. Reilly Danvers, MD. A fast survey of the face registered a shock of unruly dark hair tumbling over slightly unfocused gray eyes, and a wide, generous mouth open in stunned surprise. Liz held out her hand. "Dr. Danvers, please forgive me. Are you hurt?"

"Do I know you?" Reilly muttered, unable to decide whether to be pissed or to laugh. She hadn't been dumped on her ass by a woman, or anyone else for that matter, since she'd stopped competitive sparring three years earlier. After her eyeballs stopped ricocheting around in their sockets and she was able to focus on the figure leaning over her, she decided that being pissed might not be the smart road to take. The woman who had knocked her flat was beautiful. Wavy, shoulder-length coppery-brown hair. The milky complexion of a classic redhead accompanied by deep green eyes. At the moment, those eyes were so sharply focused on Reilly's face, so penetrating, that for an instant she thought the woman was reading her mind. Considering that her thoughts were about to veer in directions they hadn't taken in a very *very* long time, that might be a bad idea. Realizing she was staring at a perfect stranger while sprawled on the floor, Reilly took the outstretched hand and pulled herself to a sitting position. Tentatively, she touched the back of her head and smothered a wince when her fingertips landed on a lump the size of a walnut.

"You're hurt, aren't you?"

"No," Reilly said quickly, automatically. "I'm okay. Just surprised."

"That seems to be the order of the day," Liz muttered. "Listen, we're creating a hazard in the middle of the hall. Let me help you up."

Before she could protest, Reilly felt long, cool fingers thread through hers, and she followed the gentle tug until she was standing upright. Hands still linked, they both shifted toward the wall, out of the steady stream of hospital personnel and visitors crowding toward the elevators.

"Let me see your head," Liz said, dropping Reilly's hand, but not before registering the natural, almost familiar way Reilly's fingers had closed around hers.

"I'm fine," Reilly protested. "Believe me, I'm a doctor."

"And of course, that means you're never wrong," Liz commented dryly.

"Not a fan, huh?"

"I'm a lawyer."

"Ouch."

Liz shook her head. "Sorry. I am a fan, actually. Well, at least most of the time. Turn around."

Deciding that acquiescing was easier than arguing, Reilly pivoted. "How did you know my name?"

"Name tag. Stand still."

"Yes, ma'am," Reilly muttered.

"Try Liz. Liz Ramsey." Liz gently parted Reilly's short, thick hair. "Well, I don't see any blood."

"Told you."

"But," Liz went on as if Reilly hadn't spoken, "you're getting an impressive hematoma."

"You sound like a doctor, not an attorney," Reilly said over her shoulder.

"Malpractice attorney."

"Double ouch."

"For the defense, so I expect you're safe. The hospital retains my firm, in fact."

Reilly angled around until they were facing one another again. "Glad to hear it, and I hope I never need your services."

"Me, too. How much does that hurt? Honestly."

"Nothing a few aspirin won't cure."

Liz rummaged through her Hermes shoulder bag. "Damn, I usually have some."

"No matter. I'll get some at the gift shop."

"You're kidding. Can't you just ask someone in the pharmacy? Or a nurse?"

Reilly started to shake her head, then abruptly stopped when the throbbing escalated. "Not anymore. Everything is unit dose and accounted for."

"Then at least let me buy them for you. The gift shop's on this floor, isn't it?"

"Yes, but—"

Liz sighed. "Do we really have to debate this? It's an aspirin, not a date."

The instant the words left her mouth, Liz regretted them. She was practically flirting with a woman she didn't even know. Not only did she never flirt, the furthest thing from her mind and the last thing she needed in her life was a new woman.

Reilly grinned. "At least let me buy you a cup of coffee."

Liz made a show of checking her watch, mentally backpedaling. "I've got another appointment—"

"And I need to be in the OR in forty minutes. We'll make it a quick coffee. What do you say?"

Thinking ahead to her bi-weekly lunch date with her two best friends, Liz knew exactly what their first question was going to be, and suddenly, she didn't want to answer it. That told her just how badly she'd been thrown by the news herself. Avoidance wasn't her style. No matter what the disappointment, no matter how much something hurt, no matter how hard the situation appeared to be, she threw herself at it, into it, until she beat back the pain and won, somehow. Except lately that strategy hadn't been working so well. She checked Reilly Danvers's calm gray eyes, felt her quiet assessment, and wondered if her own bewilderment and uncertainty showed in her face. She doubted it.

"Twenty minutes. I could use a cup of…" *You're pregnant.* "Tea." Liz suppressed a groan. "Decaffeinated tea."

"Somehow," Reilly said, cupping Liz's elbow for a second to direct her toward an adjoining hallway, "I didn't figure you for the tea type."

"Yes, well, looks can be deceiving."

❖

"Do you think we should call her?" Candace Lory asked the petite brunette seated across from her at the corner booth at Smokey Joe's, a restaurant bar on the fringes of the Penn campus that had been their hangout since their student days. She sipped her martini, appreciating one of the many perks of working for herself. She didn't have to worry about having a drink at lunchtime, or taking an extra long midday break if after the business was done she wanted to review the "details" with a client who happened to catch her eye. Thank God, commodities trading wasn't like so many professions. She could sleep with a client now and then without destroying her reputation, if she was careful. A little risky, maybe, but if there was no risk, where was the fun? For some reason, sex made her think of Liz, and she asked again, "Bren, should we call her?"

"She'll be here," Brenda Beal said. "She's never missed a lunch date with us in—how many years has it been now? Seven—almost eight years?" She groaned. "God, I feel old."

"Thirty isn't old."

"Say that in three years when you get there," Bren complained good-naturedly, although she doubted Candace would ever fret about her age. Candace was one of those women who looked as good in jeans with no make-up as she did in haute couture. Even when Candace had arrived on campus that first day as a freshman, she'd stood out from the others in the dorm where Bren was the RA. She might have been fresh off a farm in Lancaster County, but she hadn't looked like the stereotypical farmer's daughter. Blond and blue-eyed, true, but there the resemblance ended. At five-ten, she was willowy and model-pretty, with an air of subtle sensuality even at eighteen that had heads turning. Candace's wide-eyed innocence had disappeared in the last nine years, somewhere between girlfriends number two and twenty. Now she looked the part of her high-powered, fast-paced job—a job that suited perfectly her wild, risk-loving nature. Her raw silk blouse was cut low enough to entice while still remaining within the bounds of professional good taste. When she was working, Bren noticed, Candace wore her long ash-blond hair pulled back and clipped at the nape of her neck, giving her an almost austere appearance. She probably thought that made her clients more comfortable handing over big bucks to her, as she bought and sold and rode the margins. She was probably right.

"Liz is only five minutes late," Bren pointed out reasonably, falling into her role as the voice of calm just as she had back when Candace was still a student and bemoaning the latest crisis in her life.

"She's always on time," Candace fretted. "One of us should have gone with her."

"She didn't want us to. You know how private she is."

"I ought to," Candace replied, her smooth features tightening. "I went out with her for almost a year and didn't have a clue why she wanted me, and then...didn't."

Since Bren was far from an expert on relationships, never having had one, she refrained from suggesting that the reason Liz broke up with Candace might have been because Liz had found her making out with a soccer player at a party one night. Since Bren tried not to take sides where her friends were concerned, and since Liz and Candace had weathered that particular storm years ago, she just repeated, "Let's give her a few more minutes. Then if she doesn't show, we'll go find her and drag her butt over here."

Candace smiled wanly. "Okay. I'm just...you know, worried."

"I know," Bren said softly. "Me too."

"Why orthopedic surgery?" Liz munched a stale peanut butter cookie and washed it down with a revolting sip of tepid floral-flavored tea. God, was *this* what she had to look forward to for the next seven months? She pushed the thought away and concentrated on the woman sitting across from her. Dr. Reilly Danvers was what Candace so frequently referred to as melt-in-your-mouth-hot. With her nice tight body, slightly husky voice, and kiss-till-you-drop mouth, the surgeon was an attractive package. Six years ago, Liz thought, she might have been tempted, even though Reilly was very different than the usual urbane objects of her desire. She had a casual, almost unconcerned air—as if she never worried about others' opinions of her—and Liz found the attitude refreshing. And at one point in time, she would have found Reilly Danvers downright sexy. But now, she was just grateful for the company and, she admitted, the diversion.

"I picked ortho because I was a jock." Reilly swallowed two aspirins with a sip of coffee. "And I wanted to work with other jocks, at least that's what I thought when I started my training. I ended up doing ortho trauma, instead."

"So what seduced you away from sports medicine?"

"I like never knowing what's coming through the door next," Reilly replied, chipping the edge off her Styrofoam cup as she thought about the question. There were other reasons, ones she didn't want to talk about. Emergency surgeries kept her busy, kept her mind occupied and her body tired. When she fell into bed after hours of relentless tension, she closed her eyes and rarely dreamed. When she got up the next morning or rolled out in the middle of the night to handle some crisis, she had no time to reflect on the empty space beside her and her emptier life.

"Ah," Liz said teasingly. "An adrenaline junkie?"

Reilly nodded, not offended. That was the simple answer, and partially true. "Maybe. I get a charge out of being in the hot seat, I guess. Thinking on my feet, knowing that there's no time to do anything except follow your instincts."

"You enjoy the challenge."

"Yeah, I guess I do," Reilly said. "Don't you, doing what you do? Duking it out in court?"

"I like pitting my mind against my opponent, outmaneuvering them mentally," Liz replied contemplatively. "I like finding the weak point in the argument and turning it into a weapon."

Reilly chuckled. "You sound like you enjoy winning."

"I suppose I do." Liz wondered at the personal turn in the conversation. She had lunch with her colleagues at the firm several times a week, and she didn't think in almost eight years she'd ever had more than half a dozen personal conversations. And here she was, having one with a stranger. Maybe that explained her willingness to talk about herself—after today she'd never see Reilly Danvers again, so she didn't have anything to fear.

"What did I say?" Reilly asked, pushing her cup and the pile of white Styrofoam chips aside.

"What do you mean?"

"You look upset. I'm sorry, I didn't mean to—"

"No. Sorry. Just a lot on my mind." Liz schooled her expression to relax. "You asked about my work. In many ways, it's like an elaborate game of chess. The aspect I enjoy most is uncovering the subtle facts in a case that will make the difference in the verdict."

"And the truth?" Reilly asked quietly. "Is that part of it, too?"

Liz searched Reilly's eyes, looking for reproach, but found none. "I like to think so."

❖

Candace half-stood as Liz slid in opposite her in the booth, next to Bren. "We were about to send out a search party!"

"I'm only fifteen minutes late," Liz said with a wry smile. Candace was always volatile, but she didn't usually hover. For the last two months, though, she'd been hovering quite a lot. Most of the time, Liz didn't mind, but today her nerves were raw. "I had a bit of an accident—well, not really an accident," she hastened to add when alarm flashed across Candace's face, "more like an encounter." She laughed. "I collided with a surgeon and knocked her flat. I only thought it was right to buy her a couple of aspirins by way of an apology."

"You left us sitting here worrying while you bought some surgeon…" Candace narrowed her eyes. "Was she cute?"

Brenda groaned softly.

"Yes," Liz said indulgently, recognizing the Candace she knew and loved coming to the surface, "she's very cute."

"Still, even if she was hot…was she hot?"

"Yes," Liz replied, thinking that Reilly Danvers was definitely hot, if you went for the intense, darkly attractive types. Which she didn't. She had always been drawn to the brightly burning extroverts like Candace and Julia. At the thought of Julia, her heart ached. Even as she struggled to push the sorrow aside, she wondered as she had so frequently over the last eight weeks, if the pain was from missing Julia or just from knowing she had lived six years of a lie.

Brenda, with her usual quiet sensitivity, touched Liz's arm. "You okay?"

Liz clasped her friend's hand. "Yes, I'm fine. Thanks."

Candace, seemingly having forgotten her interest in Reilly Danvers and whether she was a potential bedmate, reached across the table and took Liz's other hand, joining the three of them in the old familiar circle. "So, honey, what did the doctor say?"

Liz looked from one expectant face to the other. Brenda, who spent her days directing the rare books department in the Temple University library and her nights in some sort of scholarly pursuit that Liz had yet to completely understand. At five-foot-four, raven-haired, doe-eyed Brenda had women following her at any kind of gathering, but she rarely dated. And Candace. Candace, who had stolen Liz's heart when Liz should have been old enough to know better, and who had casually, innocently broken it on her way to the next effortless conquest. Her two best friends. One ex-lover. So different, and yet together, forming a whole.

For nine years they'd shared secrets, heartbreaks, the joy of new beginnings and the pain of breaking up. The three had forged something that went beyond friendship and created a family in a far more intimate way than anything Liz shared with most of her blood relatives. Her friends looked at her now, with worry and expectation.

A few minutes earlier, as she had crossed the campus from the University Hospital to the bar where they had hung out in their carefree student days, she had considered what she would say when they asked the inevitable question. What would she tell them, when she herself wasn't certain how she felt about the news? She wanted to give herself time, time to examine a future that was so very different than what she had anticipated just three months before. But now, sitting with her friends, the family she had made, she knew that time would not change her answer.

With a tremulous smile that for once she could not control, Liz said, "You're both going to be aunts."

CHAPTER TWO

W hat are you going to tell Julia?" Brenda asked softly.
"Not a damn thing," Liz said sharply. Brenda's gentle smile never wavered, but Liz made her living, and quite a successful one, reading the subtle expressions and body language that most people missed. Her tone had stung, and her misery wasn't Bren's fault.

"I'm sorry, Bren." Liz squeezed Bren's hand and then let go of both Bren's and Candace's. She settled back in the booth with a sigh. "I'm jumpy today. Sorry."

"That's okay. You're allowed," Brenda said.

"I'll tell you what you should say to that miserable two-timing bitch," Candace seethed. "You should tell her to take the next train back to Hoboken, or wherever the hell she came from, and to take her little graduate student girlfriend with her."

"It's Hackensack," Liz clarified, "and since Julia just got tenure last fall, I don't think she's planning on moving anytime soon."

"Maybe we can get her fired," Candace said, leaning forward with a feral glint in her sky blue eyes. "Don't they have some rules against fucking your graduate students?"

"Uh, Candace," Bren interjected, "maybe we should just celebrate Liz's news right now and plan our smear campaign later."

Liz ordered a Sprite from the waitress who stopped beside the table, and felt some of the bleak pall that had surrounded her lift a little on the wave of her friends' unstaunchable support. "Julia isn't involved with one of *her* graduate students, at least not that she mentioned. And even if she was, that's not our problem."

Candace snorted and took a healthy gulp of her martini. "I hate that bitch."

"Thank you," Liz said.

"So," Bren said into the sudden silence. "What do we do now?"

We. Liz liked the way that sounded. She could count on these two. When she was lonely or scared, they would be there, and that was a big reason why single motherhood didn't loom quite so dauntingly. Her friends would help her, even though they couldn't heal the betrayal of discovering that her lover of almost six years hadn't been in love with her for a long time. Julia had informed her of that at the same time as she had announced that she was currently involved in a passionate affair with a woman more than a decade younger than either of them. Almost worse than Julia's infidelity was Liz's loss of faith in her own judgment, because she hadn't suspected Julia was on the verge of leaving. Oh, on some level, subconsciously, she had sensed something was wrong. They didn't make love as much as they used to, especially not in the last year. Julia seemed to have more committee meetings and evening academic obligations than ever before, so they saw less and less of one another. In retrospect, it hadn't been the best time to start a family, but at thirty-five, Liz was running out of time. They'd always planned on having children, and in the midst of actually preparing for the reality of it, she hadn't noticed that Julia wasn't really involved. Obviously, she hadn't noticed a lot of things.

"Stupid," Liz muttered.

"No you're not," Bren said, as if she'd read Liz's mind. "Trusting. Not stupid."

Liz fixed Bren with a stare. "Actually, I think they're one and the same."

❖

Reilly's head snapped back and she bit down hard on the rubber mouth guard clamped between her teeth. She kept her gloved hands raised in front of her chest and tucked her elbows tight to her sides, dropping back with one leg in anticipation of the roundhouse kick she knew was coming. Blocking the kick with one arm, she snapped a back fist and caught nothing but air.

"Halt," Master Drew Clark called, and Reilly immediately shifted into her ready stance, fists extended in front of her, legs spread shoulder width apart.

"Come with me," her tall, blond instructor ordered.

Reilly followed her friend and teacher to the far corner of the room, away from the other students. "Sorry."

"For what?" Drew asked, indicating Reilly's gloves with a tilt of her head. "You can take those off. You're done for tonight."

"Yes ma'am." Reilly jerked loose the Velcro on the wrist of her right glove with her teeth, clamped the glove under her left arm, and pulled her hand free. Then she rapidly removed her left glove and placed them both on the bench against the wall.

"I thought we agreed you wouldn't train if you'd worked all night," Drew said.

"Yes ma'am, we did," Reilly said, confused. As usual, she could read nothing in Drew's face beyond the usual intense focus she displayed in the *dojang*. A few inches taller, Drew was a good twenty pounds lighter but all muscle, and the fiercest fighting machine Reilly had ever seen. If she didn't know the ex-Marine sergeant outside the confines of this twenty-by-forty-foot room where Drew taught women to defend themselves and to trust *in* themselves, Reilly might have thought Drew had no more feelings than a machine. But Reilly knew otherwise. "I didn't work last night. Well, I did, but it was quiet and I slept five hours. That's plenty for me."

"Then what happened today?"

"Nothing."

Drew didn't object, but Reilly felt her probing gaze. Nothing had happened—if she didn't count being taken out by a femme in heels, which surely didn't warrant mentioning at the moment. The rest of the day had been typical—an MVA with two patients requiring urgent fracture reduction in the OR, a delayed bone graft on another, and a few washouts on patients waiting for flap closure. It was true, she'd thought about Liz Ramsey every now and then, in between cases—waiting for the patient to come up in the elevator from the surgical ICU, waiting for a room to be cleaned, waiting for anesthesia to put her next patient under. Hurry up and wait was the order of the day in the OR. She'd had fleeting glimpses of Liz's all too infrequent smiles, her melodic but oddly weary voice, and the brief glimmers of her sharp wit and bright mind. It had been a long time since a woman had occupied her thoughts, even for a few seconds. A long time since Annie.

Involuntarily, Reilly shuddered. She knew Drew would see it and hurried on. "Nothing happened. But maybe I am tired. I missed that block, didn't I?"

"The one where I could have taken your head off?" Drew asked levelly. "Yes, you missed it completely. That's a dangerous lapse, Master Danvers."

"Yes ma'am, I know."

Drew's eyes flickered to the rest of the room, then she rested a hand on Reilly's shoulder. She wouldn't have done it if any of the students could have seen the personal gesture. She never even touched her own lover intimately within the walls of the dojang. "Are you okay, Reilly?"

"I am, thanks. I had an interesting *accident* earlier. Nothing serious." Reilly grinned. "I'll tell you about it later, over a beer. Are we going out?"

"I think Sean plans to. Why don't you take the under-belts through their forms for the rest of the class."

Reilly snapped her arms to her sides and bowed. "Yes ma'am."

❖

"Let me get this straight," Sean Gray said, leaning close to Reilly so that the students at the adjoining table wouldn't overhear. Her deep hazel eyes sparkled with amusement. "You got taken off guard and dumped on your ass?"

Reilly knew she would take some ribbing if she told her story, especially from her friend and friendly rival Sean, Drew Clark's lover. When Reilly had started training at the dojang four years earlier, Sean had just earned her second degree black belt, putting Sean two levels below Reilly's fourth dan. And even though Reilly's rank automatically placed her in a senior position to Sean, that had not prevented them from becoming friends. She was especially grateful that both Sean and Drew never pushed her for personal details that she didn't want to reveal. The dojang had become her refuge, and in those early, difficult years, she'd spent more time there than anywhere else except the hospital.

"She came out of the stairwell like a torpedo," Reilly said in her own defense. "It wasn't just a question of being unprepared, she was right on top of me before I could blink. Splat."

"Splat," Drew mused. "I can see how that offensive tactic would work."

"The splat attack," Sean laughed while shifting her chair closer to Drew and curling one hand around the inside of her leg, just above her knee.

Reilly noticed the familiar gesture and felt a pang of longing. Sean didn't look anything like Annie—Annie had been small and blond, whereas Sean was dark-haired and solidly muscled from years of training, but Sean had the same ready smile, and she touched Drew with the same easy familiarity that Annie had used to touch her. She missed that connection, despite everything else. She wondered why she was thinking about Annie more today than she had in months. To her surprise, Reilly realized that she didn't think about her every waking moment the way she had the first couple of years. A little disturbed, she wondered when that had changed.

"Maybe you need some more time sparring," Drew said seriously.

Sean looked as if she was about to disagree, then quickly fell silent. Reilly was always impressed with the way Sean balanced her personal relationship with Drew and her role as Drew's student. Not an easy line to walk.

"I don't mind more workouts if you think I need them," Reilly said. "It's just the competition I need to avoid. I can't afford another broken finger, especially not now that I have a staff position."

Drew nodded, covering Sean's hand where it rested on her thigh. "Of course, you're probably not going to be attacked by attorneys in full battle mode too frequently."

Laughing, Reilly caught the glint of amusement in Drew's eyes. As serious as she knew Drew to be about the importance of training and self-defense, she had grown to appreciate Drew's subtle humor. "I don't know, maybe I'll get lucky again."

"Oh ho," Sean said softly. "So it wasn't an altogether unpleasant experience."

"Unpleasant?" Reilly thought back to the twenty minutes she had spent in the cafeteria over coffee and conversation with Liz Ramsey. Liz was a stranger, but she had felt comfortable with her, even relaxed. She had been curious about her, too—wondering what caused the sadness that hovered just below the surface of her appraising green eyes. She hadn't been curious about a woman, about anyone, in a long time. "No. If you don't count the bump on my head and the blow to my pride, it was—sort of nice."

Sean gave Reilly a long look, then just nodded. Reilly was grateful that she didn't have to elaborate, because she didn't have an explanation for why she had thought more about Liz Ramsey in one day than she had about anyone else in years.

❖

When her cell phone rang at a little after eleven p.m., Liz checked the readout before answering. She didn't do the kind of legal work where emergencies arose in the middle of the night, and if it was some eager or anxious young associate, then they could email her and she'd check it in the morning. When she saw the number, she answered. "Hi, Candace."

"Were you sleeping?"

"No," Liz said, laying the paperback romance novel aside. "I was reading."

"Something serious or something trashy?"

Liz laughed. "Something hot. Melanie Richards' latest."

"Fallen Angels?"

"You read it already?"

"I've worked my way through the good parts," Candace said. "A couple of times each. God, that woman delivers more orgasms per page than any writer I know. I can hardly make it through a chapter without stopping to—"

"I get it," Liz interrupted, not wanting any further incentive to recall exactly what Candace liked to do while reading something hot. Not while she was lying alone feeling completely unaroused and unarousable. Nothing like getting dumped and feeling faintly nauseous a good part of the day to kill one's libido. "Something wrong?"

"No. Just restless. Wanted to hear a friendly voice. You know."

"Uh-huh. No one to keep you company tonight?"

Candace laughed, a satisfied purr. "You know I never let them stay all night. Besides, she had an early meeting in the morning, so I had an excuse to send her home after round three."

"So why are you really calling instead of basking in the afterglow?" Liz felt Candace's hesitation. "Confess."

"I was thinking maybe you'd like me to go with you on your next visit. To the doctor's."

Liz closed her eyes. She should simply say yes. It would be good to have company, and Candace and Bren were going to badger her until she let one or both of them come with her. But right now, she just couldn't make the leap from what she had expected this experience to be like to the new reality of her life. She needed a little more time to create a revised picture of her life as a single, working mother. And she would, soon. Just, not tonight.

"I'll let you know when I need you, okay?"

"I could kill her for doing this to you," Candace growled.

"It's done," Liz said, suddenly tired. "Julia's gone, and it's time to move on."

"And you're okay with that?"

"I'll have to be. I don't have any other choice."

"What about our lunch dates?" Candace asked. "You'll still make them, won't you?"

"I wouldn't miss them. I'll talk to you soon," Liz said, forcing lightness into her tone. When Candace disconnected, Liz reached for her book. Maybe she could read herself to sleep.

After a few pages, when she realized she was picturing the series' main character Jae Blackman—an enigmatic, devil-may-care gambler turned undercover agent—with Reilly Danvers' piercing gray eyes and tight, fluid body, she was taken aback by the twinge of excitement low in her belly. Recognizing it, she tossed the book aside and snapped off her bedside light. Reading obviously wasn't going to put her to sleep, and the last thing she needed was a dose of mindless lust. Resolutely, she closed her eyes and willed herself to sleep.

❖

"You're very good, but I know you're cheating," a low sultry voice murmured in Jae's ear.

Jae pushed her chips across the table to the dealer. "Cash me out."

Taking her time, Jae folded the hundred dollar bills and slid them into the front pocket of her silk tuxedo pants. The stranger was standing close behind her, close enough that Jae felt the press of the firm breasts against her back. Not exactly an invitation, more of a challenge.

And the hard, heavy heat in her pelvis made her think a challenge was just exactly what she needed.

Bren rubbed her eyes and leaned back in her desk chair, rereading the last few paragraphs. Jae was headed for a fall, but then, it was time. She'd been skating the edge of her need throughout three books, and Bren knew it was time to push her to face what she really wanted.

"I hope my editor thinks so," Bren muttered, envisioning the rest of the scene. Jae on her knees, a pale slender hand gripping her hair—

The phone rang, shattering the image.

"Hell." Bren checked caller ID, then grabbed the phone. "Hi."

"Hi," Candace said. "What are you doing?"

"Getting ready for bed. It's midnight." Bren hadn't told Candace or Liz or anyone when she'd gotten her first book accepted for publication. Back then, she told herself she was keeping it a secret because it was probably just a fluke. Maybe no one would buy her book or like her book and she'd never write another one. Now, five years later, she was one of the most popular erotic romance novelists working, and she couldn't use that excuse any longer. She hadn't told her best friends because her writing, the characters she created, were just so private, so personal, she didn't know how to share them. How could she ever explain to them that the fictional world she fashioned sometimes felt much more satisfying than the one she lived in every day. It would only hurt them, and she cared about them too much to do that. "What's going on?"

"I just talked to Liz. She doesn't want me to go with her to the doctor's."

"How did she sound?"

"About how you'd expect when your cheating lowlife girlfriend walks out on you."

"Candace," Bren said gently, "I know you love her..." *still in love with her, Cand?* "...and you're worried, but Liz is going to be okay. What she needs is for us to help make the next seven months the wonderful, happy time it should be. She'll get over Julia."

"You're right," Candace sighed. "I never thought Julia was right for her."

"Maybe she wasn't. Maybe this will turn out to be the best thing that could happen to Liz."

"I hope you're right."

Bren laughed. "Aren't I always?"

"Yes, damn it. Usually. All right, go to bed so you won't fall asleep in the stacks tomorrow."

"Night."

Bren hung up and saved the file she was working on. Sex was out of the question now—if she started, she wouldn't be able to stop until she was finished, and she'd be too keyed up or too aroused to sleep, and she had an early morning meeting. She clicked over to her email to take one last check before she went to bed. Smiling, she opened one of the recent messages.

Dear Melanie – When is Jae going to fall in love?

When indeed, Bren thought, and decided to leave the answer to another day.

CHAPTER THREE

If Liz heard the phrase "fecal contamination" one more time, she was going to vomit. In fact, she was going to vomit no matter what the next words uttered by the VP of Risk Management.

"Excuse me," Liz blurted as she shoved back her chair. Registering the expressions of surprise on the men and women gathered around the conference table, she jumped up and bolted from the room. Praying she would make it, she fled down the hall toward the restroom.

Mercifully, both stalls were empty and she swerved into the nearest one just in time. Hot and dizzy, she dropped to her knees and braced her forearms on the cool white porcelain. Eyes closed, she surrendered to a second wave of the all too familiar nausea and vomited.

At first, she thought she imagined a hand gently drawing her hair away from her face. But the wonderfully cold paper towel against the back of her neck was real enough. So was the quiet voice.

"Take a breath, nice and slow."

Liz sensed someone kneel beside her and felt an arm curve around her shoulders. Helpless to do otherwise, she leaned into the embrace.

"God, this is embarrassing," Liz whispered, eyes still closed as she took one breath after another until she started to feel a little better.

"Oh I don't know, I can think of a lot worse things."

Liz wanted to laugh, but the effort was still too much. "Thank you for...oh," she said when she focused on the face so close to her own. The eyes she remembered as the color of winter sky were darker now, nearly black with...worry? "Reilly. God. Thanks."

"How are you feeling?"

"I'm fine," Liz said as briskly as she could manage, realizing she was still on her knees in a toilet stall being held by a near stranger. Could she possibly be any more humiliated? She braced a hand against the gunmetal gray divider separating the two stalls and pushed herself up.

"Take it easy," Reilly said immediately, sliding her arm from Liz's shoulder down to her waist.

Liz was acutely aware of Reilly's body pressed against hers in the cramped space. They were almost the same height, a little above average, and she had always considered herself to be in good shape—at least as good as twice weekly workouts in the gym and the occasional early morning run could keep her when so much of her time was spent behind a desk. But it didn't take more than fleeting contact for her to recognize that Reilly's body was hard, hard in the way only serious athletes were ever conditioned.

"Still a jock, huh," Liz murmured.

"Comes with the territory." Laughing, but her face still creased with concern, Reilly stepped back while keeping both hands lightly on Liz's hips. "Steady?"

Liz straightened her shoulders. "Yes. I'm all right. I just need to—" she gestured toward the sinks.

"Sure." Reilly released Liz almost reluctantly and moved aside to allow her to reach the sinks. Folding her arms, she studied Liz as she leaned over the sink and ran cold water to freshen up. Her naturally pale skin was ashen. Sweat beaded on her forehead and soaked the hair at her temples, making the deep red-brown appear nearly black. "When you're ready, we'll get you something to drink."

Liz waved a hand in her direction. "You must be busy. You don't need to babysit me now." Blotting her face with a paper towel, Liz smiled a "I have everything under control" smile. "Thank you for coming to my rescue."

"Hardly." Reilly shrugged, watching Liz's eyes, which she had learned during their brief conversation the week before were the true barometer of how she was feeling. Right now, their lustrous green was cloudy. "How long have you been feeling ill?"

"I…" Liz fumbled for the words. She hadn't told anyone other than Candace and Bren yet. Over the last week, she'd started planning for the changes in her life that were right around the corner. She'd have to arrange for maternity leave, find a nanny, and then negotiate with her law partners how best to adjust her work schedule when she returned—not to even mention doctor's visits, baby clothes, nursery furniture. If she let herself think about it, she'd panic over how much there was to do. But structuring the future assuaged her anxiety and helped restore her confidence in herself. Still, she wasn't ready to face the explanation and the inevitable questions that would follow. Not now, not to Reilly. Not when she already must appear so pathetically weak. "I'm not sick, in fact, I'm already feeling much better. Maybe it's something I ate or a twenty-four-hour bug. Really, Reilly. Go back to work."

"I worked last night so I'm off today. The only reason I'm still here at eight-thirty in the morning is that there was a staff meeting." Reilly pushed away from the wall and took a step closer. "You're white as a sheet, Liz. And you're shaking. Do you have a car here?"

"No, I usually take a cab. Saves the time of parking."

"Then let me drive you home."

"I'm not going home," Liz said incredulously. Spying her purse on the floor, she busied herself retrieving it. She didn't even remember grabbing it on her flight from the conference room, but she was glad she had. Avoiding Reilly's slightly unnerving scrutiny, she searched her purse for the mints she always carried and slipped one into her mouth. "I'm in the middle of a meeting with the hospital administrators, and I have a dep to prepare for this afternoon."

"You need something to drink and a little bit of food in your stomach. And you need to change your clothes."

"What?" Liz glanced down at her navy slacks. Both knees were marked by perfect damp, chalky ovals.

"I think that's cleanser," Reilly observed. "And I think emergency dry-cleaning is required."

"God damn it," Liz muttered. "I *do* need to go home." She eyed Reilly. "But I'm just a ten minute cab ride away. I really don't need you to go out of your way."

"Liz, stop being so stubborn."

"I'm not being stu—" Liz caught the flicker of amusement on Reilly's face and grinned despite her acute embarrassment. She hated that Reilly had witnessed her debacle. She also hated to admit that the subtle sickness still churned in her stomach. "All right, maybe I am a little…resistant. I'd love a ride, thank you. Let me get my briefcase and make up some excuse."

"Why don't you just tell them you're not feeling well?" Reilly asked as she followed Liz out into the hall.

Liz shot her a look. "What is it you surgeons say? To ask for help—"

"Is a sign of weakness," Reilly finished. "I doubt anyone would ever consider you weak. And being under the weather is hardly a sign of weakness."

"Just give me a minute," Liz said, heading down the hall. Despite what Reilly had said, she doubted that if Reilly were ill, she'd ever admit to her fellow surgeons that she couldn't do her job. No matter how natural that circumstance might be, women in positions like theirs still didn't admit to their predominantly male colleagues that there was anything, short of death, that could interfere with their work. And then *they'd* better be the ones dead. She took a deep breath, settled her expression into one of calm control, and stepped into the conference room.

"I'm so sorry," Liz said. "The office just paged and I'm afraid I have to go. I'll check in with you later, Tom, in case there's anything we need to go over."

Then, before anyone could respond, she gathered her briefcase and walked out. It was always much better to leave with the last word.

"Ready?" Reilly asked.

"Yes," Liz replied, although she wondered what she was doing letting a woman she barely knew take her home. Reilly's quiet insistence was very persuasive, but she certainly didn't need anyone taking care of her. Hormones. That's all it was.

❖

Five minutes into the ten minute ride from West Philadelphia to Rittenhouse Square, Liz realized she was experiencing another of those unnerving transitions that were becoming all too frequent. She wasn't nauseous any longer. She was starving. Starving as in if she didn't eat something in the next few minutes, she was likely to attack innocent bystanders on the street.

"Are you tired?" Liz asked. "You said you worked all night."

Reilly glanced over as she maneuvered her red Chevy Camaro through the relatively sparse midmorning traffic. "Not really. I'm usually keyed up after being on call and I don't like to sleep during the day. Why?"

"I'm hungry. There's a great bagel shop a few blocks from my building. If you don't mind taking a detour, we can grab some. That is, if you haven't had breakfast or—"

"Sounds great. Brenner's?"

"That's the place. I guess everyone knows it."

"Probably. At least everyone in the neighborhood." Reilly turned down Twenty-first Street. "We're practically neighbors."

"Really? Where do you live?"

"I've got an apartment on Pine. One of the old brownstones near Twenty-second."

"Nice."

"Yeah," Reilly said flatly. She pulled over to the curb, switched off the engine, and turned toward Liz. "You want me to go in?"

"Obviously, my appetite is back and I'm feeling fine." Liz glanced down at her stained slacks. "But I look a little worse for the wear."

"Just give me your order. I'll take care of it."

Liz hesitated, then bowing to common sense, acquiesced. After giving Reilly her order, she watched out the window as Reilly sprinted around the front of the car and loped toward the bagel shop. Like most surgeons Liz knew, Reilly didn't walk when she could run. On the other hand, the sensitive way Reilly had comforted her that morning wasn't something Liz was used to when dealing with surgeons, who frequently seemed if not self-centered, at least fiercely focused to the exclusion of almost everything else. Remembering the way Reilly had held her in her arms when she'd been too sick to stand up, Liz felt a rush of gratitude—and a flush of pleasure at the memory of Reilly's hard body. That was a reaction she didn't care to examine too carefully, especially not when her emotional state resembled a rollercoaster off its tracks.

Catching a glimpse of movement out of the corner of her eye, she studied Reilly returning. Even though she wasn't Liz's type, Liz had to admit that in her low-slung, boot-cut jeans, sneakers, and scrub shirt, with the hot summer breeze ruffling her hair, Reilly looked plenty sexy.

"God," Liz muttered, "no one mentioned this was going to turn me into someone completely unrecognizable."

"Talking to yourself?" Reilly asked as she slid into the front seat and handed Liz a bag. "Hot out of the oven."

"Delirious from hunger. Hurry." Liz clutched the warm bag. If she *had* been taken over by aliens, there was nothing she could do about it now.

Laughing, Reilly gunned the big engine and followed instructions.

❖

"There's soda and juice in the refrigerator, if you want something to drink," Liz said as she held open the door to her ninth-floor condo. "As soon as I change, I can make coffee, if you'd rather."

"I'll have whatever you're having," Reilly said.

Liz indicated the living room on the right. "I'll be back in just a minute."

"Take your time."

When Liz disappeared in the opposite direction down a hallway that ran through the rest of the apartment, Reilly slid her hands into her jeans pockets and strolled around the large room that took up the entire width of that end of the condo. Tall windows faced out toward Rittenhouse Square, the small Center City park that was a focal point for tourists and residents alike. Two sofas sat at right angles to one another on an oriental carpet, a gleaming dark wood coffee table between them. Neat and orderly and barely lived-in. She gravitated toward the far wall where built-in bookcases held an assortment of books, photographs, and an occasional vase.

These weren't the legal tomes that Reilly imagined Liz kept in her office, but an eclectic array of literature—popular fiction, biographies, nonfiction. She noticed a photograph of Liz with a man who looked about Liz's age. They were both dressed in white shorts and polos with a logo Reilly couldn't read over the left breast, and carrying tennis rackets. The dark-haired man, well built and what most people would consider handsome, had his arm around Liz's waist, and Reilly felt a pang of disappointment which she quickly pushed aside. Looking for other photographs, she was surprised that there were no others in the room. In fact, the entire room looked slightly barren, as if something or some *things* were missing.

Reilly returned to the photograph. She guessed that Liz was a decade younger in it, and although she was smiling, her expression was shuttered. Whatever she was feeling, she wasn't going to reveal it for posterity.

"Do you play?" Liz asked from somewhere behind Reilly.

"Not tennis," Reilly said, turning. Liz had changed into sage slacks with an off white shell, beneath which the barest hint of her lace bra showed. Reilly quickly averted her gaze. "I was more of a sandlot baseball kind of kid."

Liz smiled. "Hence your interest in sports medicine."

"When I figured out I wasn't going to be an Olympic caliber softball player, I had to do something." Reilly indicated the photograph. "Do you still play?"

"No," Liz said abruptly. "I've graduated to squash. Do you? Still play ball?"

"Yep. In the city league in Fairmont Park," Reilly said. "The hospital has a team. Well, several actually, but I play on the all women's team. I never liked mixed teams."

Liz eyed the photograph. "I know what you mean."

"Is he your, ah...husband?"

"Stepbrother."

Relieved, Reilly almost grinned before reminding herself that could mean anything. Liz might still have a husband, an ex-husband, a boyfriend—or several. Liz stood only a few feet away, but suddenly the distance between them felt heavy with unspoken questions.

"I'm gay," Reilly said.

"So am I."

"I could use one of those bagels."

"Come on out to the kitchen. I'll fix you one."

CHAPTER FOUR

The kitchen was bright and sleek and spotless, like the rest of the condo. A round wooden table big enough for two sat in front of a window that also overlooked the park. A stack of newspapers—all from that morning, Reilly was willing to bet—was piled neatly on the wide window ledge. A coffee pot and a single mug sat upside down in the dish drainer next to an otherwise empty sink. Reilly took that to mean Liz lived alone. Of course, it could simply be that her girlfriend, or partner, was traveling or had worked all night and wasn't home yet. And why she was even speculating, Reilly grumbled mentally, she didn't know.

"Do you want your bagel toasted?" Liz asked, her back to Reilly as she took plates down from the cupboard.

"However you're making yours is fine," Reilly replied. "Can I do anything? I'm pretty handy with a knife."

Liz looked over her shoulder and smiled. "Sit. You must be tired."

Reilly pulled out a chair at the small table, although she wasn't tired. Usually when she came off an overnight shift she was too keyed up to sleep, even though mentally and physically she was often drained. This morning she wasn't worn-out at all, and she couldn't credit that to an easy night. She'd operated until almost five a.m. on a young man who had tangled with a jet ski and lost. No, being with Liz made the difference. Reilly hadn't spent time alone with a woman in years, and she'd forgotten the simple pleasure of watching a woman move comfortably around her own kitchen, and the way a quick smile could feel like a gift.

Liz worked quickly and efficiently, aware but not minding that Reilly was watching her. That surprised her, because ordinarily intense scrutiny made her wary. Usually, close observation in the courtroom meant her opponent was looking for a weak point in her argument or some telltale sign in her expression that she was not as certain as she wanted to appear. It was nice not to be on guard, although she couldn't quite decide why she felt relaxed with Reilly. She didn't know her very well, but then maybe it was because Reilly had already seen her at her absolute worst. On her knees, helplessly vomiting.

"God," Liz muttered in disgust.

"What?"

"Oh," Liz said quickly, wondering when she had started talking out loud to herself. "Nothing." When Reilly raised a quizzical eyebrow, she added, "I was merely bemoaning the fact that you saw me in a less than shining moment this morning."

"It was just a human moment. It happens to all of us."

"Yes, well, there are some things some of us would like to pretend we aren't susceptible to."

"Like getting sick once in awhile?"

"You know what I mean," Liz said, carrying the food to the table. She passed one plate to Reilly.

"I know you don't like it when you're not in charge, and you probably prefer to do everything for yourself," Reilly said.

"Don't you?" Liz countered, deciding not to question how Reilly had come to that conclusion about her. It might be accurate, but deflecting the conversation was better than going down a road that might result in personal disclosure.

"Like to be in charge? Pretty much. I think it's an occupational thing."

"Maybe. But I think we choose our occupations because they suit our personalities, and not the other way around."

"That's what the psychologists tell us." Reilly munched the bagel. "These are the best in town. Can I get some of that soda you mentioned?"

"Oh, sorry," Liz said, rising quickly. "My entertaining skills are a little rusty."

"Can't be any worse than mine."

When Liz opened another cabinet to retrieve glasses, Reilly noticed empty shelves. The same had been true for the cabinet with the dishes. It looked like someone had recently moved out. Liz turned and must have seen the question in her expression, because she answered before Reilly could comment.

"I live here alone, but until a few months ago, I didn't."

Reilly took the drink Liz held out to her. "Thanks."

Liz nodded and sat down.

"I never know what to say to something like that," Reilly said. "Sorry seems natural, but maybe you threw her out. Or she could have been just a roommate, in which case I'd be presumptuous."

"Neither is the case," Liz said without inflection. "She was my partner, and she left me."

"Then I'm sorry."

"Thanks. I'm not sure if I am or not," Liz mused.

"That's good."

"Maybe." Liz shrugged. "I *am* pissed that she left me for a younger woman, though."

"Younger? Like what—twelve years old?"

"Smooth. Very smooth."

"Not usually," Reilly said, "but thanks. And I wasn't kidding. What are you, twenty-eight? Thirty?"

"I'm thirty-five. Julia took up with a twenty-three-year-old."

"Julia has judgment problems."

"That's kinder than what I've called it."

Reilly grinned. "Well, I don't know her. If I did, I might not be so nice."

Liz laughed. "My best friends are outraged for me, and I love them for it. But neither one of them has made me laugh about it yet. I appreciate it."

"You're welcome." Reilly added seriously, "And I really am sorry. I know it's tough."

"Yes…well." Liz stood with the pretense of taking her plate to the sink when she felt the sting of tears threatening. What was wrong with her? Confiding in someone she'd just met and now on the verge of crying in front of her?

Hoping to redirect the conversation, Liz rinsed her dish, and when she had herself under control again, turned back to the table. "How about you? Got a girlfriend, or are you the swinging surgeon type?"

"Neither one."

Liz had asked the question casually, but she caught a flash of pain course through Reilly's eyes. "I'm sorry. I didn't mean to get personal."

"That's okay." Reilly took a breath and seemed to visibly force the tension from her shoulders. "We seem to get personal when we talk. It's strange."

Liz nodded, but said nothing, having learned that there was much to be heard in silence.

Reilly met Liz's gaze. "She died."

"Oh Reilly," Liz murmured. "I'm so sorry."

"It was quite a while ago." Reilly stood, having come to a place she couldn't revisit or explain. "I should let you get back to your day. Thanks for breakfast."

"You're welcome." Liz didn't know what to say, an occurrence so rare she was momentarily stunned. Reilly hurt, she knew that, and she wanted to…what? Comfort her? Make the sadness in her eyes disappear? Touch her? With a start, she realized they were standing a few feet apart, staring at one another. "Are you all right?"

"Yes." Reilly smiled a slightly crooked smile that made her look at once wistful and sexy. "You need a ride to work?"

Liz glanced at the clock. "I'm not going right back to the office. I have a standing lunch date with friends on Mondays and Thursdays."

"Nice," Reilly said, looking relieved at the change of subject. "The best friends who are outraged for you?"

"They're the ones," Liz said as she led Reilly through the condo. "We've known each other since school and dubbed ourselves *The Lonely Hearts Club*. We used to sit around commiserating about our dateless status or our most recent break-up." She stopped abruptly. "God, I can't seem to get off this subject."

"Understandable."

"Well obviously, I need a diversion. I'm beginning to bore myself."

Reilly laughed. "Come to the softball games if you need a change of pace. Friday, Sunday, and Wednesday nights."

"When's *your* next game?" Liz asked impulsively.

"Tomorrow night. Six o'clock. The field at the top of the plateau," Reilly replied slowly.

Liz realized she hadn't even thought about work or Julia or the uncertain future for the last hour. Even at her most relaxed with Candace and Bren, she was always aware of time passing and of all the things she still had to do. When she was with Reilly, though, she lost track of everything else. "Who knows. Maybe I'll take you up on your prescription, Dr. Danvers."

"If you do, be sure to say hello."

"I will," Liz said lightly, while silently asking herself what she was doing.

When Liz said goodbye to Reilly on the sidewalk in front of her building, she watched Reilly walk away and decided there was nothing wrong with allowing herself a pleasant uncomplicated diversion.

❖

"Oh my God," Candace announced dramatically as she dropped into the booth across from Bren and Liz. "I've been running around like a madwoman all morning. Can you believe it? I overslept and almost missed the opening of the market."

Bren laughed. "Let me guess. Wednesday night. Probably wasn't bingo. Not bowling. Ballroom dancing?"

Liz tried unsuccessfully not to snort.

Candace looked aggrieved. "I'll have you know, I worked late at the office updating portfolios. And then..." She paused for effect and waited until she was certain that she had Liz and Bren's total attention. "I went home, had a leisurely bubble bath, and...read a book."

"Let me guess," Liz said. "Melanie Richards."

"I hate that woman," Candace said vehemently. "First I stayed up half the night finishing her damn book, and then I...well...you know, I was wide awake and horny."

"I thought we promised we wouldn't discuss work at these lunches," Bren said. "And books qualify as work where I'm concerned."

"I don't think Melanie Richards' books quite fall into the category of your typical rare book," Liz pointed out.

"That's an understatement," Candace agreed, waving to the waitress. "Bloody Mary...a double." Turning her attention back to her companions, she added, "Her books are everywhere you look, now. You should try them, Bren."

"Still, books are books and I see enough of them all day," Bren insisted, feeling uncomfortable as she always did when someone mentioned Melanie's books. She usually didn't feel guilty about keeping her secret, except when she had to employ subterfuge with her friends. Then it felt like her privacy came at a price she didn't want to pay.

"I'd give anything to have one night with Jae Blackman," Candace went on, oblivious to Bren's discomfort. "God she's sexy. I *know* there's something about her that Melanie isn't telling us, some deep dark secret. And I know it has to do with sex."

Silently Bren agreed. Jae was more than sexy. She was everything Bren found attractive in a woman—and it wasn't just that she was darkly handsome and knew her way around a woman's body. She was also secretly wounded and uncommonly sensitive, and she wasn't afraid to acknowledge her raw physical needs. As Bren explored Jae's complex character more deeply with each successive book, she became even more enthralled.

"Candace, honey," Bren said lightly, "almost everything has to do with sex for you."

Candace fixed her with a stony glare. "And your point would be?"

"Okay, okay," Liz said. "We've had this conversation before. Cand and I will discuss what we'd like to do with Jae Blackman some other time."

"God, you're no fun," Candace said, pretending to pout. Then she reached across the table and tapped Liz's hand, an almost-caress. "So. How are you feeling?"

Liz grimaced. "Most days like I woke up in someone else's body."

"Morning sickness?" Bren asked.

"It's a little more like morning, noon, and night sickness." Liz toyed with the straw in her glass of lemonade and tried to look more upbeat than she felt. "But the good news is, I only have a couple more weeks of it, at least according to everything I've read."

"What did the doctor say?" Bren countered.

"What could she say? It's normal."

Candace and Bren sighed simultaneously.

"You didn't call her, did you?" Candace said.

"I have another appointment next week. And besides, I know what she's going to say. Avoid spicy foods. Eat crackers before a meal. Drink lemonade—it helps settle your stomach."

"Baby," Candace said, using an endearment Liz hadn't heard her use in years, "this is one thing you can't be in charge of. You've never been pregnant before and, well, you're…older."

"Thank you, Candace, for reminding me of that," Liz said dryly. "I think Julia made that very point very nicely already."

Bren interjected, "Candace cares about you, Liz. So do I. You have to promise you won't take chances."

"I won't. I promise not to worry you."

"Liz," Bren said cautiously after a quick glance at Candace, "do you want this baby? Because we all know it's not happening the way you planned."

Liz looked from Candace to Bren. "Oh hell. I really have worried you two, haven't I." She leaned forward intently, making eye contact with each of them in turn. "I absolutely want this child. I wanted it before Julia walked out, and I want it now. It's just that the circumstances have kind of temporarily overshadowed the 'Oh, hallelujah, I'm having a baby' part."

"Good." Bren bounced a little in her seat. "Because we already have all kinds of fun things planned, like baby showers and fixing up the nursery and a naming party and…things."

"Thank you," Liz said, brushing her fingertips over her cheeks to wipe away the quick flood of tears. "God, this is the second time today. This is ridiculous."

"What?" Candace demanded.

"I'm all over the place emotionally. And you know it's not like me at all to get weepy."

"What else happened today?"

"Oh, nothing. I was just telling Reilly about Julia and I got…never mind." Liz recognized the hawk-like glare in Candace's eyes. Part was likely Candace's natural curiosity, but the other looked a little bit like jealousy, and Liz wasn't in the mood to deflect Candace's questions.

"Reilly. Reilly." Candace played with the name as if it were some exotic flavor, then lasered in on Liz. "Would that be the surgeon from last week?"

"Yes," Liz confessed.

"You didn't tell us you were seeing her."

"I'm not *seeing* her."

"But you saw her. Today."

Bren murmured, "Candace. Your claws are showing."

"Oh, bullshit," Candace snapped. "Nothing exciting is happening in our lives, Bren. We might as well get off on Liz's."

All three laughed and the tension dissipated.

"So tell," Candace demanded.

"It's hardly sexy. Unfortunately, Reilly witnessed my early morning bout with morning sickness and was nice enough to drive me home afterwards. We got to talking. That's all."

"I don't remember," Candace said conversationally. "Did you say she was hot?"

"Yes," Liz said, grinning at the memory of Reilly's tight body in jeans and a scrub shirt. "She's hot."

"So when are you seeing her again?"

"Oh my God, Candace. I'm pregnant, in case you've forgotten. The last thing I want is a date." Despite her protests, Liz thought about Reilly's casual suggestion that she drop by the ball fields. Casual. She could do casual.

"What?" Candace pounced.

"Nothing. Nothing." Liz picked up her lemonade and drained the glass. "So how would you two like to go to a softball game tomorrow night?"

CHAPTER FIVE

O h my God, oh my God," Candace moaned breathlessly. "Why am I just finding out about this place now?"

Laughing, Liz watched Candace's head swivel rapidly and finally slapped her playfully on the arm. "Stop that, you're going to hurt yourself."

"I don't care. *Look* at the women. I feel like I've died and gone to heaven. Do you think they need more players?"

"When's the last time you did anything more athletic than hefting your briefcase?" Bren teased. She closed the top on her black Mazda RX 7 convertible, her one indulgence. Liz and Candace, who had driven to the softball fields in Liz's Audi, waited by her door. When Bren climbed out and surveyed Belmont Plateau, she finally got the full effect of seven softball fields filled with women. "Oh. Oh my God."

"That's what *I* said," Candace replied archly. She threaded her arm through Bren's and added conspiratorially, "Besides, doesn't fucking Angela Howard blind last night count as exercise?"

"It certainly does in my book," someone replied in a low, husky voice.

Liz jumped at the familiar sound and spun around. There couldn't be two women in the world with that voice, and one glance confirmed her assessment. Parker Jones, an associate in her law firm, stood behind them, a saucy grin on her face and a predatory glint in her eye. If possible, Parker looked even better in athletic shorts and a tight tank top than she did in her always elegantly tailored business suits. With her windblown chestnut hair, blue eyes, and summer tan, she was model-gorgeous. Liz knew Parker was a lesbian and had always thought her attractive, but their only interaction had been strictly professional. Parker worked in the real estate and property group, so their paths didn't cross very often, and during business hours, the only thing Liz generally thought of was business. And of course, she had been married. And unlike Julia, she didn't break her vows.

"Hi Liz," Parker said, her attention riveted to Candace. "I was just on my way over to the field and I saw you drive in." She held out her hand to Candace. "I'm Parker."

Candace did a slow survey before raising slightly hooded eyes to Parker's. "I'm Candace. I gather you play ball."

"I'll play any game you're interested in," Parker replied. "I already like the sound of your exercise program."

"I'll be sure to keep that in mind," Candace said throatily. "If I'm looking for a workout partner."

Liz glanced at Bren, who rolled her eyes.

Parker switched her attention to Bren, who still looked amused, and launched another mega-watt smile. "I didn't get your name—an unconscionable oversight."

"Hi," Bren said, extending her hand. "I'm Brenda."

"Good to meet you," Parker replied, holding Brenda's hand for an extra second. "So, what brings you all out here?"

"A friend is playing," Liz said, suddenly feeling protective of her relationship with Reilly and not knowing why. Maybe it was because she suddenly realized every unattached woman on the wide expanse of playing fields, and some of the not-so-unattached ones, was probably looking for a summer fling. And she didn't want to be relegated to that category. "I didn't know you played on a softball team, Parker."

"It's a secret vice." Parker fell into step as they climbed the slope to the fields. "Actually, about half my team is lawyers." She laughed. "It's amazing we get anything decided, what with all the debate that usually goes on."

"And what position do you play," Candace asked, edging closer to Parker as they walked.

"I pitch. Fastball."

"I just bet that you do," Candace murmured.

"Who are you playing tonight?" Liz asked as she realized they were all headed up the grassy expanse toward the diamond at the very top of the rise. Other playing fields were scattered over the lower part of the plateau.

"A team from University Hospital—Angels of Mercy."

"You're kidding," Liz said. "That's really their name?"

Smiling, Parker nodded. "Ironic, too, because they're just about the most competitive team in the league. Except, of course, for the Just Hammers." Her grin widened and she glanced at Candace. "That would be my team."

"Is that the team Reilly plays on?" Bren asked Liz. "Angels of Mercy?"

"I'm not sure. I didn't ask her."

"Reilly Danvers?" Parker asked.

Surprised, Liz said, "Yes. She's my...our...she invited us."

"Then you came on the right night. Reilly's the star hitter for the Angels, and our teams are tied for first place." She leaned closer to Candace, her voice dropping bedroom low. "And tonight I'm pitching."

"Well, I just won't know who to cheer for, then will I?" Candace said sweetly. She turned to Liz. "After all, we *are* here for Reilly, aren't we?"

"Oh, absolutely," Liz said lightly. Candace had been probing her for more information about Reilly, and so far she had refused to take the bait. Thinking about introducing Candace to Reilly, she wondered if Candace was Reilly's type. Almost every woman she'd ever known had been dazzled by Candace's natural beauty and her playful, seductive manner. Suddenly, Liz was glad they'd run into Parker. At least for a night, Candace might have someone to focus on besides Reilly. Although, of course, if Reilly was interested, there was absolutely no reason why she shouldn't date Candace. No reason at all.

❖

Reilly swung through the pitch, feeling loose and comfortable with her swing, and easily knocked her last warm-up pitch into far left field. As she shouldered her bat, she idly checked out the opponent's bench. When she saw Liz standing with Parker Jones on the Hammers' sideline, she stopped so abruptly she blocked the path of the next batter coming around the backstop toward home plate.

"Hey, Reilly," Sean protested, "out of the road."

"Oh, sorry." Reilly side-stepped but kept her eyes on Liz.

"You okay? We need you on your game tonight."

"I'm fine. I just...never mind." She had wondered all day if Liz would come tonight, and had been looking for her since she'd arrived at the ball field forty-five minutes ago. But they hadn't exactly agreed to meet, and she should have figured Liz would be there with another woman. But, Jesus, Parker Jones? Not only was Parker the best pitcher in the league, she had a different woman on her arm every week.

"You sure?" Sean asked.

"Sure I'm sure." Reilly frowned at her own brief lapse in concentration. Liz was single. It made sense she'd be dating someone. "Don't worry."

"Okay." Sean didn't sound convinced and her expression changed to concern. "We all want to win, you know, but it's just a game. If you're tired—"

"I'm great. And I know it's just a game." Reilly grinned. "Just a game where we're going to kick their asses."

Sean grinned back. "Damn right."

Reilly hustled back to the Angels' sideline and knelt by the players' bench to make sure all her gear was still together. The Angels were in the field first, and she didn't want to have to search for her glove when the game started. Pulling off her batting glove, she stuffed it into the back pocket of her shorts. When she stood, Liz was beside her.

"Hi, Liz!"

"Hi yourself. You didn't tell me you were an ace hitter," Liz teased.

"I've had a few lucky games," Reilly said, trying not to stare. Liz's hair looked lighter in the sunlight, almost as if strands of gold had been spun through the dark auburn. Her green eyes were warm and unabashedly welcoming. In navy shorts and a white ribbed tank top, she looked younger and softer than she had in her business clothes. For just a second, Reilly remained silent, merely enjoying the sight of her. Then Liz tilted her head very slightly, as if in question, and Reilly said the first thing that came into her mind. "I was hoping you'd make it."

"Oh, well I…" Liz glanced over the field and down the slope to the other six fields, caught off-guard by the pleasure of Reilly's pleasure. "This is amazing. It beats the hell out of corporate dinners."

"I know what you mean." Reilly looked toward the Hammers' bench. "So I saw you consorting with the enemy."

"The enemy?" Liz frowned, then followed Reilly's gaze. "Oh. You mean Parker. I didn't even know she played until ten minutes ago.

But I understand her team has been giving you a beating."

"A beating? They're tied with us for first place," Reilly exploded. "Hell, they wouldn't even be *there* if we hadn't had to take a loss one night when we couldn't field the team. Three of us ended up getting called in for a multi-vehicle pile-up—" She narrowed her eyes as Liz burst into laughter. "Not funny. That was really not funny."

"I can see you take your softball seriously."

"What's the point of playing if you don't want to win?" Reilly liked the way Liz laughed. It was the first time she'd seen her so unguarded, and it wasn't until that moment that she realized Liz's features had been shadowed by sadness or worry or both until now. Like this, with the sunlight slanting across her face and her eyes suffused with pleasure, she was beautiful. Just plain beautiful.

"I'm torn as to who to support," Liz confided. "My associate over there, along with a bunch of other attorneys I know—or, you, over here. Maybe I just shouldn't pick sides."

"Whatever Parker's offering, I'll double it," Reilly teased. "Beer, pizza—you've got it."

"She hasn't actually gotten to the bribing stage yet. Besides, I imagine you've got lots of fans cheering you on."

For just a second, Reilly's smile faltered and then she caught her breath and forced the past back where it belonged. "I could always use someone in my corner."

Liz's eyes grew serious. "I know what you mean. So. Where should I stand?"

Reilly grasped Liz's hand and tugged her toward an open spot on the Angels' bench. "You should be able to see from here well enough. Be warned, if you get up someone's likely to steal your spot."

"I'm an attorney, Reilly. No one moves in on me." She caught herself, then shook her head ruefully. "Well, at least not until recently."

"Forget about that for tonight." Reilly realized she was still holding Liz's hand, but since Liz wasn't pulling it away, Reilly swept her thumb slowly back and forth over the smooth skin. "It's Friday night and we're about to kick some lawyer ass."

"There's something slightly perverse in me cheering about that," Liz said, "but I think that's exactly what I'm going to do."

"Good decision, counselor," Reilly said, feeling unaccountably light-hearted. "I have to warm up." Reluctantly, she released Liz's hand. Her palm felt warm from the heat of Liz's touch and she closed her fingers to hold it in. "If you're still here after the game, I'll buy you that beer."

"We'll see," Liz said. "But thanks."

Reilly backed away. "You're welcome."

Liz watched Reilly run onto the field, noting that her initial assessment of Reilly's body had been wrong. As in understatement. Reilly was more than tight and well conditioned. Her shoulders were broad and strong, her ass firm and just round enough to hold onto. Her thighs were more muscular then Liz had gleaned, even considering the way her jeans had stretched over them. Reilly was the epitome of hot, in the way of some women who were just a little rough around the edges.

"Walking on the wild side, baby?" Candace murmured from so close by Liz jumped.

"How long have you been standing there?"

"Just long enough to see her practically eye-fucking you."

Liz caught her breath, surprised at the undercurrent of animosity in Candace's voice. She'd always sensed lingering attraction from Candace, but Candace had never made a move while Liz had been with Julia. And she'd never been so overtly jealous before. "Jesus, Cand. What's the matter with you? We were only talking."

"You've been out of circulation a long time," Candace said flatly, her eyes tracking Reilly as she fielded the ball at shortstop and side-armed it hard and fast to first base. "You're not used to picking up on the signals. And she was sending them loud and clear. As in she wants to get into your pants."

"I think you're wrong," Liz said, watching Reilly now, too. "We've had a few pleasant conversations. She's refreshingly direct. And honest."

Candace cut her a look. "What does that have to do with her wanting a piece of your ass?"

"Okay." Liz blew out a breath, frustrated by Candace's obstinacy. "What is it that's really bugging you? Because I can't believe it's the fact that someone might possibly find me attractive, which I'm not saying I believe is true."

"I'll tell you what's wrong. Julia used you, and you didn't even know what was happening," Candace said emphatically. "Now you're going to have a baby and the last thing you need is someone who's going to play with your affections."

Liz laughed, then held up her hand when she saw Candace's eyes spark with anger. "I'm sorry. I'm sorry, really. I know you're just worried about me. I know you care about me. But Candace, come on! I'm thirty-five years old and hardly a blushing virgin."

"Who's a virgin?" Bren asked as she joined them.

"Actually, sweetie," Candace said, "I always thought *you* were."

Bren gave her a long contemplative look. "Not everyone announces their every orgasm."

"I certainly hope not." Candace smiled slyly. "I'd never have time to buy and sell. And don't think I didn't notice you trying to change the subject."

"And don't think *I* don't know you've been trying to get me to tell you the details of my sex life since the day you moved into the dorm," Bren said. "Keeping you guessing is the way I keep you interested."

Candace settled both arms around Bren's shoulders and leaned in close, front to front. Her few inches of extra height brought her breasts perilously close to Bren's face, and her tight stretch top made it clear she wasn't wearing a bra. "You don't have to tease me to keep me interested."

"You know," Bren said, tilting her chin up so she wouldn't have to stare at Candace's nipples, "you might fool most people, but I know you're a lot more than a pretty face and a gorgeous body."

"Don't tell." Candace brushed a kiss over Bren's cheek. "And since I can't get anywhere with you, I'm going to find some pom-poms and wave them at Parker."

Bren shook her head fondly as Candace slipped away, then glanced at Liz. "So? That's her at shortstop, huh? Reilly?"

"Yes."

"She's good-looking. Different than I expected."

"How so?" Liz suppressed an urge to wave when she caught Reilly glancing her way, before staring intently back at the batter.

"I guess I expect you to be more interested in women like Julia or Candace or…who was the one after Candace? Susan?"

"Suzanne McKenzie," Liz replied, feeling as if she were looking back into a different lifetime. "My first and last love affair with a straight girl. God, she kept me on the line for a long time."

"Well, she *was* pretty. And she had great breasts."

Liz chuckled ruefully. "She did."

"Reilly looks a little more…complicated than the others."

"You mean because she's more butch?"

"No. Well, she is, but that's not exactly what I mean. There's something about her," Bren mused, "that makes me think there's a lot going on under the surface. Not like Parker, for instance."

"Oh, don't sell Parker short. Maybe she just *acts* like she's only interested in sex."

"Maybe. But I bet it's Reilly who has the secrets."

"Don't we all?" Liz asked.

"Yes. But some secrets have the power to hurt."

"What's hurting you, sweetie?" Liz slipped her arm around Bren's shoulders.

"Nothing that a night out with you and Candace won't cure."

"Did anyone ever tell you," Liz said, "that you've got a way with words?"

Relaxing into Liz's embrace, Bren replied, "A time or two."

Liz jumped at the sharp crack of a bat and watched a ball rocket across the infield. Reilly was nothing but a blur as she dove headlong toward the ground, both arms outstretched. Everyone nearby gave a collective gasp as Reilly rolled several times and came to a stop on her back, then lay motionless. Heart pounding, Liz took one step forward, then halted abruptly as Reilly's arm rose straight up into the air to display the ball captured in the web of her mitt.

The umpire called the third out, and Reilly's bench broke into loud cheers as Reilly jumped up.

"Hot dog," someone muttered, and Liz noticed Parker beside her, frowning toward the field. Candace stood with her, her fingertips grazing Parker's arm.

"Pretty spectacular catch," Liz countered.

"Yeah yeah," Parker grumbled good-naturedly. "Let's see how she'll do against my fastball."

Candace put her mouth close to Parker's ear and murmured loud enough for Liz to hear, "I can't believe anybody can beat you when you're on your game. And I bet you'll be on your game tonight."

Parker gave Candace a long look. "Why don't you stick around after and find out."

"Why don't you show me what you've got," Candace suggested, "and I'll let you know."

"Watch me," Parker growled, then broke away and ran out onto the field.

"Why didn't you tell me you were hiding *that* at your office," Candace chided Liz. "I would've come to more of your office parties."

"That's what I was afraid of," Liz muttered, remembering Candace disappearing for an hour with one of the bartenders at the Christmas party. "You ogle Parker. I'll be right back."

Liz skirted around the equipment bags and knelt down behind the bench where Reilly was seated with some of her teammates. "Nice play."

Reilly swiveled around until she faced Liz. When she spread her legs to lean forward, her bare knees were almost touching the outside of Liz's arms. "Lucky catch, but don't say I told you that."

"Your secret is safe with me," Liz said.

"Thanks," Reilly said solemnly.

"You're welcome," Liz replied, certain they weren't talking about softball any longer.

CHAPTER SIX

I'll be back in a few minutes. Bathroom," Bren said, although she doubted Liz would actually miss her. Liz's attention was totally focused on Reilly. Thinking back, she couldn't remember Liz ever having been so into Julia, not even during those first few weeks of romantic psychosis. Liz *had* been crazy about Candace at the beginning—so crazy that she'd denied the insanity of getting involved with an inexperienced but sexually avaricious 18-year-old—and that had predictably ended in disaster. Not that Brenda thought Liz was contemplating a relationship with Reilly, at least not consciously, but Liz definitely seemed to be intrigued.

"And maybe that's just what she needs," Bren murmured as she threaded her way through the crowd and climbed the slope to the park building in search of restrooms. Liz hadn't seemed happy in a long time, and now that her life was in such turmoil, maybe a crush would take her mind off Julia and help ease her through the transition.

"It's not like she's going to get involved or anything."

Confident that Liz wouldn't be *that* crazy, Bren concentrated on following the narrow, overgrown path around the perimeter of the sprawling, cement block structure for some sign of the restroom. The side of the building facing the ball fields had once been a concession stand, but that was now boarded over and clearly no longer in use. Continuing through the ankle high, scraggly grass, she turned a corner and discovered an open archway with faded green letters above that read Women. She was happy she hadn't waited until after dark, because even in the waning daylight the area looked deserted and mildly foreboding. She felt even less comfortable when she stepped through the archway into a large, dimly lit room with concrete walls and floors. The only light came through two narrow rectangular windows high up on the far wall. Four doorless stalls lined one wall, and two cracked, dirty porcelain sinks occupied the near corner. "Rustic" was a kind descriptor.

Taking a tentative step deeper inside, Bren drew up short at the sound of a soft moan. Her first inclination was to flee, but another part of her was curious. Cautiously she crept forward and peered into the recesses of the first stall. A blond woman, a little older than Brenda, leaned with her shoulders against the cinderblock partition that separated the space from the next stall. When she turned her head and smiled faintly at Brenda, her eyes appeared slightly dazed. Bren could tell her breasts were larger than average and her legs long and shapely since her blouse was unbuttoned low enough to expose her hard nipples and her skirt was hiked up to her hips. A short-haired brunette in grubby blue jeans, biker boots, and a sleeveless black T-shirt knelt between her legs, licking her.

Bren caught a glimpse of a moist pink tongue disappearing into the apex of the creamy thighs and heard soft sucking followed by another throaty moan. Instinctively, she took a step back.

"Don't go," the blonde whispered and even though her words were faint, they held a hint of command.

Captivated by the tone and the scene, Bren stared as the blonde drove her fingers through the kneeling woman's short, slick black hair and directed her mouth where she wanted her.

"Lick me there. That's right," the blonde murmured.

Bren could just make out the line of the bottom's jaw as she intensified her efforts, alternately sucking and tonguing the blonde. *Jae, oh God, it's Jae*, which she couldn't be, of course, because Jae wasn't real. At least not to anyone except Brenda. Except—except this woman kneeling on the filthy floor with her hands clasped between her tight denim-sheathed thighs, pleasuring a woman whom Bren was sure was a stranger to her, was exactly as Bren had seen her countless times in her mind's eye.

"Ahhh," the blonde sighed, her eyes on Bren, her thighs trembling. "She has a talented tongue. She's going to make me come."

"I know," Brenda whispered, her gaze alternating between the blonde's face and Jae's mouth devouring her.

The blonde's breasts lifted and fell with each panting breath, and her hips writhed restlessly. She stared down at the woman between her legs, and Bren knew she was on the verge of coming.

"You can masturbate, if you must," the blonde gasped, and Bren wasn't certain to whom she was speaking—her or Jae. Keeping her hands by her sides, she watched Jae fumble with her jeans. When Jae shoved a hand into her gaping fly and groaned, Bren turned away. She wouldn't watch Jae come while making love to another woman. Not unless *she* dictated it.

Stumbling outside, Bren blinked at the sudden assault of lingering daylight and struggled for breath. A thin wail followed her and she half-ran down the slope, chased by the ghosts of her own making.

❖

"How's it going?" Bren asked when she rejoined Liz, who hadn't moved since Bren last saw her.

"They're tied with two innings to go." Liz glanced at Bren, then frowned. "Are you okay?"

"Yes, of course."

"You sure? You look…upset."

"No. I'm not. I…" Bren shrugged. "I walked in on two women having a *moment* in the restroom."

"You're kidding." Liz laughed. "Although I'm not sure why I'm surprised. You can practically see the pheromones in the air around here. God, I haven't walked in on a hot make out session since we lived in the dorms. I feel old."

"They weren't making out." Bren saw Jae on her knees, heard the scene play out, knew just the way Jae's face would look as she brought herself to orgasm seconds after making the blond stranger come. She ached to write it, capturing the instant when the pleasure made her blind.

"Bren?"

"Hmm?" Bren asked, feigning interest in the game being played in front of her rather than in her mind.

"What were they doing?"

"Oh. Uh, one of them was going down on the other one."

"Well," Liz said almost reverently. "I'm sorry I missed that. Did you know them? Oh God, it wasn't Candace was it?"

Bren laughed. "No, it wasn't Candace. If it had been, I'd probably still be watching."

"Watching what?" Candace said, bumping her hip against Bren's as she joined them.

"Bren walked in on a bit of oral sex in the bathroom," Liz confided.

"Really?" Candace said with interest. She pivoted, surveying the field. "Where is it?"

"Never mind," Bren said, slipping her arm through Candace's. "I'm sure they're done by now, and besides, it's not your kind of place. I think there was mold growing in the cracks on the floor."

"Okay, that's yech. But was it hot?"

"Yes," Bren said quietly, remembering Jae's tight, slender body and the way her mouth moved with such certainty over the blonde's pumping sex. "She was very hot."

"I don't suppose you got her name?"

Bren smiled. "No. I didn't need it."

❖

"I never realized I'd find dirty, sweating women such a turn on," Candace announced as she stood between Liz and Bren on the Angels' sideline. "I bet Parker plays just as hard in the bedroom as she does out there, too."

"Why do I think you're going to find out?" Liz teased. She barely heard Candace's laughing reply as Reilly strode up to bat. "Quiet now. The Angels are down a run and this is Reilly's last at-bat. She's only managed to get a single off Parker all night."

"You talk like a veteran already," Bren said.

"Just listening to everyone else," Liz replied nonchalantly.

"Uh-huh. And of course, Reilly's been giving you an instant replay every time she's come off the field."

Liz didn't answer as Reilly straddled the plate, looking relaxed even though the muscles in her forearms stood out in stark relief as she gripped her bat and angled it over her right shoulder. Her face was a study in concentration as she regarded Parker on the mound going through her elaborate pitching routine—rolling her shoulders, checking the runner at first base with a quick feint throw, squinting at Reilly as if she were an insignificant speck on the horizon.

"They're really cute, aren't they," Candace murmured. "All bristly and competitive."

"Reilly said she played in college, but I think it was a little more than recreational."

"Parker told me she had a sports scholarship, too." Candace chuckled. "While we were partying and picking up girls, they were probably studying their playbooks."

"*You* were picking up girls," Liz reminded her. "I was doing my fair amount of studying."

Parker fired a pitch. Reilly swung and missed.

"Oh, Parker smoked her," Candace crowed.

"Lucky," Liz muttered.

"Oh sure. She's been lucky all night, which is why Reilly's team only has two runs."

"Parker's team hasn't done much better."

Bren interjected, "You two sound like sports wives. Cut it out, it's scary."

Parker rifled another fastball. Reilly swung and missed.

"Damn," Liz exclaimed.

"I wonder if winning makes Parker horny," Candace mused. "Whenever I close a big deal, the first thing I want to do is have sex."

"She hasn't won yet," Liz reminded her.

"You always want to have sex," Bren noted.

"Of course," Candace went on, "I have to figure out how to get her away from her teammates after the game."

"There's always the bathroom," Bren said helpfully.

"Thank you so much," Candace said. "I had something a little more elegant in mi—"

Parker's arm blurred. Reilly swung, her bat slicing the air as her body uncoiled like a snapped spring. A sharp crack split the air, and the ball streaked into deep left field.

"Yes!" Liz cried. "Go, Reilly!"

Reilly raced around first and rounded on second base. The runner ahead of her scored. The game was tied. Reilly headed for third. The left fielder caught the ball on the bounce and fired it to third. Reilly slid under the tag. Safe at third.

"Oh yes," Liz said. "Reilly is the winning run. All we need is a hit."

"I wonder how Parker feels about sex if she loses," Candace grumbled.

"Maybe you'll find out," Liz replied. "If I don't strangle you first."

Candace laughed. "I never knew you were so competitive."

Liz caught herself before she could say there were a lot of things about her that Candace didn't seem to know. Their ill-fated love affair was a thing of the past, and it surprised her to realize she still harbored some resentment. Maybe it was the recent pain of Julia leaving her, and the realization that once again she had counted on someone to be there for her, and she'd been wrong. Maybe it was her damn hormones. She was edgy and moody and, although she wouldn't admit it with Candace around, horny. When she didn't wake up nauseous, she woke up horny. And the smoldering arousal didn't appear to be limited just to the morning, either. The last week or so she'd found herself thinking about sex in the middle of the day. Another change she definitely didn't welcome. And watching Reilly all night didn't help. She had to agree with Candace—dusty, sweaty, adrenaline-charged jocks were definitely hot.

"Mindless lust," she muttered. "Like I really need that now."

"Anytime is a good time for that," Bren whispered.

Liz colored. "Just tell me no one else heard that."

"I think you're safe. There's too much screaming going on."

"Thankfully." Liz gripped Bren's arm as the next batter settled in at the plate. "Two outs. Reilly on third. Pray for a hit."

Beside her, Candace screamed, "Strike her out, Parker! Come on, baby. Blow one by her."

"Candace, honey," Liz warned. "You might not want to yell that on this side of the field."

"You'll protect me."

Liz might want to strangle her, but Candace was right. She loved her. They were friends.

"All the same," Liz said, sliding her free arm around Candace's waist. "Let's not tempt fate."

Parker stared down the batter while Reilly crouched at third, ready to spring as soon as the ball was struck. Liz focused on Reilly, fascinated by her intensity. It was just a game, but Reilly threw herself into it as if it were the most important thing in her life. Liz imagined Reilly was that way about everything, and for just an instant, she allowed herself to envision what it would be like to be the focus of that kind of attention. A restless stirring inside immediately warned her away from such dangerous thoughts.

The ball rocketed from Parker's hand. The bat flashed golden in the slanting rays of the evening sun. The batter connected, the ball shot towards second, and Reilly surged toward home plate. Parker dove and intercepted the ball in the infield, then rolled to her knees and fired it toward home.

"Slide, Reilly, slide," a dozen voices screamed.

Reilly hit the dirt just as the catcher snagged the ball and swept her glove across the plate.

Silence fell over the field, then the umpire waved her arms and shouted, "Safe!"

Cheers erupted. The Angels had won.

Liz clapped, caught up in the jubilation as Reilly was swamped by her teammates. Then, Reilly broke free and ran toward her, a huge grin on her face.

"I think you brought me luck," Reilly panted.

"Oh, I don't think so," Liz replied. "You were great."

"Thanks."

Liz glanced down, then exclaimed, "Reilly, your leg is bleeding."

"Huh? Oh—that's just a little turf burn from sliding. No big deal."

"Is that just you being tough, or is it really okay?"

Reilly smiled. "It'll be fine when it's cleaned up."

Bren appeared next to Liz. "Great job, Reilly. I thought for sure you'd get tagged at the plate. Nice slide."

Liz raised her eyebrows. "Are you a closet softball player, Bren?"

"I played in high school," Bren admitted.

"You think you know your friends…" Liz teased.

"Well, how much do we ever really know anyone?" Bren smiled at Reilly. "Anyhow, great game."

Parker jogged up and clapped Reilly on the shoulder. "Nice running, Danvers."

"Nice pitching. Good game. Especially considering the score."

"Well, we'll get a rematch in the playoffs."

"Looking forward to it," Reilly said.

"Me too," Parker said before looking to Liz and the others. "So—

are you all up for beer and a burger? A bunch of us are heading over to the Elm Street Pub."

Liz hesitated. Reilly was probably going to the pub, and she wasn't certain that spending more time with her was wise. Even though Reilly hadn't intimated she was interested in her in any way, really, Liz didn't want to give her the wrong idea. On the other hand, the prospect of spending the rest of the evening at home in her half-empty condo, surrounded by reminders of her most recent failure, was depressing. She turned to Bren and Candace. "What do you say?"

"I've got some work I've been putting off," Bren said. "I think I'll head home. You can give Candace a ride, right Liz?"

"I'll take care of Candace," Parker said quickly.

Candace gave Parker a slow once over. "I guess I'm going to the pub, then." She grasped Liz's hand. "Come with. It'll be fun."

Liz glanced at Reilly.

"Come on," Reilly said with a smile, although her eyes were unexpectedly serious. "You have to help us celebrate whipping the Hammers."

"Hey!" Parker protested.

"Okay," Liz agreed, deciding there was no harm in a friendly get-together. And after all, there was safety in numbers, and Candace would be there.

After Liz and Candace hugged Bren goodbye, Candace sidled over to Liz while Reilly and Parker gathered their gear. "Does Reilly know about the baby?"

"No. Why should she?"

"If you're thinking of dating—"

"I'm not."

"Okay. But maybe you should let her know that."

"Don't worry. I will, if I need to," Liz said irritably. "Sometimes, two lesbians can just be friends, you know."

"Uh-huh." Candace linked her arm through Liz's. "Then I guess we should go join our *friends*."

"You know, sometimes you're a real pain in the ass."

Candace laughed. "I know, but you still love me."

Liz watched Reilly shoulder her equipment bag and tried not to think about friends and lovers and the shifting boundaries that divided them.

CHAPTER SEVEN

Reilly leaned back in her chair across the rickety scarred wood tabletop from Liz and watched her laugh at something Candace was telling her. Parker had squeezed onto the bench seat next to Candace and Liz, and all the adjoining tables were filled with players, from their teams and others. The baseline noise level in the crowded, dimly lit sports bar was so loud that ordinary conversation was a challenge, and Reilly couldn't hear the joke. She didn't mind, though, because being on the edge of the action gave her the opportunity to observe Liz without being obvious about it.

Ordinarily, she didn't stay for more than one beer—just long enough to keep Sean and her other teammates from bugging her about never going out. Work and softball and her nights at the dojang were plenty to fill up her time. She didn't go to parties. Being single was pretty much like having a blinking sign on her back saying "hit on me," and she got tired of saying no. She got tired of asking herself why she was still saying no, too. Tonight was unusual. Getting a win off the Hammers was always a high, but that wasn't the only reason she was feeling so good. Liz tilted her head back and laughed again, emphasizing the long, smooth column of her neck, and Reilly was reminded of how deceptively fragile a woman's body could appear. She imagined if she skimmed her fingertips along the angle of Liz's jaw and over her throat she'd discover the steely strength of tight muscles beneath satin skin. Her gaze drifted lower to the swell of Liz's breasts and her hands trembled. Quickly, she lifted her gaze and found Liz staring at her with a half-smile.

Nonplussed, Reilly drained her beer and only then remembered she had come right from the hospital after spending the entire afternoon reconstructing an open shoulder from a gunshot wound. She hadn't had time for dinner, and now she had a bit of a buzz on. That probably explained why she felt flushed and just a little bit shaky. Her pulse was racing, too. She looked at the empty bottle clenched in her fist. It was only her second, at least, that's what she thought. Or had Parker bought another round for the table a while ago? Jesus, it wasn't like her not to pay attention to what was going on around her.

"You okay?" Liz asked, leaning across the table. "You looked like you were a million miles away."

"Just winding down," Reilly said as she edged forward to close the distance between them. At least Liz hadn't said she'd looked like she was undressing Liz in her mind, which she hadn't been. Not exactly. Although she could still almost feel the hot pebbling of hard nipples against her palms. "Did you enjoy the game?"

"It was great." Liz chuckled. "Just what I need, a little more competition during my off hours because I don't get enough during the day."

"Didn't you say you play squash? Now *that's* a tough game."

"Oh sure. And from the looks of the scrapes on your leg and the gash on Parker's elbow, you play softball just for the social interaction."

Reilly grinned, and although her head might be a little fuzzy, she noticed that Liz had very neatly diverted the subject away from herself. "Playing it safe never gets you anywhere. Nothing to lose, nothing to win."

For a second, Liz's smile faltered and Reilly wondered what it was she had said. She replayed the conversation in her mind, and other than realizing that she very rarely had any kind of conversation with a woman, she couldn't put her finger on anything amiss. Nevertheless, Liz seemed upset. Reilly slid her hand across the table and rested her fingers on Liz's. "Are you okay? You're not still feeling sick, are you?"

"No," Liz said quickly. "I feel great. It's just been a long week. I think I'll call it a night."

Ignoring the surge of disappointment that came out of nowhere, Reilly said, "I'll walk out with you."

"Just give me a minute to make sure Candace has a way home."

Reilly signaled good night to Sean, who sat at a nearby table with Drew, and stood as Liz half-crawled over Candace and Parker to squeeze out between their table and the one next to it.

"All set?" Liz asked.

"Yes. Candace taken care of?"

"Parker is giving her a ride."

Reilly didn't comment as she wended her way single-file behind Liz through the boisterous crowd. Once outside, she breathed deeply and tried to decide if her head was clear enough to drive. At just after nine p.m., the sky was dark but the air still warm. A night breeze carried the lingering scent of cut grass and hot earth. The smell of summer always made her think of being a kid, and how damned easy it had all seemed then. Endless summer—if she'd only known it would end someday. But then, life was like that—you couldn't go back when you were finally smart enough to appreciate what you had.

"Where did you park?" Reilly asked, pushing aside the familiar melancholy.

"Around the corner on Lincoln Drive."

"I'll walk you."

"You don't have to," Liz said. "Isn't that your car across the street?"

"Yes, but I'm going to take the train. One beer too many."

Liz shook her head. "You most certainly are not. I'll take you wherever you want to go. Will your car be all right here tonight?"

"It should be. This is a residential area. But you don't need to—"

"And who was it who gave me a ride home not so long ago when I was a little off my game?" Liz grabbed Reilly's hand. "Don't argue. We're practically neighbors, so you know it's not out of my way."

Reilly tensed as Liz's fingers curled around hers. It was a friendly gesture, nothing more. She tried to remember the last time anyone had touched her and couldn't.

Liz looked down at their joined hands and let go. "I'm sorry."

"It's okay, I'm just jumpy."

"Come on, my car's over here," Liz replied, looking as if she didn't believe Reilly's explanation.

Reilly couldn't think of a reason to refuse, and she didn't really want to. She'd enjoyed Liz's attention while she was playing earlier. Every time she'd looked across the field, their eyes had met. The connection was probably only in her mind, but it felt good in a way she'd forgotten. Her enjoyment in fielding a ball or getting a hit had been heightened because Liz was watching. Foolish, maybe, but pleasurable, just the same.

"I appreciate it, thanks."

"You're welcome." Liz walked around the driver's side of her car and regarded Reilly with a smile. "Besides, I owe you for introducing me to the guilty pleasure of softball voyeurism."

"Hell, if you think tonight was good, you'll have to come to the Tournament Ball at the end of the season."

Liz quirked an eyebrow. "You mean ball as in dance?"

Reilly nodded.

"You're not kidding?"

Reilly shook her head.

"Candace is not going to believe this."

❖

"I guess this isn't your usual Friday night fare," Parker said, sliding back into the booth next to Candace and placing a martini in front of her.

"Thanks," Candace said, taking a sip. She'd been pleasantly surprised to find that the bartender did a nice job with the mixed drinks, even though almost everyone was drinking beer. "What do you think I'm usually doing on Friday night?"

"Dinner, the theater, drinks after at the Chelsea Lounge."

Candace smiled at the reference to the city's newest watering hole, where the in-crowd went to see and be seen. And Parker was right, it was one of her favorite places to end the evening if she hadn't already found a companion for the night. The mix was refreshingly metro, and she never had any difficulty finding a female partner. She didn't worry about marital status or even primary sexual identity, because she wasn't in the market for a relationship. She was pleased that Parker seemed to be on the same wavelength. "Correct on all counts."

"So I should consider myself lucky you ended up here," Parker replied.

"Are you feeling lucky?" Candace teased.

"I usually am."

Parker pulled on her beer bottle and stretched one toned and slightly dust-smudged arm out along the back of the bench behind Candace's shoulder, looking nothing like the high powered attorney Candace surmised her to be. What she did look like was a very confident and sexy woman. About Candace's height, putting her several inches above average, Parker had a rangy build with long lean legs, small breasts, and nicely developed shoulders and arms. Her medium length chestnut hair was in disarray but managed to look stylishly attractive nevertheless. Expensive haircuts would do that for you.

"I'm surprised you didn't have a cheering squad tonight," Candace probed. Interest had been signaled, now it was time to set down the ground rules.

"I don't tend to cultivate the kind of relationships that generate fans."

"How about a wife who prefers staying home with a good book?"

"Nope."

"No steady girlfriends?"

"Not a one."

Candace laughed. "But a few not so steady ones?"

Parker grinned. "It's been my experience that repeat performances usually carry strings, and I'm more of a woodwind type myself."

"As in you blow hard and fast and then you're gone?"

"Something like that," Parker acknowledged. "How about yourself?"

Candace reached under the table and smoothed her palm up and down the inside of Parker's bare thigh. She let her fingertips stop just beneath the edge of her shorts. "What would you say?"

"Snare drum," Parker said immediately, covering Candace's hand and easing it a little higher until Candace felt the heat pouring from her skin. "A blast beat that takes your breath away."

"I'd say we're well-attuned." Candace considered sliding her fingers just an inch or so higher and investigating how much hotter, and wetter, Parker was. She hadn't made a woman come in a public place in a long time.

"I have very good control," Parker said, as if reading Candace's mind. Her voice had dropped what seemed like an octave at the same time as her hand had drifted from the back of the bench to Candace's shoulder. She stroked Candace's arm and brushed her lips over the rim of Candace's ear. "In case you were thinking of taking advantage of me."

Candace turned her head just enough to whisper against Parker's mouth, "I intend to take everything you have to offer."

Parker's thigh twitched beneath Candace's fingers. "Are you ready to leave?"

"I've been ready since the minute I saw you tonight."

❖

"Lick me there. That's right," the blonde murmured.

Jae caught the distended clit between her lips and swept her tongue back and forth against the sensitive spot underneath, the spot that made the standing woman bite back a whimper every time she touched it. She thought she heard the staccato click of heels against the marble floor of the casino lounge, but didn't slow her pace, sensing the orgasm gathering in the hot pulsing flesh against her mouth. The tile was cool beneath her knees and her tuxedo pants were a vise against her throbbing crotch.

"Ahhh," the blonde sighed, her thighs trembling. "She has a talented tongue. She's going to make me come."

"I know," Jae heard someone whisper. Not alone then. Eyes closed, she sucked and teased until the fingers gripping her hair shook violently. Above her, the blonde panted for breath while her hips writhed restlessly. Yes, she would come soon. Very soon.

"You can masturbate, if you must," the blonde gasped, and Jae wasn't certain to whom she was speaking—her or the unknown observer—but she didn't care. Permission had been given, and she needed it. Needed it so much. She fumbled with her trousers and finally got the button open. Jae shoved a hand into her gaping fly and gripped her clit, hard and slippery and aching. Groaning, she vibrated it between her fingers and sucked harder. She would come, had to come, because her flesh was burning, bursting, but it wasn't coming she cared about. She felt her mistress harden even more, filling her mouth, and she devoted herself to only one thing, delivering the pleasure she had been entrusted to give.

"Oh yes," the blonde keened, her voice a thin high wail. "Yes. I'm coming."

With the cry of pleasure enveloping her, Jae squeezed and twisted until her swollen flesh released her. Drained, she sagged forward, her cheek against the smooth thigh. Warm fingertips briefly caressed her face. Then the blonde shifted and Jae was alone on her knees in the empty stall.

Bren leaned back from the keyboard, sipped her wine, and slowly reread the passage. The entire time she'd been writing, she'd held the image of the dark-haired woman from the bathroom in her mind. At some point, the Jae she knew almost as well as she knew herself and the flesh and blood rendition she'd seen earlier became one, and the scene unfolded with perfect clarity. The mistress was blond, large breasted and luscious, commanding and so sensuous. Everything Bren was not. But the blonde's orgasm, her sweet surrender to Jae's talented mouth, had been Bren's.

"Jae," she whispered. "What are you doing?"

❖

"Are you working this weekend?" Liz asked as she took the exit from the Vine Street overpass onto Twenty-third Street. As she headed south of Market into a more residential section of Center City, the traffic eased and she glanced at Reilly in the passenger seat. Reilly sprawled, legs apart, head back, forearms resting in the bend of her thighs. She gave the appearance of being utterly relaxed, but Liz felt a thrum of barely suppressed tension vibrate in the air between them.

"No," Reilly replied. "I'm back-up call on Sunday, and it's probably fifty-fifty that I'll get called in, but I'm not on first call again until Monday. There are five of us, so it works out to about once every four days, considering vacations and things like that."

"How about I pick you up in the morning and take you back to your car?"

Reilly rolled her head to the side and regarded Liz for so long Liz thought she was going to refuse. Then she said, "Only if I buy you breakfast."

"The Downtown Diner?" Liz asked.

"Is there any other place?"

"Not that I can think of." Liz hoped her stomach would be settled enough to do the place justice.

"So we have a deal?" Reilly asked.

"Deal," Liz repeated. Not a date, she immediately added silently as Candace's warning that she should tell Reilly about the baby echoed in her mind. She would tell her, if the right moment came along, but the topic wasn't something that just popped up in casual conversation. And that's all that was really happening between them—a few casual meetings. They were neighbors, but she needed to know someone a lot better than that before she confessed her secrets. "Is eight o'clock too early?"

"I'm a surgeon, remember? That's lunch."

Liz laughed as she turned onto Pine and double-parked in front of the address Reilly gave her. "I keep early hours, too, but Saturday *is* Saturday. You're allowed to sleep in."

Even with Reilly's face partially in shadow, Liz could see her expression change. For a brief instant, sadness washed across her features, blunting the sharp clear planes of her face and leaving a shimmering after-image of loss. Liz leaned closer and touched Reilly's hand. "I wish…"

Liz hesitated, surprised both by her actions and her uncertain sentiment. What was she doing? Reilly grew very still, her hand slowly closing into a fist beneath Liz's fingers. Liz fought the urge to wrap both her hands around Reilly's, as if she could take away the hurt with something as simple as a touch. Foolish, because she should know better than anyone that wasn't possible.

"You took such good care of me the other day," Liz said. "I wish I could somehow return the favor."

"Well," Reilly said, her voice husky, "you did cheer for me tonight, and I'm pretty sure I got that last hit because you were louder than anyone out there."

Liz recognized the evasion, but respected Reilly's right to her privacy. God knew, she protected her own. "Then I'll have to do it more often."

"That should work." Reilly turned her hand over and squeezed Liz's fingers, a fleeting connection that nevertheless felt to Liz like a caress. "See you in the morning."

"Good night," Liz said. She waited in the car and watched as Reilly climbed the stairs to her building, keyed the lock, and finally disappeared inside. Only then did she recognize the odd feeling in the pit of her stomach as disappointment. She had hoped Reilly would ask her in.

"Crazy, that's what that kind of thinking is," Liz muttered as she drove away. "You have got more than enough to handle without complicating it with someone, even a very nice someone like Reilly Danvers."

Reilly Danvers. Liz liked the sound of her name. She liked the way she traveled around the bases, sleek and sure. She liked the way she occupied space, as if she owned it. She especially liked the way Reilly had gently held her hair back and wiped her face when she'd been sick. She liked a lot about Reilly Danvers. Enough that it was time to be extra careful.

CHAPTER EIGHT

R eilly stared at the ceiling, watching dawn chase the night shadows away. Even as the room lightened, unease lay heavily in her chest.

Saturday is *Saturday*.

Liz had made the observation lightly, as if everyone would understand the meaning. Weekends were mini-holidays, after all, two days in which to do something special. Two days to relax and enjoy life. Except that wasn't true for her. Weekends were no different than any other days of the week. Saturday wasn't a day to sleep late, make leisurely love, and drink coffee in bed with the newspapers scattered across the covers. Sunday wasn't a day to take an early morning run, go back to bed after a quick shower, and awaken a woman with soft kisses and murmured promises. Those intimate moments were no longer part of her life.

She had accepted the emptiness in her life, even welcomed it, because even though she missed Annie, she also took comfort in knowing she could not repeat her past mistakes if she remained alone. She would always miss Annie's smile, her laughter, and even the anger that so often ended in kisses. But just the same, her thoughts of Annie had faded these past few years—until meeting Liz. Odd, that Liz made her think of Annie. They were nothing alike. If anything, Annie had been more like Liz's friend Candace. Annie had charged through life, a little wild, a little reckless, wanting to experience everything on the edge. Life with Annie had been a crazy ride filled with delirious pleasures and unexpected pain and hidden secrets. Secrets, Reilly had learned, that could kill.

Reilly threw aside the sheet and sat up on the side of the bed, hating that the memories had come back to haunt her now, when she had finally succeeded in burying them. She couldn't change the past, couldn't undo the mistakes she had made, and she still had nowhere to go with her fury. Annie was not here to answer the question that haunted her. Why? Why hadn't Annie trusted her?

Annie wasn't here to answer, but one thing Reilly knew with certainty—she had failed the woman she loved, and she never wanted to be in a position where it could happen again. If that meant being alone forever she didn't care. Loneliness was a small price to pay for her sins.

Reilly glanced at her bedside clock, wondering what the hell she was doing. She was supposed to see Liz in just a few hours. Liz was somehow responsible for the past plaguing her so ferociously these last few weeks, and that alone should have been reason enough to avoid her. But it wasn't. Liz was warm and open and refreshingly direct—exactly the opposite of Annie, and the kind of company Reilly hadn't realized she craved.

She grabbed a T-shirt and shorts from a pile on a nearby chair, pulled on socks and her running shoes, and lifted her house key from a hook by the door. A run would clear her head. Having breakfast with a woman she liked wasn't a crime, not when she knew what she needed to guard against.

❖

"Sun's coming up," Parker murmured, cradling Candace in her arms as she slowly stroked inside her. "I think that's my cue to leave."

"Oh God," Candace moaned. "If you stop, I'll kill you."

"I don't want to overstay my welcome."

Candace wrapped both arms around Parker's neck and pressed her face against her throat. Her hips undulated with the building pressure. "Just shut up and make me come."

Parker laughed. "Aren't you doing that right now?"

"Uh-huh." Candace bit down on the thick muscle at the base of Parker's neck as she closed around Parker's fingers and her orgasm spilled out.

"Beautiful," Parker whispered, her clit jumping as Candace shuddered. "You make me so hot."

"Keep going," Candace gasped weakly, caressing Parker's face, then her breasts. Parker groaned and Candace slipped her hand lower, drawing teasing circles on Parker's stomach. "I want to come again. Want to come with me?"

"Oh yeah, please."

"What…what do you want?"

Parker lifted her hips. "Just stroke me."

Candace pushed herself up and straddled Parker's stomach with Parker's hand still inside her. She reached back, gripped Parker's wet center, and squeezed. On the verge of climaxing herself, she laughed wildly as Parker stiffened and her eyes rolled back.

"Yes, oh baby yes." Parker arched her back, her free hand grasping air.

"Parker," Candace snapped. "Don't you dare come yet."

"Jesus," Parker gasped, her face a mask of pained pleasure. "What do you want from me?"

"Fuck me," Candace growled, rolling her palm over Parker's clit. Parker thrust into her, hard, and again, harder, and Candace started to come. Above the raging scream of her own orgasm, she heard Parker cry out. Then there was nothing except mind-melting pleasure.

Moments later, Candace fell over onto her back and sighed. "That was excellent."

"Yes," Parker said, her voice a husky whisper. "It certainly was."

Lazily, Candace turned her head on the pillow and regarded Parker. Her hair was damp, her neck and chest still flushed with satisfaction. The muscles in her neck that had been so tight as she orgasmed just seconds before now fluttered delicately beneath her sweat-slick skin. Candace always took pleasure in pleasing a lover, but seeing Parker so completely unguarded struck her as indescribably beautiful. Candace's chest constricted with unfamiliar emotion, and she immediately had the urge to flee.

"Feel free to use the shower," Candace said.

"You're right, I need one." Parker rolled over, kissed her until Candace was on the verge of asking her to stay, then pulled away. "Go back to sleep. It's still early."

"Thanks." Candace smiled and caressed Parker's cheek. "See you around."

Parker's eyes were dark, unreadable. "See you."

❖

Liz munched on soda crackers as she gathered her purse and keys. Happily, her stomach was cooperating for a change, and she thought she might actually be able to eat breakfast. Out of habit, she slowed in front of the mirror in the vestibule. During the week on her way to work, she checked her makeup, but today she checked her figure. Her jeans had seemed the tiniest bit tight when she tucked in her pale green scoop tee. She was just a little past ten weeks, and she didn't think she should be showing yet. Even naked she hadn't been able to discern any difference in her body. Still, she felt a little self-conscious, although she didn't know why she should. Whether or not Reilly Danvers found her attractive was not high on her "important things I need in life" list.

Resolutely, she reached for the door only to stop almost immediately as her cell vibrated on her hip.

"Liz Ramsey," she said, not even bothering to check the caller ID. It was too early on a Saturday for Candace, and Bren rarely called, not being a phone person. So it was likely the office.

"Did I wake you?" a soft, sultry voice inquired.

Liz's stomach plummeted and she braced one arm against the door as her legs threatened to go wobbly. She took in a slow breath to make sure her voice didn't quaver. "No. I was just on my way out."

"You're not working so early on a Saturday, are you?"

"Julia, you never cared when I worked before. Why are you calling?" Liz was pleased to hear that her voice held an edge. She hated that a simple phone call from Julia could unsettle her. But then, everything unsettled her these days. The other night she'd cried over a car commercial.

"I was hoping I could come by this morning."

"Why?"

"We have some paperwork to sort out—insurance policies, that sort of thing. And we should talk about the buyout on the condo."

"Today's not a good day," Liz said abruptly. "In fact, just about any day is a bad day. Have your attorney call my attorney. I really don't want to see you."

"Liz, honey—"

"Don't. Don't pretend there's anything between us. You made it very clear there wasn't."

"I know the timing was terrible—"

"You're right, it was," Liz said. "It was about six years too late. And I'm about to be late for breakfast. Goodbye."

Liz disconnected the call and closed her eyes. She was shaking. Damn Julia, or maybe, damn *her* for being so blind for so long. How had she not seen that they had become nothing more than shadows in one another's lives? How had she ever imagined that they could raise a child together? She touched her abdomen. This child would change her life in ways she couldn't begin to imagine. For the first time, she was thankful that Julia was gone. Her child would never have to bear the burden of holding together a relationship that wasn't meant to be.

With another deep breath, she left the apartment and took the elevator down to the parking garage. Even though Reilly was only a few blocks away, Liz was ten minutes late arriving. Reilly was waiting outside, leaning against a lamppost on the corner half a block down from her house. In her tight blue jeans and faded red cotton shirt, she was easy to pick out among the surprisingly large number of people already out and about. Liz drew alongside her and powered down the passenger side window.

"I'm sorry I'm late. Do I still get breakfast?"

Reilly grinned and climbed into Liz's Audi. "I'll put it on account. I have a feeling I'll be late a lot more than you."

Liz pulled away, knowing she was blushing at the inference that they would be seeing one another again. Seeing one another often enough to be late on a regular basis. Now that Reilly was closer, she noticed the shadows beneath her eyes, but didn't know how to politely inquire about them. She didn't really know very much about her at all. No facts, that is, beyond her occupation.

Although she *did* know she was competitive, and, thinking about the awful episode of morning sickness, kind and caring as well. Remembering Reilly's response to her confession about her break-up with Julia, she could add intuitive to the list. And she knew she had lost someone she loved. Come to think of it, she knew a lot about Reilly Danvers, and she liked it all. And that was without factoring in smart, funny and stop-your-heart gorgeous.

"Where are you from?" Liz asked abruptly, wanting to get her mind off *that* track immediately.

"A little town in upstate New York."

Reilly mentioned a town Liz had never heard of.

"Brothers? Sisters?"

"One brother. He still lives there. You—besides your stepbrother?"

"A sister. She's an Army major. She's flying helicopters in Iraq right now."

"Jesus," Reilly said. "That's scary."

"It's terrifying." Liz gripped the steering wheel harder. "It took me a long time to get serious about my career. I couldn't wait to go off to college and have a good time. Andi's a year younger and all she could talk about from the time she was twelve was West Point. This is her second tour."

"I understand those Army pilots are really good."

Reilly touched Liz's leg softly for a second. The brief contact was innocent and yet so comforting, Liz's throat tightened.

"Yeah. I know. She's the best."

"You're pretty close, huh?"

Liz nodded. They emailed almost every day, if Andi wasn't on a mission. Andi had been quick to tell her she'd never thought Julia deserved her and that Liz was better off without her. In the next breath, she'd made Liz promise to send ultrasound images so she could have a picture of her niece or nephew to put by her bunk. Liz blinked away tears. Oh God, she couldn't lose it now. Not while she was driving. Not in front of Reilly.

"Do you want me to drive?" Reilly asked softly.

"You know," Liz said, pulling over to the curb, "I just need a second. It's been kind of a lousy morning." She skimmed both hands over her cheeks, happy that she hadn't actually shed any tears. She laughed shakily. "I swear to you, I'm not usually like this."

"You don't have to explain," Reilly said.

"Julia, my ex, called as I was walking out the door. I was already angry at her, and then thinking about Andi over there…emotional overload." Liz blew out a breath and shifted sideways in the seat to face Reilly. "I know you don't know me at all, but there's a really good reason—"

"Liz," Reilly interrupted, her expression unexpectedly tender. "There's nothing strange about being upset that your sister is in the middle of a goddamn war. Or that your goddamn ex called first thing

Saturday morning and pissed you off. Sounds like a really good reason to cry…or swear."

Liz grinned and the moment to get into heavier topics passed. She really didn't want to talk about Julia, and talking about being pregnant meant talking about the whole sorry mess. For just a little while, she wanted to be free. Free of Julia. Free of her mistakes. Free of her heartache. And Reilly was so damn good at making her feel good. Was it so wrong to want to feel that way for a few hours? "You're right. Are you hungry?"

"Starved. I ran a few miles this morning, and all I had was half a stale Power Bar when I got back."

"Couldn't sleep?" Liz pulled back into traffic.

"Restless night," Reilly said offhandedly.

"I know it wasn't the beer, you only had two or three."

"Two more than I should have, considering I didn't have dinner."

"No wonder you're starving." Liz turned into the parking lot in front of the diner. The shiny aluminum-sided structure resembled the wingless fuselage of an airplane, right down to the rows of oval windows. "Are you one of those workaholic types who forgets to take care of herself?"

Reilly grinned as she got out of the car and walked with Liz to the revolving front doors. "Not really. But I won't complain about some TLC, if you're offering."

Liz let the comment pass because she wasn't sure if it was meant to be as flirtatious as it sounded. Inside, the diner was crowded and noisy, but they managed to snag one of the last window booths. Unfortunately, the air conditioning was far from efficient and the heat, combined with the smell of last night's fried food layered on top of breakfast, made Liz queasy. Nevertheless, she was determined not to give in.

"Coffee and the breakfast special," Reilly said to the waitress who appeared immediately by their side.

"Ice water, please, and scrambled eggs and toast," Liz added. She leaned back in the booth and thought of a dozen casual, meaningless things to say. But nothing about being with Reilly ever seemed to be casual. "So why aren't you sleeping?"

Reilly stared at her, obviously considering whether to answer or not.

"You can tell me it's none of my business," Liz said quietly. "Because it isn't."

"Ghosts."

Liz searched Reilly's eyes, trying to find a clue as to what her next question should be. She read people for a living. She was good at it. But this time, it was so much more important not to make the wrong decision.

"What was her name?"

"Annie."

"Irish?"

Reilly nodded. "Not a redhead like you, though. Her hair was lighter and her eyes were darker."

"You said it was quite awhile ago." Liz noted the quick comparison. Had Reilly been thinking about Liz and comparing her to Annie? The thought made her wonder what the result had been.

"Almost five years."

Liz listened to the timbre of her voice, judging her pain. She heard sorrow, but not raw grief. She also didn't hear a warning to back off, but she didn't want to open old wounds. "Was it an accident of some kind?"

Reilly waited while the waitress set down their drinks, and then clasped her coffee cup in both hands. "No. She had a stroke. An aneurysm."

"God, that's awful."

"Yes." Reilly shuddered, as if shaking off a memory, then smiled wryly. "I'm sorry. Lousy breakfast topic. Thanks for asking."

"I'm sorry, too." Not bleeding anymore, Liz thought, but not completely healed either.

"Annie was about your age when she died. She was nine years older than me."

"Which makes you…" Liz calculated. "Thirty-one now."

"Right."

"That's almost the same difference as between Candace and me."

"You two were lovers?" Reilly asked between bites of her breakfast. "Or…are you still?"

"God no," Liz said quickly. "I mean, we were, but we're not anymore."

"I wondered. She seems very…protective."

"Candace and Brenda and I have been best friends for years. They're as close to me as my sister. Maybe closer, because I adore Andi, but I don't understand her."

"Is your sister a lesbian?"

"She is. Single, always has been, pretty much."

"Occupational, probably."

"That's partly it." Liz nibbled on her toast and pushed her half-eaten eggs aside. Her stomach had settled but her appetite had fled. "My parents split when we were fourteen, and we did the half a year back and forth thing until we finished high school. I think it turned her off to relationships."

"But not you," Reilly stated, leaning back from her empty plate.

"I keep trying." Liz laughed ruefully. "Haven't done very well so far."

"Like I said before," Reilly murmured, "Julia's an idiot."

"She is, isn't she?" Liz smiled. "You're very good for my ego."

"Well, you're good for my game. Only seems fair."

"When's the next one?"

"Tomorrow afternoon."

The air was suddenly filled with questions, and Liz wished desperately for the answers. Had she heard an invitation? Had Reilly really been flirting with her or was the sadness that surfaced when she grew quiet a sign that her heart still belonged elsewhere? *Even more importantly, am I only pretending my interest in Reilly is casual? Am I lying to myself the way I lied about what was happening with Julia all these months?*

"Want a cheering squad?" Liz asked before the voices in her head could dissuade her.

"Yes," Reilly said immediately.

"Good." Liz welcomed the swell of anticipation, something she hadn't realized she'd been missing for far too long, not caring that all the questions still remained.

CHAPTER NINE

B ren settled in front of her computer with a cup of coffee and a raspberry cheese Danish and logged onto Melanie Richards' author blog for her Saturday morning chat. She sipped and nibbled and scanned the questions from her readers. Smiling, she answered a few of the easy ones.

What do you wear while you're writing?
It depends on what I'm writing. If I'm outlining or editing, I usually choose something old and comfortable, because that's tough work! But if Jae is going out and there's the possibility she'll have an exciting encounter, I might dress up in something slinky.
Why can't you write faster?
Then I wouldn't have time to talk to you, and I'd miss all this fun!

Bren enjoyed chatting with her readers online. While the interactions struck her as personal, sometimes almost intimate, she was comfortably shielded by the anonymity not only of her pseudonym, but by the boundaries of virtual reality. When she was writing, when she was chatting with readers about her characters or plots or future plans, she was completely Melanie Richards. She loved being able to release that other part of herself—the bold, daring, sexually adventurous part. As she read the next question, Bren slowly set down her coffee cup. Everything on the screen except that single question faded.

When is Jae going to admit that she's waiting for a mistress to show her what she really needs?

What astounded Bren about the question was that she'd barely known herself what was happening with Jae until the last few months.

But someone had understood, someone had read between the lines. Bren wondered what she had revealed in the snippets of story she'd recently posted as teasers. What had this reader sensed about her character that she had only just realized? Had she unwittingly exposed part of herself without realizing it, too? She typed, then deleted, then typed a vague response. She read it, knew it was a cop-out, and deleted it. The blinking cursor mocked her. Her own inner voice taunted her. *Are you ready to commit? Are you ready to admit where Jae is going, where you want to take her? Where* you *want to be?*

Someone had guessed her secret, and her discomfort was matched only by her excitement. Before she could think about it too much, she typed.

Jae is waiting for the only woman she can trust enough to tell her secrets to. Maybe she'll find her on the very next page.

Reilly relaxed as Liz took her Audi through the tight, twisting turns of Lincoln Drive. She often worked weekends because work was a welcome respite from too many hours with nothing to do but think. This weekend, though, she was glad she was free.

She enjoyed the sensation of someone else being in control for a while. In the operating room, even in the dojang, she was always in charge. Responsible for others. It was nice not to have to do anything for a few minutes, and although they didn't talk as Liz focused on the road, the silence was comfortable. The narrow road hugged Wissahickon Creek as it meandered northwest from Center City, and the air grew noticeably cooler and clearer as they traveled deeper into the huge stretch of parkland. At the speed Liz was going, they'd reach Reilly's car in another few minutes. Reilly didn't really want to get there. Thinking about the long day stretching before her, and the even longer night, and then almost another whole day before the late afternoon game Sunday, she felt a pang of loneliness. "What are you doing the rest of the day?" Reilly asked.

"I don't know," Liz replied, keeping her eyes on the road. "I can tell you what I'm *not* doing. I'm not going to the office. I might not even check my messages."

Reilly laughed. "Sounds pretty rebellious."

Liz flicked her left turn signal and veered onto the street where Reilly had left her car. "Actually, I expect Julia will have left messages or paperwork for me, or else had her attorney do it, considering she didn't get any satisfaction from me this morning. When she wants something done, she's relentless."

"It has to be difficult. I'm sorry."

"That's nice of you to say." Liz braked to the curb opposite the neighborhood bar and restaurant where the teams had gathered the night before. She cut the ignition and turned in her seat. "Considering I'm as much to blame as she is."

"Were you having an affair too?" Reilly asked.

"Only with my caseload," Liz said dryly, "but apparently some people consider work a form of infidelity."

"I know these situations are always more complicated than they look," Reilly said, "but I don't see how you can blame yourself."

"It's probably not a bad thing," Liz said, trying to make light of it. "A little self-reflection is good for the soul."

Liz's smile didn't hide her sadness, and Reilly had an overwhelming urge to find the insane woman who had hurt her and shake her. On the other hand, she had absolutely no desire for Julia to reappear, which left her feeling very confused. Liz's face was pale, her eyes softly wounded, and Reilly acted without thinking, spurred on by Liz's sadness and her own familiar loneliness. She leaned across the narrow space between their seats and slid her arm around Liz's shoulder. Liz's lips parted in surprise, her searching eyes filled with questions.

"Like I said," Reilly murmured, watching Liz's irises deepen from pale green to forest darkness as she slowly lowered her mouth toward Liz's.

Liz had never been so aware of being about to be kissed in her life. Her lips actually tingled. Reilly's arm behind her back was tight as a steel band, and Reilly's fingers, where they circled Liz's upper arm, were hot. Reilly's mouth would be hot, too, she was certain of it. Her dark eyes were molten, so intense that Liz shivered.

Reilly brushed her mouth over Liz's, lightly but not at all tentatively. "Your ex was crazy to let you go."

Liz skimmed her fingers along Reilly's arm and over her shoulder to the back of her neck. She twisted a thick strand of dark hair between her fingers, resisting the desire to grasp a handful and drag Reilly's body closer.

When Reilly groaned quietly, Liz parted her lips, allowing her entrance a tiny fraction. She was right, Reilly's mouth was hot, her tongue softly insistent as it slicked over the surface of her lips. Liz tasted her and was suddenly hungry. So hungry. Hungry to be touched, to be wanted.

Liz sucked Reilly's tongue deeper, cradling Reilly's jaw in the palm of her hand. Reilly tugged her closer, and somewhere in the lust-fogged recesses of her brain, Liz was aware of the gear shift digging into her ribs and Reilly's other arm circling her waist. Her breasts swelled and heat kindled in the pit of her stomach. She felt wanton, *wanting*, in a way that was far more primal and urgent than she'd ever experienced before. She wanted to climb onto Reilly's lap so that every part of her body could make contact. Her skin burned. She ached inside. In another few seconds, she would be beyond caring where she was or that she was about to make love to a woman who was supposed to be a casual acquaintance.

"God, you can kiss," Liz groaned, pulling back and bracing both hands against Reilly's shoulders.

"So can you," Reilly panted. Her hand shook as she threaded her fingers through Liz's hair. It felt so good to touch her. Liz was so alive, so real. "Maybe we can go somewhere a little more private."

"I need to put the brakes on here, Reilly," Liz said, regretting the words as soon as she saw Reilly's expression shutter closed. "God, I'm doing this all wrong. I'm sorry. Things are pretty crazy for me right now and—"

"Look," Reilly said in an even, almost toneless voice. "I was out of line. I should be the one apologizing. With what you're going through, the last thing you need is someone jumping you." She reached behind her and found the door handle, pushed it open, and slid out. "I'm sorry."

Liz leaned across the passenger seat. "I don't think you understand. I don't think I do, completely, but I didn't expect that kiss and I'm not making myself very clear."

Reilly grinned ruefully. "Believe it or not, I didn't expect it either. Thanks for the ride, Liz."

Reilly closed the car door and even though Liz wanted to call her back, she didn't. Not only hadn't she anticipated the kiss, she most definitely hadn't expected the way she had responded. She'd been ready, more than ready, to make love. And although she didn't have anything against two adults enjoying each other physically if they got the urge, she liked Reilly. Maybe if she hadn't known her at all, maybe if they'd just bumped into one another at a party, she could have had sex with her and walked away satisfied. Candace did it all the time, and it seemed to work just fine for her. But she wasn't certain that she'd want to walk away from Reilly, and what else could she do, considering that she was in no position to offer anything else?

Reilly's car sped by and swerved around the corner. Liz waited until the roar of the engine faded away, then started her car and carefully followed. Her head and her body still seemed to be reeling and her hands were shaking. Opening her cell phone, she pushed a number on her speed dial and held her breath.

"Hi, Lizzie," Bren said when she answered. "What are you doing?"

"Making an even bigger mess out of my life, if that's possible."

"Uh-oh. Do we need an emergency meeting of the LHC?"

Liz smiled, grateful for the thousandth time for her friends. "I think maybe we do."

"Should I call and see if Candace is finished with Parker?"

"What makes you think she's with Parker?"

Bren laughed. "Tell me you didn't know they'd end up together about ten seconds after Candace laid eyes on her."

"Five seconds."

"You're right, I stand corrected. Where are you?"

"About six minutes from your house."

"I'll see you in six minutes then."

"Thanks, Bren. You're the best."

"Nah, just your best friend."

❖

Reilly didn't look in her rearview mirror. She didn't want to know if Liz was behind her. She drove blindly for a few blocks, not really thinking about where she was going. She was still thinking about the kiss. She was still shocked by it. Shocked that she'd kissed Liz without giving a thought to what might happen. She'd kissed her because she couldn't think of another way, a better way, to tell her how much she didn't want her to be upset. How much she wanted to see her smile. How much she wanted to erase every hurt she'd ever suffered.

She'd kissed her because she hadn't had the words, and she needed so much for her to know.

She couldn't ever remember doing anything like that in her life. She'd been so much younger in both years and experience the first time she'd kissed Annie, or rather, when Annie had kissed her. When Annie had informed her that it was time to leave the party where they'd met. When Annie had led her home and up to her bedroom and taught Reilly how to please her. She'd followed Annie's lead because Annie burned so brightly that everything else paled in comparison, even her own needs.

A few minutes ago she'd kissed Liz because she'd needed to. She hadn't considered that Liz might not want to be kissed, probably *didn't*. Hell, Liz was clearly still struggling with her breakup and had admitted she'd been thrown by a call from her ex that morning. Obviously there was unfinished business there. And Liz hadn't given any indication that she wanted anything more than friendship when they'd gotten together.

Reilly pulled over in front of a square, two-story, stucco building and finally took stock of her surroundings. She wasn't all that surprised to find she had driven to the dojang without even thinking about it. Maybe a workout was just what she needed to get her head straightened out. She never did anything without thinking it through first. At least, not since she'd let Annie carry her away on the tide of Annie's passions and obsessions.

After locking the car, Reilly hurried up the four wide stone steps to the double front doors and was surprised to find them unlocked. Only the senior instructors had the key and no classes were scheduled at this time on Saturday morning. She climbed the wooden staircase to the second floor, her footsteps echoing in the silent building, and slowed as she approached the door to the dojang, which stood ajar. When she pushed it open a few inches more and peered inside, she saw Sean in the middle of executing a black belt form, and stood quietly until she was finished.

"You're here late," Reilly said, waiting for Sean to bow before entering.

"Hey," Sean said. "I didn't expect to see you until tomorrow at the game."

"Sorry to interrupt."

"That's okay. I stayed after class to practice a little for my test. I'm about done."

"That's coming up in a few weeks, isn't it?"

"I hope so. Master Cho hasn't set the date yet."

Reilly shoved her hands into the pockets of her jeans, uncertain whether to stay or go. She wondered where Liz was, what she was thinking. She rubbed the back of her neck where Liz had rested her hand, still aware of the pressure of Liz's fingers drawing her closer. Liz might not have expected the kiss, might not even have wanted it, but she *had* kissed her back. Reilly replayed the way Liz's lips had parted, the way her tongue had felt, welcoming her and teasing her just a little. The kiss had been good—it had been great, and her stomach still churned with the desire for more.

"What's up, Reilly?" Sean asked, studying her with a worried look.

"I…" Reilly rarely thought about the fact that Sean was a clinical psychologist. They only saw each other at the dojang or on the softball field. And those times when they had a few drinks together at the bar, they'd never had a truly personal conversation, because Reilly just didn't. Her conversations with colleagues were limited to discussions of surgery, sports, and on rare occasion—usually late at night over the third or fourth trauma case in a row—sex. *Their* sex lives, not hers. Intimate disclosures were not her style, although she'd been having revealing personal discussions with Liz since the very beginning. She sighed. Liz. Everything was different with Liz. "Believe it or not, I'm a little turned around about a woman."

Sean grinned. "Really. Is that good or bad?"

"I don't have any idea."

"Well that sounds normal."

Reilly laughed and almost immediately felt better. "Does it?"

"If she doesn't turn you upside down and inside out and pretty much fog your windshield, what's the point?"

Despite her joking remark, Sean's eyes were warm and sympathetic.

"Want to talk about it?" Sean added.

"I don't think so."

"Want to work out? I've got an extra uniform with me."

"Feel like sparring?" Reilly asked.

"Do I have to promise not to hurt you?"

Reilly grimaced, still thinking about letting her hormones call the shots a few minutes earlier. "Don't worry, my head's too hard to damage."

"Maybe." Sean handed Reilly a *gi*. "But where women are concerned, we almost never think with our heads. And sometimes, our hearts can be pretty smart, too."

"Thanks." Reilly took the uniform and headed toward the changing room. She'd followed her heart once before, and all she'd gotten was heartbreak. She wasn't going there again.

CHAPTER TEN

S ean bowed, then stepped back and pressed her gloved hands to both thighs as she bent over, panting. Sweat ran in rivulets down her neck, and the white T-shirt she wore beneath her gi jacket clung wetly to her chest. A purplish bruise blossomed on the left side of her jaw. "Had enough?"

"Maybe," Reilly gasped, sinking down on the narrow bench that ran along one side of the practice area. She pulled at the Velcro on her gloves with her teeth, and finally got her hands free. After wiping wet strands of hair off her face, she rested her head against the wall and stared at the ceiling. Her left hip ached from the fall she'd taken on the unpadded floor. "Nice leg sweep."

"Thanks. Pretty slick back fist from you, too." Sean sagged onto the bench beside Reilly. "I don't know how I'm going to spar four or five black belts, all of you outranking me, when I test for third dan."

"You'll be fine. You'll be so pumped, you won't even know you're tired."

"Easy for you to say."

Reilly swiveled her head and grinned at Sean. "Yeah. True. Drew will probably wipe the floor with you."

Sean smiled. "Not if I can help it."

"She's about the best I've ever seen."

"I know," Sean said with evident pride. Briefly, her face clouded. "She taught hand-to-hand combat in the marines. She hasn't been out that long."

Reilly considered Drew's probable age. Still young enough to be recalled. Reilly respected Drew's position as their senior instructor, as well as Sean's lover, and didn't want to tread into private areas. "I guess she hasn't heard anything?"

"Not officially, but she's been in touch with people she knows who are still in. If things go on much longer, recalls are likely."

"Let's hope it ends soon," Reilly said, thinking of Liz's sister and all the other countless troops in the war zone.

"Yeah, let's hope." Sean shifted sideways on the bench and rested her chin on her knee. "How's your head?"

"You dumped me on my ass, which hurts. My head is fine. How's your jaw?"

"Stings."

"Sorry."

"Don't be, you did me a favor. I'll be looking for that counter in the future."

"In that case, you're welcome," Reilly said.

"I don't remember ever seeing you with a date," Sean said after a minute of silence.

"You haven't."

"I just always figured you were a lesbian because you're too good looking not to be."

Reilly laughed and Sean joined her. "Thanks."

Sean continued to regard her thoughtfully and Reilly knew she was waiting for her. She appreciated that Sean wasn't pushing. "I'm not much into dating."

"Confirmed bachelor?"

"No, just a wary one."

"I was married once, to a guy," Sean said.

"Really. I never would've thought that."

"Neither would I, looking back from where I am now."

"You and Drew just seem like you've always been together."

Sean's expression softened. "When I got divorced, I really wasn't looking for anything, or anyone. I certainly wasn't looking for a woman, even though my twin sister's gay."

"That might have been a clue," Reilly said dryly.

"You think so?" Sean chuckled. "Well, then I met Drew. Actually, I *saw* Drew, and that was about it for me."

"So you think this love at first sight thing can happen?" Reilly considered her first night with Annie. It hadn't been love, it had been lust. No, more than lust…a compulsion, a need so fierce she hadn't been able to do anything but follow. *Moth to a flame.*

"Instant attraction? Sure. Love? I don't know, I think so sometimes—the beginnings of it anyway," Sean mused. "It wasn't just that I thought she was gorgeous, which I do, but the first time I saw her was here. I watched her training for two hours, and by the time the night was over I was hooked."

"If you watch Drew train you can tell a lot about her," Reilly said.

"Yes. And everything else I imagined about her was true."

"You're lucky."

"I am."

Reilly looked at the ceiling. "I was with a woman for three years and most of the things I thought I knew about her turned out not to be true."

"She lied to you?"

"No, not really. She just didn't tell me things." Reilly gazed back at Sean. "And I didn't pick it up, or maybe I didn't want to. Either way, I was partly responsible."

"For what?" Sean asked gently.

Her death, Reilly thought. "It not working out."

"Feeling gun-shy?"

Reilly grimaced. "I wouldn't have said so a few weeks ago. I was pretty content with the way my life was going. I wasn't looking for anything."

"And then something shook it up."

"Someone." Reilly sighed. "I'm not sure what I'm doing, and the timing sucks."

Sean laughed. "Like I said, that sounds about right. The redhead I saw you with after the game?"

"Yes. Liz."

"She's nice looking."

"She's gorgeous."

Sean laughed again. "True, but I was trying not to sound shallow. So are you dating?"

"No. I'm not sure I'm going to be seeing her again at all." Reilly stood up and stowed the sparring gear in the cabinet. "Thanks for the workout. And for...listening."

"Any time. And thanks for punching me in the face."

"Any time."

Reilly changed back into her street clothes, said goodbye to Sean, and headed down to her car. The workout had been rough, mentally and physically. She was tired and sore. But not tired enough or sore enough to have calmed the unrest stirred by Liz's kiss.

❖

Candace, wearing a tight pink T-shirt, baggy jeans, and strap-sandals, flopped onto the nearly threadbare sofa in front of the open windows in Bren's West Philadelphia Victorian and propped her feet up on the steamer trunk that stood in for a coffee table. She'd arrived with her blond curls still damp from the shower half an hour after Bren had called.

"God," Candace sighed, balancing a glass of wine on her stomach. "Sometimes I wish I still lived here. I think I might have had some of the best sex of my life on this sofa."

"Thank you for that image," Bren said, curling up with a cup of coffee in an equally worn armchair across from the sofa. It wasn't yet noon and a bit early for her and wine. She had changed out of her holey sweats into a decent pair before Liz had arrived, but hadn't bothered with shoes.

"Well it's no secret," Candace scoffed. "You walked in on me in the throes enough times."

"I kept my eyes closed." Bren grinned mischievously. "Most of the time."

Sometimes, Bren agreed with Candace about turning back the clock. The three of them had rented the house for four years until Liz and Candace could afford to move into their own places. Bren had purchased the house then and renovated it to suit her needs. She'd kept some of their old furniture for her office, a tall-ceilinged room with walnut floors and deep bay windows, a fireplace on one wall, and a view of the brick-walled rear garden. She made enough money from her book royalties that she could have re-furnished the entire house, but she didn't want to. The office, where she slipped into another world to write and dream, was her sanctuary and her favorite room in the whole house. Sometimes she'd look up from her computer, expecting to see Candace wrapped up in her latest flame on the sofa and Liz bent over a lawbook, a glass of red wine in one hand. Seeing the empty room always hurt a little until she remembered they would always be there.

"Some memories never go away," Bren teased.

Carrying a glass of iced tea, Liz sat down next to Candace and nudged her with her knee. "And you still hog the couch. Move over."

Candace shifted an inch and patted Liz's thigh. "So let's hear it. I can't imagine how you managed to get yourself into trouble since we just saw you..." She glanced at her Piaget. "Thirteen hours ago."

"I won't ask what *you've* been doing for the last thirteen hours," Liz grumbled.

"I'll be happy to tell you. In detail. But you first."

"You don't have to tell us," Bren cut in. "You've got a love bite on your neck."

"I don't. God damn it. Where? I *told* her not to..." Candace broke off, her eyes narrowing as she lasered in on Bren. "That is not funny, Brenda Louise."

"Sorry." Bren glanced apologetically at Liz. "So what happened?"

Candace had made Liz promise on the phone not to say anything until she arrived, and the wait hadn't helped Liz clear up her confusion. "I don't even know where to start."

"Okay," Candace said brightly. "Let's start with rough and rowdy Reilly. Would that be a good guess?"

"She isn't." Liz thought of how Reilly always seemed to know exactly what she needed without her even asking. Without her even knowing, sometimes. "She's tender and thoughtful." At Candace's raised eyebrows, Liz said, "I mean it. She's a lot more gentle than she looks."

When Candace feigned a yawn, Bren kicked the bottom of her foot. "Cut it out."

"Okay, sorry. Sorry," Candace said, looking not the least bit chagrined. "But really—with the way she came on last night? All sweaty and aggressive and competitive?"

"She is," Liz said, "but that's not all she is." She sipped her tea and added quietly, "This morning she kissed me."

"Wow," Bren said, genuinely surprised.

"Really," Candace said coolly. "And just how did that come about."

"Cand," Bren said with a bit of heat in her voice, "do you think you can be quiet long enough for Liz to tell us?"

Candace shot her a look, but obediently pressed her lips together.

"After breakfast I—"

"You spent the night with her?" Candace shot upright.

"No," Liz said patiently. "I drove her home last night because she had too much to drink. When I offered to bring her back to her car this morning, she wanted to take me out to breakfast. Are you with me so far?"

Candace made a hurry up motion with her hand.

"Well, that's it really. I drove her to her car and she kissed me." Liz shrugged. "I guess it really isn't that big of a deal."

"Except for the fact that you hardly know her," Bren pointed out reasonably.

"And she's not your type," Candace added quickly.

"And you just broke up with Julia—the bitch," Bren chimed in.

"And you're pregnant," Candace said darkly.

Liz sighed. "Okay. Reasonable points."

She pulled her legs up onto the old, nappy sofa and curled her arms around them. Resting her cheek against her knees, she wished she were back in law school, still living here, when everything had seemed so critical but in retrospect had been far simpler than she'd ever realized. Candace had been fresh-faced and so filled with life and spirit that even when she was breaking hearts, including her own, Liz couldn't help but love her. Bren had always been there, sturdy and solid and strong. She was the rock, despite being the smallest of all of them in size. And Liz had known just what she wanted in life. A career, a partner, a family. It had never occurred to her that the things she wanted would be at odds.

"Was it a good kiss?" Candace asked grudgingly.

"Terrific," Liz muttered.

"Do you like her?" Bren asked

"Yes." That was one thing Liz was certain of. She knew there were things about Reilly she didn't know, almost certainly important things. Things about Annie, for sure. Whenever Reilly spoke of her something dark, something more than the pain of loss, surfaced in her eyes. But even though Liz knew there were secrets, she trusted her.

"Let's look at this logically," Bren suggested.

"Have you ever considered that kind of approach might be the reason you never accept a date?" Candace said. "There's nothing logical about lust. You see, you want, ergo, you screw."

Liz laughed wryly and Bren smiled.

"That's your formula," Bren replied. "Some of us actually think about things like who and why and what happens the next day."

Candace tilted her head contemplatively. "That sounds a lot like pouring cold water on flames to control a fire. If you're not careful, all you end up with is ashes."

"Maybe." Bren couldn't disagree too strongly, because she had a feeling under the right circumstances she just might take Candace's route. If she'd had the opportunity to take the blonde's place in the bathroom a few nights before, if she could have been the nameless woman dictating her needs, controlling the events, she would have done it.

"You know," Liz said wearily, "I wish I could be more like you, Cand. I actually even thought about you this morning, when I was kissing Reilly and what I really wanted to do was tear her clothes off— or have her tear off mine. I knew you would do it, and love it, and I wished I could too."

"You wanted to tear her clothes off?" Candace sounded stunned.

Liz nodded. "For a few seconds, yeah. I did. God, she's got a beautiful mouth."

"Uh-oh," Bren murmured.

"What?" Liz said, turning to Bren.

"I never heard you say anything like that about Julia."

"Sure I did. When we first met. I said she was hot and sexy and—"

"No you didn't," Bren and Candace said simultaneously.

"Well, I'm sure I meant to."

Candace ran the tip of her open-toed sandal up and down Liz's calf. "You did used to say that I had a great tongue."

Liz almost said that every woman in Philadelphia could probably testify to Candace's skills, but held back because she knew what very few others ever realized. Underneath Candace's seductive bravado, some part of that insecure farm girl still remained, and Liz would never hurt her.

"In the positive column," Bren interjected, "what do we have besides the fact that she's…ah…got a beautiful mouth." Silently, she contemplated the phrase and found it perfect. She couldn't wait to find a place for it in her next chapter.

"She looks really good when she sweats," Candace supplied helpfully.

"She's smart and listens and…" Liz laughed. "She turns me on."

"Debit column?"

Liz sighed. "I just came out of a long, complicated, unsatisfying relationship with Julia, and that's not even really over. And of course," she placed her hand on her abdomen and smiled crookedly, "there's the little matter of Junior or Junior-ess."

"So what do we have," Bren said thoughtfully. "You're attracted to her but there are complications." She glanced at Liz's hand where it still lay on Liz's belly. "That pretty much changes everything, doesn't it?"

"It certainly does," Liz admitted.

"What are you going to do?" Bren asked.

"The only thing I know for sure is that I'm going to apologize and explain to her why I cut and ran in the middle of a kiss I let go too far."

"You don't have to see her again, you know," Candace said.

"Yes I do. She kissed me first, but I kissed her back. That's reason enough to explain." Liz felt better for having made the decision. "There's a game tomorrow. I'll talk to her afterwards. Parker is probably playing, Candace."

"Probably," Candace said casually, "but I don't plan on seeing her again. We had our night of ecstasy. I'll go to keep you company, though."

"Me too," Bren said, wondering if Jae, as she now routinely thought of the dark-haired stranger, would be there.

Liz took Candace's hand and stretched the other out to Bren, who took it.

"Thanks. I think I'm going to need you two tomorrow."

CHAPTER ELEVEN

Liz tucked the Audi into a narrow spot between a Hummer and a Harley hog. "Gotta love lesbians," she murmured.

"I'm doing my part," Candace said from the passenger seat.

Bren leaned forward between the bucket seats. "Everybody's on the field. Did we miss the start?"

"It's warm-ups, I think," Liz replied, cutting the engine and checking her watch. She'd wanted to arrive early enough to talk to Reilly. She hadn't been able to think of anything else for the last twenty-four hours, and she'd slept poorly. Unfortunately, traffic had been backed up along the River Drive because of an early evening concert at the open air theatre in the park, and it had taken longer than anticipated to reach Belmont Plateau. Now, cranky and anxious to find Reilly, she exited the car and shaded her eyes as she scanned the playing fields.

"Can you see where the Angels are playing?"

"There's a team with black jerseys right over there," Candace pointed to her left.

"I don't see…no, that's not them. The Angels' shirts have white lettering."

"Parker's team is straight across from us," Bren noted.

Candace looked disinterested. "There's Reilly's team—on the far side, just down the hill from the building."

"Right next to the field where Parker's playing," Bren added, searching the figures stretched out on the slope behind the playing fields and seated in groups under the scattered trees, hoping to see a familiar stranger.

"I'm going to see if I can catch Reilly before the game," Liz said, starting onto the grassy expanse that stretched for a quarter of a mile in all directions.

Bren grabbed her arm. "You can't cut across the fields, not while they're warming up. You could get hit with a ball or run into by a fielder who isn't looking where—"

"I can see," Liz said irritably. "And the last time I checked, my legs were working. I can get out of the way."

"Bren's right," Candace put in. "You need to walk around the outside of the fields."

"It'll take an extra ten minutes," Liz griped.

Bren patted her arm soothingly. "Reilly is going to be here all night."

"All right," Liz acquiesced. "Fine. But can we get go—"

"Isn't that Parker?" Bren asked, indicating two people coming toward them with a large cooler swinging between them.

"Go ahead you two," Candace said. "I'll catch up in a minute."

"Sure?" Liz asked.

Candace shrugged nonchalantly. "Go."

Liz and Bren waved to Parker, then hurried off.

"Hey," Parker said, slowing as she drew alongside Candace. "We've got cold beer here thanks to Mandy, if you're ready for one."

Candace glanced at the young blonde wearing skimpy shorts and a bikini top that barely covered her nipples, who she assumed was Mandy. "Looks like you've got a little bit more than beer."

"Yeah well, maybe." Grinning, Parker shrugged, but her eyes searched Candace's intently.

"I'll pass," Candace said. It was always important to establish the rules, and the rule had always been one night, and one night only. Oh, she'd broken her own rule a few times and gotten away with it, but it was never smart. She had learned very quickly not to trust a woman who said she didn't want anything other than a good time, because too often, the next morning she wanted more. Liz had been the only woman with whom she'd been tempted to change the game, but she hadn't been able to. She'd fucked it up and almost lost one of the most important people in her life. She wouldn't make that mistake again.

"You sure?" Parker asked. "I can save you one. Come collect it later."

"No," Candace said, careful to keep her voice light and her smile friendly. "Something tells me you'll have plenty of takers. Have a good game, Parker."

"Thanks, I will." Parker turned her grin on Mandy. "Ready to haul this across the field, baby?"

"Anything ya want, ya got it."

Candace watched them go, Mandy's tight little ass swaying with every step. *"Anything ya want." I'll just bet. God, Parker, have all your brains dropped into your crotch? Jesus.*

Annoyed as much with herself as with Parker's undiscriminating tastes, Candace headed off in the direction Liz and Bren had disappeared. A hundred women waited on the other side of the field, and one of them would be perfect to take her mind off Parker.

❖

Reilly fielded a ground ball and underhanded it to second for the first out in a double play just as she saw Liz settle onto a wooden bench on the sidelines. Fortunately, it was only warm up and not the first inning, because her concentration immediately went all to hell. She hadn't thought she would ever see Liz again. She'd been watching the parking lot and the adjoining fields for the last hour, and had eventually decided that Liz wasn't coming. Why should she? Liz had made it pretty clear that Reilly had gone somewhere Liz didn't want to go with that kiss.

There wasn't any reason for Liz to come back to the field. Except she had. Reilly squinted, trying to make out if Liz was watching her.

"Reilly, heads up!"

A ball whizzed past her ear.

"Reilly, get your head in the game," Sean yelled from center field. "You almost got it taken off."

"Gonna get a drink," Reilly yelled to no one in particular and hustled off the field. She sprinted down the outside of the third-base line, behind the backstop, and toward Liz.

Liz watched her coming, hoping she'd see a smile or some other sign of welcome. What she saw instead was worry and uncertainty. She hated knowing she put that look there. She'd had plenty of practice in court ordering her thoughts and speaking under pressure, swaying others to her opinion, but as she stood to meet Reilly, everything she planned to say went right out of her head.

"Hi Liz," Reilly said.

"I was hoping I'd get here sooner." Liz noticed several women watching them, and stepped a few feet further away from the bench. Reilly followed. "I need to talk to you. I want to explain about yesterday."

"Liz," Reilly sighed. "You don't need—"

"Yes I do. It's important to me. Please."

"Hey," Reilly murmured, reaching out as if to touch Liz's arm, then drawing back. "Okay. Sure. That's fine. We can talk."

Liz wished Reilly would touch her. She didn't usually crave physical connection, which is probably why she hadn't noticed that she and Julia hadn't shared much for months. But the memory of the barely restrained tension in Reilly's body as she'd held her yesterday, the tight hard feel of Reilly's arms around her, kept intruding on her thoughts. For all her gentleness, Reilly was physically commanding, and Liz liked it.

"Can I take you out for a drink after the game?" Liz asked, even though that hadn't been her plan. Now that they were face to face and the game was about to start, Liz wanted, no *needed*, more than just a few minutes. She wanted to be alone with her.

Reilly rocked back on her heels, her arms folded across her chest. For a second, she gazed past Liz with a distant expression, and Liz was afraid she was going to say no. Liz held her breath.

"How about pizza at my place?" Reilly asked.

Liz felt her smile stretch across her face. "Yes. Yes, that would be perfect."

❖

Candace jostled the strangers who crowded around her in front of the Angels' bench, trying to see over their heads to the next field where Parker's team played. Now and then she caught glimpses of Parker on the mound, stretching her long body, rolling her shoulders, strutting. She smiled to herself, recalling the pleasure of that body moving sensuously over hers and just exactly what those long sensitive fingers could do to her hot and ready flesh. When she caught herself in the midst of an erotic daydream starring herself and Parker, she resolutely looked away.

She had plenty to occupy her right here in front of her. The woman crouched at third base for Reilly's team looked yummy. Short and compact and a little scruffy, she was exactly Parker's simmering, sophisticated opposite. An ice cold beer to Parker's aged, single malt Scotch. Yes indeed, what she needed was a little changeup to shift her fantasies onto the next encounter. Cocking her hip, she smiled at the cutie, who grinned back and gave her a leering once over. Candace made a bet with herself that they wouldn't make it out of the parking lot. Ms. Tough Guy would probably come while she was fucking Candace—the butch ones like her often lost it too soon. Parker hadn't though, she'd held back her own pleasure until Candace was ready. There hadn't been anything particularly submissive about Parker, but she had been content to let Candace lead. Except…except when she had been teasing her, holding her and making her beg to come. There weren't many women who could make her beg.

Candace shook herself when she realized she was back in bed with Parker again. Damn it, what was it about that woman? All right, she was good-looking. She was great in bed. She wasn't afraid to look Candace in the eye, to search for more than Candace was content to let people see. But really, was that all that special? Candace shied away from that line of contemplation and searched for her girl du jour on the field.

The game came to an abrupt halt when a woman ran onto the field shouting for Reilly. Like everyone else, Candace crowded up to the sideline to see what was going on.

"Reilly," Candace heard the woman wheeze between pants, "sorry. Sorry. We need you…on field five. Parker got hit with a…line drive. Can you come?"

"Sure." Reilly tossed her glove in the general direction of the Angels' bench and dashed off with the still-gasping woman.

Candace didn't give it a thought. She raced after them. By the time she reached the next field, a small crowd had gathered around the pitcher's mound and she couldn't see anything.

"Excuse me. Excuse me," she said sharply, shouldering her way closer. "I need to get through. Could you move please."

Maybe it was her tone of voice, or possibly her sharp elbows, but no one challenged her. After a minute of not-so-subtle shoving, she reached the center of the throng. Reilly knelt by Parker's shoulder, murmuring something Candace couldn't hear. Parker lay on her back, her arms and legs frighteningly still. Candace stepped over Parker's inert form and knelt opposite Reilly, who gently probed Parker's face.

"What happened?" Candace whispered.

Reilly didn't look up. "She caught a line drive in the cheek."

Parker's right eye was completely swollen shut and already turning purple. A thin trickle of blood ran down from the corner, and a host of butterflies took flight in Candace's stomach. She wasn't ordinarily the queasy type, but seeing Parker hurt threw her more than she expected. Candace tenderly touched the top of Parker's head and discovered her hair was wet. She gasped, thinking it was blood. When she realized it was sweat, the relief made her shaky.

"Is she unconscious?"

"No," Parker muttered. "It just hurts like hell to move." Her left eye flickered open. "Candace?"

"Hi."

Parker grinned weakly. "Some stunt, huh?"

"Impressive. Be quiet now." Candace stroked her forehead and glanced at Reilly. "Should I call an ambulance?"

"Someone already did."

"Don't need one," Parker said, closing her eye again.

"Your cheekbone feels okay," Reilly said, "but you ought to be x-rayed. You could have an orbital fracture and I'd never be able to tell."

"Can it wait until tomorrow?"

"Probably," Reilly said, "but you should do it tonight."

"Don't be an ass, Parker," Candace said sharply. "Go to the ER like Reilly says."

"What happened to you being all comforting and nice?" Parker asked.

Candace snorted. "That was before I knew you were faking most of it."

Eye still closed, Parker grinned. "Damn."

"Someone should go with you," Candace said. "Which one of these little groupies did you settle on?"

"The blonde."

"Got a thing for blondes," Candace muttered, searching the crowd.

Mandy and at least six other blondes stood around, all of them looking like they'd love to be in Candace's position. That was enough to make her say, "Never mind, I'll go with you."

Sounding oddly serious, Parker said, "You don't need to. I'll be fine."

"Probably. But I've had enough softball for tonight."

In the distance, sirens sounded and rapidly became louder.

Candace reached down and squeezed Parker's hand, surprised when Parker gripped it and didn't let go. "Our ride's here."

"Good. I'm not…feeling so great."

"Uh-oh," Reilly said, instantly sliding a hand behind Parker's neck. "Candace, hold her head steady, would you?"

Without a word, Candace shifted around and gently put both hands on either side of Parker's head. Reilly rolled Parker slightly to her side just as she vomited.

"Oh, poor baby," Candace murmured, glancing anxiously at Reilly. "Is she all right?"

"Yeah," Reilly said, taking a bandanna someone held down to her and wiping Parker's face with one hand while continuing to support her neck with the other. "Let's roll her back. Slowly. Good. It's probably just a reflex from the bang to her head. But she definitely needs a CAT scan now."

"Will you come with us?" Candace asked, suddenly frightened. She knew what emergency rooms could be like for someone who didn't have an edge in the system. And more than that, Reilly made her feel safe. "I know you don't…"

Reilly met Candace's eyes, and then beyond her, saw Liz and Bren among the onlookers. Liz watched Candace with a worried expression. Reilly liked Parker, and she heard Candace's concern, and she knew Liz would be upset for her friend. The decision wasn't even a decision. "Sure."

"Medics. Coming through," a man shouted, and the crowd parted. A burly guy in his early twenties with a military haircut and a sunburn knelt down. "What do we have here?"

"I'm Dr. Danvers, ortho," Reilly said. "She's a twenty-something female with blunt trauma to the right orbit from a line drive. No documented loss of consciousness and she's been alert and oriented since I got here about three minutes after impact. Right pupil is impossible to examine due to swelling, but the left is round and reactive. She just vomited. Her airway is fine."

As Reilly talked, the medic wrapped a blood pressure cuff around Parker's left upper arm. A second EMT, who had arrived pushing a portable stretcher, inserted an intravenous line into Parker's right hand. Candace stayed where she was, stroking Parker's forehead.

From just behind her, Liz said, "How is she?"

"Reilly says she's okay, but she needs to go to the hospital. I want to go too."

"I'll drive you," Liz said instantly.

"What's your catchment area?" Reilly asked the medic.

"West Philly."

"Can you take her to University Hospital?"

"Sure can."

"Okay, thanks," Reilly said as the two men log rolled Parker onto the backboard. "I'll drive over there. Would you tell them in admitting I'm on my way. It's Danvers."

"You got it." The big guy scanned the fields and the clusters of women. "Who's winning?"

"We were," Parker muttered.

The EMT laughed. "There's always next week."

Reilly turned to Candace. "I can call you later, if you want. There's no reason for you to hang around the ER for hours."

"That's okay," Candace said. "I just need to tell your third baseman to hold a certain thought until the next game."

"Sure thing," Reilly said. "Although stay clear of the catcher. That's her girlfriend."

Candace raised an eyebrow.

Bren took Candace's arm. "Let's go before you start a riot."

Liz turned to Reilly as Bren led Candace away. "Thanks."

"Don't mention it," Reilly said. "I'm going to grab my gear. Maybe you can collect Parker's. Someone will know what's hers. Then I'll see you at the hospital."

"Okay."

Reilly hesitated a second, then ran off. Liz went in search of Parker's gear, feeling as if fate kept dealing her the Joker and laughing.

CHAPTER TWELVE

R eilly pulled back the curtain on the exam cubicle and nodded to the heavy-set redhead who leaned over Parker, carefully palpating her face. Parker reclined on the partially elevated stretcher, the right side of her face even more swollen than it had been an hour before. However, her left eye was open, and she seemed alert and fairly comfortable.

"Hi, Parker," Reilly said. "Doing okay?"

"Not bad."

"Tom," Reilly said to the plastic and reconstructive surgeon, "what are you doing here on a Sunday night?"

"I happened to be in the OR for an emergency trach when the consult came in." He shone a penlight into Parker's left eye, then carefully pried open her right eyelid and examined her right eye. "You got a case?"

"No. Parker's a friend of mine. I was there right after she got hit," Reilly informed him. "She wasn't as badly swollen then, and I didn't feel anything suspicious. Of course, I'm used to dealing with bigger bones."

Tom straightened and addressed Parker. "Everything feels good, but we'll need a CT scan to look at the floor of the orbit. Sometimes when the eye socket sustains blunt trauma, the increased pressure fractures the small bones underneath the eye."

"And then what happens?" Parker said.

"It depends on how badly they're displaced, if at all. Most of the time, we don't need to do anything."

"And if they are displaced?"

"Then we'll need to operate." He tapped her arm. "Let's wait and see what the films show first. There's no point talking about what we might need to do until we have some more facts. I'll check back with you after I review them."

"Okay." Parker shifted her gaze to Reilly as the surgeon left. "Did, uh, the others come over?"

"Candace, Liz, Bren, and a couple of your teammates are in the waiting room."

"You should tell them I'm okay and to take off."

"I'll give them the message," Reilly said, "but I don't think any of them are going anywhere. It might be a little while before you go down for the scan. I'll see if I can hurry that up."

"Thanks. Thanks for everything."

"I ought to be able to bring someone back here to keep you company while you wait, too. Any requests?"

Parker's grin was obvious, even though only the left side of her mouth lifted. "Only one?"

"The ER people like to keep the noise level down."

"Candace."

"Good choice," Reilly replied dryly.

"Crazy, probably."

Reilly clasped her forearm briefly. "I'll get her."

❖

"You know you don't have to stay," Parker murmured.

"You look like hell," Candace said, leaning over the side rail and squeezing Parker's hand. "Does it hurt much?"

"I've got a mother of a headache."

"How's your stomach?"

"Starving."

"Back to normal then." Candace patted Parker's midsection casually, and when the muscles beneath the thin cotton hospital gown tensed beneath her fingers, she pulled her hand back sharply. That brief touch telegraphed an image of the way Parker's stomach went rigid just before she orgasmed, and the memory brought a wave of heat surging through her. Even Liz, who had been Candace's first, hadn't aroused her so thoroughly so quickly. Danger signals flared so brightly that she wanted to walk—no, she wanted to run—from the room.

"What's the matter?" Parker asked.

"Nothing," Candace said brightly.

"You just got really pale." Parker reached through the stainless steel bars and caught Candace's hand. "Are you feeling okay?"

"You're the one who looks like a train wreck."

"Did you have dinner?"

"What I need is one of those beers," Candace said. Actually, she needed more than that. What she needed was a couple of martinis and another woman to take the edge off the intensity of her memories. Another body to replace the feel of Parker's hands, Parker's mouth, Parker's soft moans.

"Want Mandy's number?" Parker teased. "She's got the cooler."

"Pleeease." Candace rolled her eyes. "Blond airheads are not my type, even if she does have a great ass."

"I didn't notice that."

"Uh-huh. I'll just bet."

"No, seriously," Parker said with a hint of her devil-may-care spirit surfacing, "I'm just partial to blondes."

Candace leaned closer again. "I may be blond, but that's the only similarity."

"No question. Your ass is much better than Mandy's."

Candace threaded her fingers through Parker's, not even realizing she'd done it until the heat of Parker's palm seared her skin. The feel of Parker's fingers slipping between hers made her tremble inside in a way that was more than lust. The excitement was exhilarating, and terrifying.

"Well at least we know you don't have a concussion," Candace said, "since your brain is still functioning."

"Everything else is functioning too," Parker whispered.

Candace saw no point in pretending she didn't hear the invitation. Parker was too sharp for that, and despite her free and easy lifestyle, Candace didn't play games.

"I don't do repeats."

"Neither do I," Parker said.

"Good. Then we understand each other."

"Perfectly."

For just a second, Candace felt disappointed. Then, with the next breath, relief took its place and she smiled, happy to be on comfortable ground again.

"Friends then," Candace said lightly. "Nice and simple."

"Absolutely." Carefully, Parker released her hold on Candace's hand and drew hers back through the bars, letting it fall onto the bed. "Nice and simple."

❖

"Want something from the vending room?" Bren asked Liz. "It's after nine. You should eat something."

"I'm not really hungry," Liz said. The waiting room had emptied out over the last hour, and only one old man half-asleep in the corner and two teenaged girls, drinking soda and laughing along with a sitcom on the overhead television, remained. The stark white walls, eye-watering fluorescent lighting, and dingy gray tile-floor gave the place a bleak institutional feel, and Liz couldn't help comparing it to the carpeted floors, fabric chairs and soothing color schemes of the OB offices in the private clinic area of the hospital. That train of thought reminded her that if she didn't eat, she'd wake up in the middle of the night with heartburn. Another new development. "I guess I should have something. I just can't face the thought of microwaved machine food."

"You don't have to risk that," Reilly said, walking up to them. "I offered pizza, remember?"

"How is she," Liz said, standing. Bren and Parker's teammates joined them.

"The CT scan looks good. The surgeon's with her now. He saw some swelling behind the globe—the eyeball—and he might want her to stay overnight for observation."

"But no surgery?" Bren asked.

"Not likely. Not unless some problem develops with the pressure in her eye."

"That's great," Liz said.

"Excellent," one of Parker's teammates said. "We're going to make some calls and let everyone know she's okay. Thanks!"

"No problem," Reilly called as the women hurried off. Then, taking in both Bren and Liz, she asked, "So, how about it? Pizza?"

Bren hesitated, clearly waiting for Liz to make the decision.

"Yes," Liz replied. They all needed to eat, and after the hours of waiting and worrying, she had a feeling none of them really wanted to be alone. She knew she didn't. She wanted to be with her friends. And…she wanted to be with Reilly.

Reilly grinned. "Okay, why don't we—"

"Oh good, you're still here," Candace said, rushing in from the corridor. "The surgeon said Parker can go home if someone stays with her tonight. I volunteered us."

"Us?" Liz and Bren said simultaneously.

Reilly raised an eyebrow.

"Well," Candace said, cocking a hip and shrugging, "I don't know anything about edema and increased intra-ocular pressure and all those other things on the list."

"And we do?" Liz and Bren exclaimed.

"One of us does," Candace remarked, sliding a look in Reilly's direction.

"Oh, that's not fair," Liz said. "It's one thing to volunteer us, but Reilly's been here all night, and—"

"I don't mind," Reilly said. "We'll order some pizzas and I'll keep an eye on Parker for an hour or two."

Liz turned her back on her friends and lowered her voice. "Reilly, are you sure? Don't you have to work in the morning?"

"I have office hours all day tomorrow. No surgery. Besides, I'm used to getting by on just a few hours' sleep."

"You've already done more than your share."

"I like Parker." Reilly smiled. "And remember, I promised you pizza."

Liz hesitated, but it was hard to look into Reilly's eyes and argue. It was also hard to deny that she didn't want to say good night to her. She turned to Candace.

"Where are we taking her? Her place or yours?"

Candace smiled sweetly. "Well, Parker lives on the Main Line and we really don't want to spend all that time in the car. My place isn't all that big, but the sofa in Bren's office is *so* comfy…"

"My place," Bren said, shaking her head in fond exasperation. "Sure. Let's get her out of here. Then let's have a party."

❖

"Martini for me," Candace said, setting a drink on a metal tray decorated with hand-painted birds. "Thank God at last. Wine for you, Bren." She passed Bren a glass. "Ginger ale for Parker." She poured soda into a glass, placed it next to her Martini, and frowned at Bren. "Who in the world has ginger ale in their cupboard?"

"I do," Bren said, perched on a stool in front of the cook island in her large country-style kitchen. She had opened the rear sliding glass doors, and a sultry summer's night breeze wafted through the room. "And lucky for you, too."

"That's me, the lucky type." Candace lifted the tray and said to Reilly, "Beer in the fridge if you're drinking, or there's soda or…" she glanced at Liz, "whatever."

"I'll get it," Liz said, opening the refrigerator and finding another ginger ale for herself. She looked over her shoulder. "Beer, Reilly?"

"That's fine. Anything is good."

Bren followed behind Candace, wine glass in hand. "I'll make sure Parker has everything she needs up there. Do you two want to wait down here for the pizza?"

Liz wondered how it was that Bren always read the situation right. She always knew which one of them needed to be alone, or alone with someone else, and she always knew which one needed to talk, or be held, or just have someone to cry with. She wished she had been able to give Bren half the support that Bren had given her over the years. On impulse, she stopped her and pulled her into a hug. "Thanks."

"Don't worry," Brenda whispered, giving Liz's cheek a quick peck. "I'll think of some way for you to pay me back."

"Any time. Say the word." Liz opened her soda and gestured to the small deck that adjoined Bren's fenced flagstone patio. "Why don't we wait outside. We'll hear the doorbell when the pizza guy gets here."

"Sure."

Outside, the sky was unusually black and littered with stars, the moon a perfect white disc shadowed with secrets. The rear of Bren's house and all the others on her block faced the backs of the buildings on the next block over. Most of the windows in the paired Victorians were open, and from a few the sounds of muted voices, occasional laughter, and fragments of music floated down to them. For an instant, Liz had the disorienting sensation that she was twenty-six again, and she and Bren and Candace were having a party, and before the night was out, she'd end up making love with a beautiful girl who would make all her dreams come true. She sighed and sipped her soda.

"You sound sad," Reilly commented. She rested her beer can on the top rail and turned sideways to face Liz.

"Sad? No, nostalgic." Liz laughed shortly, casting Reilly a sideways glance. "The three of us lived here what feels like a million years ago. Actually, I moved out five years ago. God, there are nights when I feel old."

"You're not," Reilly said. "You left to move in with Julia?"

"Yes." Liz turned and rested her hips against the railing, glancing up at the second floor window where she knew Parker was stretched out on the sofa. She could almost see Candace curled up beside her in the big chair and Bren on the other side of the room, probably behind the big heavy oak library table that she used as a desk. There had been many a night when she'd wished she could be back in that room with decisions yet to be made. Decisions that she would make differently this time.

"Do you miss her?"

"What?" A second or two passed while Liz deciphered the question. "Oh. Julia. No. God, that sounds hard, doesn't it."

"Not really. I can tell it still hurts."

Liz sighed. "I'll tell you what hurts. What hurts is not knowing exactly when things started to go bad. Not knowing why, or why I didn't see something sooner. Do something earlier."

"Probably because you kept hoping things would work out."

"Probably, and that sounds pathetic."

Reilly sipped her beer. "Are you always so hard on yourself?"

"Are you always so kind?"

"No. Not at all." Reilly looked at the buildings behind them, but her expression said she was seeing something else. "Most of the time I'm so wrapped up in what I'm doing, work mostly, that I'm oblivious to what's happening with other people."

"I've never noticed that."

"Things are different with you," Reilly said cautiously. "Sometimes, when I know you're sad, I just want to reach out and take the unhappiness away."

"Reilly," Liz murmured.

"I know. I know it's—it's crazy. We just met a few weeks ago." Reilly took a step closer, her hand coming to rest on Liz's hip. She hadn't meant to touch her. She never touched women, not even casually. When she was around Liz, she couldn't seem to stop touching her. Words never seemed to be enough. She was never certain if she was making herself clear. "I know I jumped the gun yesterday. I just…when you talk about Julia I can see you hurting and I…I want to…I don't know. I…"

"Wait," Liz said, pressing her fingers to Reilly's mouth. "Wait."

Reilly closed her eyes, afraid she'd gone too far, too fast again. Liz's skin was so soft against her mouth. It was so easy to imagine those soft fingers slipping through her hair and brushing over her body. She shuddered and slid her other hand around Liz's waist. She hadn't known she'd wanted this, needed this. She leaned closer and her thighs touched Liz's. Liz's swift gasp was like gas to a flame, and Reilly ignited. She tossed her head and pushed Liz's hand away, then kissed her. This kiss wasn't tentative like the first uncertain taste had been the day before. This time she claimed Liz's mouth without apology, her tongue playing insistently over Liz's lips. She nibbled on Liz's lower lip until Liz whimpered, and then she soothed it with gentle licks. Holding Liz more firmly, she kissed along the edge of her jaw and down her throat. Liz's hands roamed her back, digging into her muscles, calling her blood to rise.

"I've wanted to do this since yesterday," Reilly groaned, skimming her hands up Liz's sides, then back down over her hips. Liz's thighs parted and Reilly insinuated her pelvis between them. "You feel so good. God, Liz, you feel so good."

Lightheaded, her vision hazy, Liz cradled Reilly's head in her hands, forcing her to meet her eyes. "Listen to me." Her breath was coming so quickly it was hard to form words. While Reilly's mouth had been on hers, while Reilly's body had been tight to hers, turning her liquid inside, the world had disappeared. No past, no future. Only the moment, and the moment had been Reilly and what Reilly made her feel. She wanted her. She wanted that moment of absolute perfect freedom to stretch backward through time and undo the hurts and the mistakes she'd made. She wanted the moment to continue, endlessly, dissolving all fear and uncertainty. That moment of connection, that moment when she felt herself not alone, but sharing breath and body and secret hopes, was worth almost any price. Almost.

"I need you to know something," Liz murmured.

"Julia," Reilly gasped.

"No. Yes, but not what you're thinking."

Reilly grew very still. "What then?"

Liz had thought of nothing except how to say this, how to explain, but the kisses rattled her. "I'm pregnant."

Reilly jerked her head free of Liz's hands and looked down, as if she were actually going to see something. "How…how far along?"

Even in the moonlight, Liz could see Reilly's face drained of color. "Almost eleven weeks."

"Eleven weeks." Reilly's voice sounded hollow. She shook her head as if someone had struck her, then she dropped her hands and stepped back. "How could Julia leave you?"

It was the last thing Liz expected her to say. And there was such sadness in her voice that Liz found tears filling her eyes, but she didn't know for whom she was crying. Herself or Reilly or someone else.

"She doesn't know."

Reilly laughed, a hollow, tortured sound. "I didn't know Annie was pregnant either. Not until after she died."

"Oh God," Liz whispered. "Reilly."

"You should tell her, Liz. Give her a chance."

"It wouldn't make any difference."

"You don't know that." Reilly took another step away, the shadows slowly swallowing her. "I need to check Parker."

The doorbell rang in the distance.

"The pizza. I'll get it," Liz said dully, but Reilly had already disappeared into the house.

Liz made way her through the empty, silent rooms to the front door, tipped the delivery boy, and carried the pizza boxes upstairs. Reilly knelt by Parker's side, talking to her quietly. When she straightened and turned towards Liz, her face was blank. When she smiled, Liz saw no warmth in her eyes. The absence of welcome was a new pain to add to the others.

"Parker is doing fine," Reilly said to all of them, her gaze flickering over Liz. "I'll come by to check her again in a few hours. In the meantime, I'll leave my beeper number with you. If there's any problem, anything you're not certain of, just call me and I'll be right over."

"Aren't you staying for pizza?" Bren asked.

Reilly indicated her softball shirt and shorts. "I'm going to head home and get cleaned up."

"Thanks for looking after her," Candace said, sitting on the floor by Parker with her back to the sofa. Parker's eyes were closed but her left hand lay on Candace's shoulder, a lock of hair caught in her fingers.

"You're welcome."

As her footsteps disappeared down the hall, Candace regarded Liz contemplatively.

"Something you want to share?"

For the first time in a long time, Liz shook her head no.

CHAPTER THIRTEEN

Reilly sat in her car in the dark just down the street from Bren's, her hands clamped around the steering wheel so hard her fingers were numb. She should go home. She should go home and forget about Liz. Parker was fine. Candace and Liz and Bren were intelligent enough to take Parker back to the hospital if a problem developed. She didn't need to be making house calls. She didn't need to see Liz again. She didn't need to have some distorted version of her past revisit her, mocking her for her mistakes and offering her a chance to repeat them.

Reilly jumped at the sound of tapping on the passenger side window. When she leaned over and peered out, Liz stared in at her.

"Open the door," Liz called.

"It's unlocked."

After a second's hesitation, Liz opened the door and slid into the front seat. "What are you doing out here?"

"Thinking. What are you doing?"

"Walking."

"You shouldn't be out here alone."

Liz shook her head. "All of a sudden everyone treats me like I'm infirm."

"There's no point taking chances, even if it is a pretty safe neighborhood."

"That's not what I meant."

"Oh." Reilly clenched her jaw. "That's another reason to be careful."

"Let's go for a ride."

Reilly stared. Liz buckled her seatbelt and relaxed in the passenger seat, her hands resting loosely in her lap. Her voice, though, had been tight with tension.

"Where?" Reilly asked.

"Anywhere."

"All right." Reilly started the engine and put the top down. "I've got a sweatshirt in the trunk if you need it."

"I'm not cold," Liz said.

They didn't speak again as Reilly drove through the nearly empty streets of West Philadelphia, past the darkened zoo, past the turn-off to Belmont Plateau and the ball fields, and west along the River Drive. Reilly pulled into an empty parking lot facing the river that cut through the city, and switched off the engine. The cooling motor ticked loudly in the hot, still night air. The river wound through the trees like a black velvet ribbon, the surface shimmering in the moonlight while fireflies danced along the shore.

"I didn't handle that very well," Liz said at last. "I'm sorry I didn't say something sooner."

"I think you tried a couple of times, but I obviously wasn't listening," Reilly said bitterly. Had Annie tried to tell her, too? Jesus, what was wrong with her?

"I was going to tell you yesterday, and then…that kiss. The last thing I expected was to have the slightest interest in kissing anyone," Liz confessed. "And then when I did, my common sense went right out the window."

Reilly shook her head. "I'm a doctor and I bought it when you told me you had the flu. Christ, I never learn."

"I just found out a few weeks ago—the day we met, in fact—and with Julia leaving, I haven't exactly been making announcements to the world."

"And you don't know me at all. There's no reason you should have told me."

"There's a very good reason," Liz said heatedly.

"What's that?"

"You kissed me and I didn't say no."

"Well, you've told me now."

Sadly, Liz accepted there would be no more kisses. With all that was going on in her life, she knew it was for the best. Reilly wasn't the kind of woman to have a casual fling, and as much as she might wish otherwise, neither was she. Especially not now, with a baby coming.

But she couldn't leave things with so much pain between them. "You said Annie died of a stroke."

Reilly stared straight ahead as her stomach churned and the old, deep pain surfaced. "Yes, she did."

"And she was pregnant?"

"Yes."

Liz wanted to know more, but could hear how it was tearing Reilly up to talk about it. For a long minute she considered allowing the past to remain buried, but somehow, she didn't believe it was. She sensed the specter of Annie's death walked through Reilly's life every day and night. "But you didn't know."

"No." Reilly shuddered and watched the moonlight slice over the water. She had never talked about Annie with anyone. "Annie was diagnosed as a teenager with severe diabetes. Like a lot of kids faced with a potentially lethal disease, she refused to face how serious it was. From the things she told me, she almost died a couple of times from diabetic coma because she didn't take her meds. She was a little better about that when she got older, but she was still wild. She refused to let anything get in the way of what she wanted."

"Her illness must have been hard for you—for both of you."

"Annie played hard. She lived every minute hard, and you either went along with her for the ride or she left you behind." Reilly sighed. "That wild streak also made her very attractive. I didn't do a whole lot to rein her in."

Liz wanted so badly to reach across the distance between them and take Reilly's hand. Reilly's voice vibrated with so much loss and self-recrimination, and beneath all that, with such bewilderment, that Liz ached. But she'd already crossed boundaries she shouldn't have, especially not with someone like Reilly, who'd already been so hurt.

"You were very young."

"Old enough. I was twenty-three when we met." Reilly leaned her head back. The black sky, pinpointed with stars, stretched endlessly to some time and place she could barely imagine. Beneath it, she felt small and alone and just a little lost. "I didn't see the signs. I didn't see that she was in trouble. I didn't take care of her." She turned on the seat and stared at Liz. "I didn't take care of her, and she died."

"She didn't *tell* you, Reilly."

"She didn't trust me, because she knew I didn't want her to get pregnant."

Liz closed her eyes, Reilly's words cutting through her now as cleanly and brutally as Julia's had that morning Julia had called from California to tell Liz to cancel the appointment with her OB. *I don't want a baby, Liz. I don't want you to get pregnant.*

The message had stunned her. Hearing it repeated now only drove home how right she had been to stop the kiss, no matter how much her body had wanted more. Now, she had to think, plan, make decisions for two—herself and the child she had decided to bring into the world. She was alone, and yet she wasn't.

"I'm sorry," Liz murmured, and she was. For Annie, for Reilly, and for herself, knowing she would never have a chance to find out what might have been between her and Reilly.

"Ready to go back?" Reilly asked, as if reading Liz's mind.

"Yes, I am."

❖

Bren turned on her desk lamp and angled it so that the cone of light fell only on her computer screen. She'd already turned off the room lights when she'd realized Parker and Candace were asleep. Candace, curled up on the end of the sofa with Parker's feet in her lap, had one hand resting on the inside of Parker's knee. They looked connected even as they slept, and young enough to be teenagers. Parker shifted and moaned quietly, and Candace immediately opened her eyes.

"You okay, baby?" she whispered.

Parker mumbled something unintelligible and then her breathing returned to the even cadence of slumber. Candace closed her eyes.

Bren smiled to herself, imagining that Candace would be embarrassed if she knew how tender she appeared in her unguarded moments. Candace had always cultivated that tough girl façade, but it wasn't hard to see beneath it if you took the time to look. Almost no one ever did, or ever wanted to. Parker didn't seem to be bothered by Candace's bravado, or she wasn't buying it. Bren wondered how long it would be before Candace realized Parker was different, and that she was different with her.

Once Bren was certain they had both drifted off again, she

opened her Melanie Richards email account to check the afternoon and evening's messages. She answered a couple of technical questions from her editor, transferred deadline dates to her calendar, and then scanned the message headers from senders she didn't recognize. Halfway down the screen, one header caught her eye.

Re: Jae's mistress

Bren didn't recognize the email address. DarkRider@freemail.com. The message was short.

What is Jae afraid of?

Bren swept the cursor to delete, then hesitated, staring at the question. *It isn't Jae who's afraid.* But she couldn't reveal herself that way—not about something she had never even told her friends. Why then, did it seem that this stranger already knew? Her finger trembled on the mouse, knowing she should ignore the message and move on, safe in her anonymity. Instead she answered, pushing against the walls of her own making.

Jae isn't afraid. She's waiting for the mistress brave enough to free her.

She pushed send, then closed her eyes and fervently wished for the message to dissolve in midair before it ever reached its target. What was she doing?

Her email alert beeped and Bren jumped, her heart racing. She was almost afraid to read the message. She opened her eyes and laughed at her own foolishness. A CNN news bulletin. Just to prove to herself she was being silly, she pushed send/receive again, knowing there would be nothing there. She was wrong.

I'm not afraid. Are you?

A minute passed. Two. Four. Bren didn't move, her fingers completely motionless on the keyboard.

Afraid of what? she typed.

Her email program was set to download mail every five minutes. She could trigger it herself, but she didn't. She had five minutes to get up and walk away from the computer. She could turn it off, and by morning, she'd be herself again. Not Melanie Richards caught in a shadow world populated with faceless women who knelt before her, waiting on her pleasure. Waiting for her pleasure. She didn't move. The only sounds in the room were the quiet sighs of two women sleeping.

Her mail downloaded.

To free me. I'm waiting.

As each minute ticked away and Bren resisted the invitation, she breathed easier. She enjoyed games, even solitary ones, and she recognized this one. She wasn't about to be seduced into revealing anything about herself, but she admired the attempt. Her mail automatically downloaded again.

The Blue Diamond Lounge. Any night after 10.

Bren gasped and quickly closed her email program, then pushed her chair back from the desk as if she could somehow escape the words on her screen. The Blue Diamond Lounge was on Delaware Avenue, a twenty-minute ride from her house.

❖

Liz tiptoed into Bren's office, Reilly close behind her. The ride back had been as silent as the trip to the river. Despite the distance between them, she'd been acutely aware of Reilly less than two feet away, rigidly staring straight ahead. The tight line of her jaw and the rigid set of her shoulders suggested anger, too, but Liz couldn't fathom its source. The sadness and regret and even remorse she understood. There was more going on than she knew, but there were only so many wounds either of them could stand to open in one night, so she had kept silent.

"Hi," Liz whispered to Bren, who sat behind her desk with an oddly blank expression. She might almost be sleeping with her eyes open. "Bren?"

Bren swiveled toward them in her chair and blinked, as if coming back to herself. She smiled. "Did you come to wake the sleeping beauties?"

"Beauty isn't sleeping," Candace murmured. "Only the beast is."

Parker grunted and made a feeble attempt to dig her toes into Candace's midsection. "The beast is awake and ornery."

"You're not allowed to be horny in your condition," Candace warned.

Parker laughed, and then immediately moaned. "Jesus, don't make me laugh. Ow. Damn."

Reilly skirted around Liz to Parker's side. She knelt by the sofa and rested her hand on the top of Parker's head. "Breathe through your mouth and try not to laugh again. It increases the pressure in your head."

"Sorry, I didn't mean that," Candace said quickly. "Is she all right?"

"Can someone turn the lights up?" Reilly asked. "Parker, close your eyes."

Liz reached behind her and raised the dimmer switch, slowly increasing the illumination from the brass chandelier in the center of the high ceiling. "Enough?"

"It's good, thanks." Reilly spent a few minutes examining Parker's face. "Does your eye hurt? Not your eyelids or your cheekbone, but the eyeball itself?"

Parker hesitated and Candace leaned forward, her expression anxious.

"No," Parker finally said. "Everything around it hurts, but my eye feels normal."

"Is it moving beneath your eyelids? I don't want to try to open your lids because at this point it's only going to put more pressure on your eyeball."

Again, Parker hesitated, and Candace slid her hand underneath the leg of Parker's sweatpants and rubbed her calf. Bren had offered her the navy sweats to replace her softball shorts upon their arrival, and the pants were tight and too short for her.

"If you're not sure, Parker," Candace said, "we can go back to the emergency room."

"No, no. I can tell. I'm okay." Parker started to sit up and Reilly gently restrained her.

"Stay down," Reilly instructed. "Changing position like that can also increase the pressure. If you want to sit up, roll on your side and ease up slowly with someone helping you."

"How long is this going to go on," Parker grumped. "I have to go to work in the morning."

Liz laughed. "Parker, honey, you're not going to work this week. You'll scare the clients away."

"Well, I at least have to work from home. I've got a dozen open files on my desk right now."

"The swelling will increase for forty-eight hours, and then start to subside," Reilly said. "We'll get some more ice on it tonight, and the longer you ice it, the faster it will resolve. You *might* be presentable with sunglasses by the end of the week."

"Better." Parker closed her eyes, obviously exhausted.

Reilly stood. "I think everyone can relax. She looks fine. If anything changes, call me."

Candace extricated herself from the tangle of Parker's legs and stood. "Thanks."

"Hey, I'm just glad she won't be pitching this weekend. We ought to be a couple games ahead of them by the time she gets back."

"Don't count on it," Parker muttered darkly.

"Well," Reilly said, suddenly uneasy. "I better go." She glanced at Liz. "Good night."

"Good night," Liz said, although she was quite sure they were saying goodbye. She watched her go, then slumped into the big overstuffed armchair. "What a night."

"So where did you go?" Bren asked.

Candace looked from Bren to Liz. "What did I miss?"

"Nothing," Liz said. "I went for a walk and ran into Reilly. We took a ride for a few minutes, that's all." She shot Bren an apologetic look. "I'm sorry. Were you worried?"

Bren blushed. "I should have been, but I got caught up doing something and didn't realize until I heard you come back how long you'd been gone. You do keep your cell phone with you all the time, right?"

Liz rolled her eyes. "Yes, I have it. I promise I will never be out of contact."

"So," Candace said slowly, "I sensed a little…tension between you and Reilly."

Liz studied Parker, wondering if she was listening.

"She's out of it," Candace said. "I can tell from the way she's breathing."

Bren smiled.

"We finally had our talk," Liz said bleakly. "Let's say there's nothing like a good dose of reality to put the brakes on one's libido."

Candace shook her head. "Darling, haven't you learned by now that you should never subject your libido to too much thought or introspection?"

"What did Reilly say?" Bren interjected.

"It's complicated," Liz said.

"Now there's a news flash," Candace muttered.

"Candace," Bren said, her tone softly warning.

Candace held up her hands. "Okay. Okay. I'll be quiet. It's painful, but I'll manage."

Liz couldn't help but laugh, which felt strange when so much of her resonated with sadness. "Long story short—she's still got some unresolved issues with a former lover who died suddenly."

"Oh, that's too bad," Bren said.

"Definitely trouble there," Candace said.

"How long ago?" Bren asked.

"Quite some time. A few years."

Bren nodded thoughtfully. "Well, sometimes we're more ready than we realize to move on, and it takes meeting someone to recognize that."

Liz studied her, wondering who besides Reilly she was referring to. "And then there's the little matter of her not wanting children."

"Deal breaker there," Candace said nonchalantly.

"Yes," Liz agreed.

Bren said nothing.

"So," Candace said, obviously ready to change the subject. "What are we going to do to celebrate your birthday, Bren? You haven't told us where you want to go yet."

Bren smiled slowly. "Anywhere I want, right?"

"Sky's the limit."

"Okay then. The Blue Diamond."

Candace gaped, for once without a comeback.

"Bren, sweetie," Liz said carefully. "The Blue Diamond is a strip club."

"I know."

CHAPTER FOURTEEN

"C omfortable?" Dr. Marta Thompson asked.

"Oh, absolutely." Liz tried not to grit her teeth. "Of course, I'm about to wet my pants. If I were wearing any."

"She's grumpy this morning," Candace said, perched on a stool by Liz's side.

"I'm not grumpy," Liz grumped.

Marta laughed. "You're allowed. This won't take very long, and then you'll be able to get rid of all that water in your bladder."

"How about all the water in my feet," Liz complained.

"How much swelling are we talking about?" Marta walked to the end of the examination table and pushed back the sheets. She pressed her thumb into Liz's ankle. "I don't see much right now."

"Usually by the end of the day my shoes feel tight."

"But not in the morning?"

"No."

"It's normal to have a little swelling in your legs after you've been active all day, particularly with the kind of heat we've been having. Try to prop them up whenever you can."

"Oh, that'll be easy," Liz muttered, "when I'm in court all day or meeting with doctors and hospital administrators."

"Liz, honey," Candace murmured, leaning close to Liz's ear, "you're going from grumpy to bitchy."

Liz glowered. "Just wait until you're in this situation someday and see how much sympathy you get from me."

Candace laughed, looking horrified. "Oh no. Never."

The doctor smiled and exposed Liz's abdomen, neatly folding the sheet across her pelvis. "Are you two ready to get a look at the baby?"

Liz nodded, suddenly anxious, and reached for Candace's hand.

"Don't worry," Candace whispered. "This is going to be wonderful."

The doctor adjusted the fetal monitor so Liz and Candace could hear the heartbeat as she moved the ultrasound probe over Liz's uterus.

"It's beating so fast," Liz murmured.

"Fast is good," Marta assured her. "Right now it's around 150 beats a minute. Ah, here we are." She pointed to the screen, her fingertips circling over an amorphous white blob about two inches long. "That's the fetus."

Liz stared, her chest tightening. It was so small, this foreign thing growing inside her. It didn't look like anything. It could almost be a trick of the imagination. But seeing it, knowing it was there—a part of her, made her feel protective. "Can you tell anything about it?"

What she wanted to ask was *Can you tell if there's anything wrong with it?*

"Can you tell if we're having a girl or a boy?" Candace asked.

Liz smiled, despite the flash of sadness that this was not happening the way she had imagined.

"It's a bit early to determine sex," the doctor said, "although with this equipment we often get good enough resolution to do it. I'm actually looking at something called fetal nuchal translucency, which is a developmental sign that things are going along okay so far."

"And?" Liz asked.

"Everything I've seen looks great. I don't see a penis, but that doesn't mean there isn't one. And twelve weeks is just a little bit too soon to base sex on the three line sign."

"Three lines?" Candace asked.

Marta put the probe away and covered Liz's abdomen. "The labia will show up as three parallel lines. By sixteen to twenty weeks, I'll feel very comfortable calling the sex if I see that or the penis."

"But everything is all right so far?" Liz repeated.

"Everything is fine. Do you want a picture?"

"Two," Liz said, her voice catching. "I want to send one to Andi— my sister."

"You got it. After you get dressed, stop by my office and we'll talk about what you can expect between now and the next visit."

"Thanks." Liz took the Polaroid prints and sat up on the side of the table. She studied them as Marta left the office. "Andi is going to love this."

Candace leaned against Liz's side, one arm around her waist. "That is so cool. I can't believe your stomach is still so flat with all this going on inside it."

Liz snorted. "Believe me, it doesn't feel flat. I'm not even halfway there and I already feel like a water balloon."

"Well, you don't look it. You look great." Candace kissed her cheek. "In fact, you look sexy as all hell."

Suddenly, Liz was acutely aware of Candace's breast against her arm, of the softness of her lips, of the subtle exotic scent of her perfume. Candace's breath was warm against the side of her neck, and the heat streaked down and settled into the pit of her stomach.

"Liz. God, Liz." Candace's mouth skimmed the edge of Liz's ear. "I miss you so much sometimes."

Body memories surfaced—Candace holding her close in the middle of the night, teasing her awake with her knowing mouth and her clever hands, arching above her with a wild cry of exultation. Liz couldn't help but respond in the arms of a woman who knew her, a woman who loved her. She'd been inside this woman, and Candace had been inside her—deeper than flesh, but it was her flesh every bit as much as her battered heart that cried out for more. Her nipples tightened and a ripple of excitement pulsed through her sex. She moaned softly.

"Oh yes," Candace murmured, gripping Liz's shoulders as her mouth brushed Liz's.

Liz's eyes flickered closed as want coiled in her depths, but the image she saw behind her trembling lids was not Candace's face. She dragged herself free of the hot, lush sea of sensation and tried to focus. Candace's eyes were a hazy blue, half lost to desire already. Liz eased away, stroking Candace's cheek.

"Sweetie. No."

"Why not," Candace rasped. "You know I love you."

"I know, but we can't go back."

Candace rested her forehead against Liz's. "God, why not?"

"I don't know." Liz laughed shakily. "I can't be called upon to think deep thoughts right now. I have to pee."

"Well God." Candace stepped back, breathing unevenly. "We can't let a little seduction get in the way of your bathroom break."

"Are you okay?" Liz averted her eyes from the hard knots of Candace's nipples tenting her sheer silk blouse. Liz still throbbed in places that she didn't want to be throbbing, and the thin hospital gown wasn't much of a barrier. She hadn't had sex in months, and her body ached more than she could ever remember not just for touch, but for release.

"I can live with being turned on until I can find a fix." Candace smiled uncertainly. "Are you mad?"

"No," Liz said instantly. She climbed down from the table and started to dress. "I'm flattered."

"I'd prefer you were dying to go to bed with me."

Liz kept her face turned away because she didn't want Candace to know just how aroused she really was. "Why ruin a beautiful friendship with something as tawdry as sex."

Candace laughed. "Tawdry. True. But it feels so good when you're doing it, and we were good. Remember?"

"Nope," Liz said lightly, buttoning her blouse. "I can't remember a thing about it." She turned just as Candace put her hands on her hips with an indignant expression. "But I know I can't imagine my life without you in it."

"Oh, I hate it when you do that," Candace pouted.

"What?"

"Remind me about all the important things in life just when I'm trying to have a little fun."

Laughing, Liz grabbed Candace's hand. "Come on, walk me to the bathroom."

"I guess there's no chance of making out in the stalls like we used to do in the dorm, huh?"

"Candace."

"Okay. Okay. I'm zipping."

After Liz finished with the doctor, she and Candace met Bren for their Thursday afternoon lunch.

"I ordered drinks for us when you called," Bren said as Liz and Candace settled across from her. "So tell me everything."

"Look at this," Liz said, passing the Polaroid across the table.

"Oh, will you look at that." Delighted, Bren beamed at Liz. "It's wonderful!"

"It's pretty amazing," Liz agreed.

"And everything is okay? Right on schedule?"

"Perfect." Liz was aware of Candace silently downing her martini beside her, but didn't know how to ease her obvious discomfort. She was still a little shocked at her own response to the unexpected kiss. That seemed to be happening a lot lately, too. First Reilly, now Candace. But even though she'd responded to Candace's kiss, it seemed now more like just another memory from their past. She didn't feel the urgent need to repeat it that she'd felt with Reilly, but maybe that was just because kissing Reilly was a new experience. Even as she thought it, she knew she was deluding herself. She'd felt a connection, an intimacy, with Reilly that she hadn't felt with Julia in years. But it didn't matter, because she wasn't going to be kissing Reilly *or* Candace again.

"Liz?" Bren asked, looking puzzled.

"Hmm? Sorry."

"I was asking about the birthing classes? When do we start?"

"Not until the last trimester. We've got a ways to go yet."

Abruptly, Candace finished her drink and slid from the booth. "I'm sorry, I've got to run." She leaned over and pecked Bren on the cheek. "We'll pick you up at nine tomorrow night, okay?"

Surprised, Bren nodded. "Okay. Sure. Did you forget about a hot date or something?"

Candace didn't look in Liz's direction. "Just something I need to take care of. See you both tomorrow. Then we'll party!"

Bren stared after her, then looked questioningly to Liz. "Is she okay?"

"She'll be fine," Liz said, hoping it was true.

❖

Candace made it to the Main Line in twenty minutes. She pulled into the circular drive in front of the elegant brick colonial and jumped from the car. Moving quickly so she wouldn't have to think about exactly what she was doing, she hurried up the flagstone walk and rapped the brass knocker on the Wedgwood blue door. A minute later, Parker answered.

"Hello," Parker said leaning against the door and grinning. "Just happen to be in the neighborhood?"

"This is a sympathy call." Candace took in Parker's bare feet, blue jeans, and faded blue oxford shirt. She looked good even though her face was badly discolored. Her right eye was open now and she regarded Candace quizzically. "How are you doing?"

Parker held the door open wide. "A lot better right now. Come on in."

Candace took in the tasteful antique furnishings in the foyer and what she could see of the library and formal sitting room as she followed Parker down the wide hall. Parker turned into a study in the rear and said over her shoulder, "Can I get you something to drink?"

"No, thanks." Candace paused in the doorway. She hadn't come to socialize, but she wasn't selfish enough to risk interfering with Parker's recovery. "Your face looks better."

"It is." Parker turned to study Candace, who looked wired, as if she were high. Parker knew that wasn't it. She stepped closer and deliberately surveyed the length of Candace's body. "Something else I can do for you?"

"Maybe there's something we can do for each other."

"I'm not at my kissing best." Parker stepped behind Candace and pulled her against her. She cupped Candace's breasts and whispered in her ear, "But everything else is working just fine."

Candace leaned her head back against Parker's shoulder, swaying as Parker massaged her breasts. "I want you to make me come."

Parker laughed, wondering who had gotten her so worked up and why they hadn't taken care of her. Foolish of them. For a second, she resented whoever it was, but then, Candace was here now. She had come to *her*, and at the moment, that was enough. "I think I can take care of that for you."

"You better," Candace panted, covering Parker's hands and squeezing Parker's fingers around her breasts even harder. "I feel like I'm going to explode if I don't come soon."

"Let's go," Parker said sharply, grabbing Candace's hand and spinning her around. She practically dragged her down the hall and up the stairs to her bedroom. Whoever had started this, she was going to finish it. And when she did, Candace wouldn't be thinking of anyone except her.

"Are you sure it's all right?" Candace asked again.

"Shut up." Parker halted by the side of the bed and kissed Candace hard. "I'll tell you if there's something I can't handle."

"All right," Candace said with a predatory gleam in her eye. She put her fingertips in the center of Parker's chest and pushed her backward toward the bed. "Lie down."

Wordlessly, Parker complied.

"You're not supposed to do anything strenuous." Candace climbed onto the bed and straddled Parker's thighs. She unbuttoned her blouse and dropped it by the side of the bed, then reached behind her and unclasped her bra. She let it fall from her arms and cupped her breasts. "So you can just watch."

"Not on your life," Parker muttered.

"All right then," Candace whispered. "You can direct."

"Anything I want?"

Candace smiled, trailing her fingers over her breasts. "Name it."

"Get naked." Parker's gaze locked on Candace's face as she unbuttoned her own jeans. "And take my pants off, too."

Candace unzipped her slacks, then shifted from side to side to remove them and her panties. When she was nude, she grasped the waistband of Parker's jeans and pulled them down her thighs, murmuring appreciatively when she saw that Parker wore nothing underneath. While Candace got Parker's jeans off, Parker unbuttoned her shirt and yanked it off, then lay down with her back propped against several pillows.

"Anything else I can do for you?" Candace asked, her breasts flushed and her pink nipples hard as marbles.

"Sit in my lap, facing me."

"Butterfly. Nice," Candace purred, settling into the cradle of Parker's pelvis and wrapping her legs behind Parker's hips. She tilted forward and rubbed herself over Parker's stomach. "I'm wet."

"Tease your nipples," Parker said, sweeping her thumb back and forth over Candace's lower belly.

Candace caught her lower lip between her teeth as she pulled both nipples between her thumbs and forefingers. She glanced down, watching Parker's thumb move closer and closer to the base of her clitoris. Her hips undulated in a slow circle against Parker's hard stomach.

"Pinch them." Parker dipped her thumb lower for a second, then skipped away.

"Oh God." Candace squeezed her breasts and pinched her nipples with her nails. "I want you to play with my clit."

"Who's in charge here?" Parker grunted. Watching Candace become more and more excited, feeling the hot slick of her arousal paint her stomach, was making her crazy. It took all her willpower not to thrust her fingers deep inside Candace and make her come, right now, but she sensed Candace wanted to be controlled for just a little longer. She moved her hand away from Candace's center. "You play with it."

"I'll come."

"No you won't. You're not going to come until I make you, and if you do, it's the last time I ever will."

"Oh come on, baby," Candace whined, pressing two fingers to the base of her clit. "I need to come."

"Too bad." Parker watched first Candace's face, then her fingers circling between her legs, her own clitoris so hard it hurt. "Use two hands."

Candace's eyes slammed shut as she tilted her pelvis and slid two fingers deep inside herself. Her fingers jerked over her clitoris, faster and faster.

"I'm going to come," Candace blurted.

Parker grabbed her wrists and pulled them away. "Slide up here."

"Be careful of your face," Candace gasped. "Oh God I'm so close."

"Play with your breasts again." Parker cupped Candace's ass and eased her higher up on the bed. "And watch."

Candace stared down, her body bowed, as she rubbed and tweaked her nipples. Parker gently kissed her clitoris and she started to come. She held herself perfectly still as Parker kissed her again, her orgasm unfurling like a flower beneath the sun, reaching, stretching, bursting with heat and life deep inside her.

"Kiss me again," Candace whispered.

Parker did.

Candace's breath shuddered from her. "Again."

Parker tenderly circled her lips around Candace's clitoris and sucked slowly until she had her all the way inside her mouth. Then she flicked her tongue back and forth.

Candace threw her head back, pulsing against Parker's mouth, exploding beyond pleasure, coming again and again. She fell forward, barely able to catch herself on her trembling arms. "Oh God. God. God, I needed that."

"No kidding." Grinning, Parker stretched her arm out as Candace collapsed next to her and cradled her against her side. "Catch your breath. Then I want to come in your mouth."

Immediately, Candace propped herself up on an elbow, sweeping her hair back from her face with her other hand. "Fast or slow?"

"Doesn't matter," Parker said. "I'm only going to last about two seconds."

Candace worked her way down the bed and settled between Parker's thighs. "You're wrong about that. I can make it last as long as I want."

What seemed to Parker like hours later, after she'd almost come a half dozen times but somehow Candace had stopped her orgasm before it could crest, she finally gave in and begged. "I can't take it anymore. Please let me come."

"Soon, baby." Candace eased her fingers inside her and teased the circle of muscle below with her thumb.

Parker groaned and raised her hips, inviting Candace deeper. "I'm going to come. Oh yeah, fuck me. Fu…"

Candace pressed deeper with both hands as Parker climaxed in her mouth. Candace didn't think of Liz. She didn't think of anyone or anything except how open and trusting and exquisitely beautiful Parker was in that moment. When Parker finally went slack with a long sigh, Candace nuzzled her face against Parker's stomach.

"So, did you get what you came for?" Parker teased, stroking her hair.

"Oh yeah," Candace whispered. What she didn't say, what she didn't even want to think about, was that she'd found more than she'd ever expected.

CHAPTER FIFTEEN

Reilly's beeper went off just as she slammed her locker, finally ready to leave for the night. Grimacing, she checked the readout. She'd been on call the night before and should have gone home first thing in the morning. Instead she'd ended up working an extra ten hours because the ortho trauma service had a dozen cases scheduled for the day, and she knew if she didn't stay and do some of them, the patients were likely to get bumped until the next day or even Sunday. And besides that, she hadn't had any good reason to go home, other than to sleep, and she'd been too restless all week to do much of that. Every time she lay down and the quiet closed in around her, she thought of Liz. Funny, once Annie had occupied her thoughts in those moments between waking and slumber, but now it was Liz, and that was as disturbing as it was different. No, it was much better to work and keep all those confusing ruminations at bay.

She frowned at the four digit number. It was the phone at the security station in the lobby. A visitor? Her heart rate soared. Liz. She grabbed the wall phone and punched in the extension.

"Danvers," Reilly said immediately, before the caller had even finished saying hello.

"Reilly? It's Parker."

Reilly swallowed her disappointment. "Hey. How're you doing?"

"I just had my follow-up appointment. All systems go."

"That's great."

"Listen, how about I buy you dinner? I owe you a lot more than that, but hey—it's a start."

"You don't owe me anything," Reilly said. "I appreciate the offer, but…"

"You got a game tonight?"

"No, Sunday."

"So then, how about dinner," Parker insisted.

Reilly couldn't think of a reason to refuse, and maybe an hour or so of socializing and a drink or two would help her relax enough to sleep.

"Okay," Reilly said. "I'm in scrubs, though. I need to go home and shower and change. Why don't I give you my address and you can meet me there. Have a drink while you wait."

"Great. We'll make a night of it. Grab dinner, go to a club, maybe run into some interesting ladies."

"Sure. Why not. I'll be right down." Reilly hung up the phone. Maybe that was exactly what she needed, a little dose of Parker's prescription for a good time.

❖

"I can't believe I don't have anything to wear," Liz complained, whipping the clothes back and forth along the rack in her bedroom closet in frustration.

"We're going to a strip club," Candace pointed out as she lounged on the bed in tight, white hip-huggers and a navy halter top. "Jeans and some slinky little top will work just fine."

"My jeans are too tight and my breasts are too big."

"Don't tell me you don't have at least one pair of jeans tucked away somewhere that will fit," Candace said.

"Maybe."

"And your breasts are fine." Candace wiggled her eyebrows. "In fact, I like the busty look on you."

Liz glowered. "C-cups are hardly what I'd call busty."

"Is this just normal pregnancy grumps or is something else going on?" Candace asked.

Liz sat next to Candace, holding a red silk blouse in her hands. "I miss Reilly."

"I guess you haven't heard from her."

"Not since she left Bren's last weekend."

"Maybe that's not such a bad thing."

"Why don't you like her?"

"It's not that. Hey, I'm all for having a little fun. But from everything you said, Reilly seems way too complicated, you know?"

"I know. I know." Liz sighed and went back to the closet to search through a stack of clothes on the top shelf. She probably did have *something* that would fit. Without turning around, she said conversationally, "So, where did you run off to yesterday in the middle of lunch?"

"Parker's," Candace replied.

"How is she?"

"In prime form."

Liz turned around with a pair of blue jeans that she had put away after losing ten pounds her first year in practice. They would have been loose on her three months before, but now they would probably fit just right. "Prime form as in she's recovering or…?"

"As in she's much better, and she can make me come so hard I feel like I'm seeing God."

"Ah," Liz said, for some reason both embarrassed and a little turned on. She almost envied Candace having someone to go to, someone she desired and trusted to take care of her physical needs, whereas she had been restless and semi-aroused all week with no options except of her own making. Not that she minded that, but it just wasn't taking the edge off.

"Ah, what?" Candace said, suddenly cranky herself. It wasn't like her afternoon with Parker was anything other than convenient.

"Nothing, I just think it's…I don't know, nice."

"Nice?" Candace laughed. "Okay, it was nice."

"Are you seeing her again?"

"No," Candace said rapidly. "Not as in *seeing* seeing. I did mention we were going to the Blue Diamond tonight." Candace looked away. "I didn't invite her or anything. I think it just slipped out when I was still a little mellow."

"Don't you mean dazed and disoriented from your out-of-this-world orgasm?" Laughing, Liz tucked in her blouse and breathed a sigh of relief when she could button her jeans. Her waistline had expanded at least an inch, except now that she actually studied it, she had a little bit more of a tummy rather than a bigger waistline. "I think it's fine if she joins us. I like her, and so does Bren. And God, it's a strip club. It's not like we're going to be having any deep personal conversations."

"Well, if she does show up, it's not like we're going to be together or anything."

"Of course not." Liz gave Candace a quick hug. "Stop being so afraid of having a relationship. They're not life-threatening."

"How do you know? They could be lethal for some of us."

Liz paused by her bedroom door and regarded Candace seriously. "Do you actually believe that?"

"They just don't work for me. I proved that with you, didn't I?"

"I think the only thing you proved with me was that you were young and you weren't ready to settle down. It doesn't mean you're not relationship material."

Candace studied her hands, unusually subdued. "I was in love with you. If I could fuck that up, I could fuck anything up."

"Maybe we moved too fast," Liz said, leaning against the doorjamb with her hands behind her back. "Maybe we weren't right for each other."

"We were great together."

"We had great sex. And we cared about each other." Liz didn't know herself why that wasn't enough. Shouldn't it be? Maybe they should try again. She wasn't even certain why she'd said no to Candace's kiss the day before. They loved each other. Candace was gorgeous and sexy and just about irresistible. Suddenly, Liz thought of Reilly and how when Reilly touched her, she felt Reilly in a place so deep, so fundamentally *her* that the connection made her ache. No one had ever made her feel quite like that, not Candace whom she had adored, or Julia whom she had wanted so desperately to love. She sighed. "And I love you to pieces, but maybe it just wasn't meant to be."

Candace raised her head and met Liz's eyes across the room. "Do you believe that? Some things are meant to be?"

"Maybe. Sometimes I think so." Liz smiled ruefully and shrugged. "Although right now, I'm batting zero."

"No you're not." Candace bounced up off the bed and slunk across the room, her eyes glittering. She kissed Liz soundly on the mouth, then wrapped her arm around her waist. "You've got Bren. And you've got me. And if you need to get laid, you've got my number."

Laughing, Liz threw her arm around Candace's shoulder. "Good to know, since you're on speed dial."

❖

Bren checked the time. 8:59 p.m. Candace and Liz would be downstairs to pick her up any second. She should check her make-up one last time and go downstairs to wait for them, but instead, she sat staring at her email. At exactly nine p.m. she pushed send/receive and watched her mail download. A message appeared—the same message that had appeared every night at nine p.m. for the last four nights.

I'll be there tonight. Will you?

This time, instead of deleting the message as she had every other night, Bren immediately typed *What makes you think I know where it is?*

You write the city like you know it.

Bren smiled. Nothing caught a writer's attention faster than someone who paid attention to their work. The doorbell rang, but Bren ignored it. She should go. This was a game that was becoming too real. Instead of signing off, she asked,

How will I know you?

Ask the bartender. He'll have a note for you from Jae.

"Bren?" Candace shouted from downstairs. "Hey? You ready?"

"Just a minute," Bren called back as she typed. *Jae isn't real.*

Are you sure?

Bren closed the email program and stood up. Enough. The game was over. All she had to do was ignore the whole thing. It was probably just a prank anyhow. She could be getting an email from someone in Iowa who'd Googled the names of bars in Philadelphia. There was no reason to think that this person would actually be there tonight, and even if she was, there was no reason to meet her.

"Bren?" Candace asked again.

"On my way."

Bren hurried downstairs. Nothing would happen that she didn't want to happen, because she was in control. She slowed, considering that. Jae—no, the stranger—understood her need to be in control. Even though it seemed like the stranger had been making all the overtures, she'd set everything up so that ultimately, Bren would make the critical moves. Bren would be in charge, just the way Bren wanted it. Interesting.

"Happy birthday!" Candace pulled Bren into her arms and kissed her exuberantly. "You ready for some adventure, baby?"

Bren tightened her arms around Candace's neck and kissed her back. "Could be."

"Oh my God," Candace said, stepping back and eyeing Bren incredulously. "Where did you get leather pants?"

"The usual place. A clothing store." Bren smiled, enjoying Candace's astonishment. Her lightweight dark brown leather pants were cut low, and she'd chosen a sleeveless black shirt that dove between her breasts and rode high enough to expose a few inches of her belly. She had a lot of skin showing—well, for her anyhow—but it *was* her birthday. A girl was entitled to be daring on her birthday.

"You look so hot."

"Well don't say it like it's such a shock," Bren chided.

"No. I don't mean that. I mean you look...different. Good. Great."

"Come on before you say anything else and really get in trouble," Bren said, laughing. "Let's not keep Liz waiting."

"Where have you been hiding this side of yourself," Candace complained as Bren closed the door behind them and they started down the steps to the sidewalk.

"I guess you could say between the covers."

"You've got some explaining to do," Candace grumbled.

"Maybe, maybe not," Bren teased. But maybe it was time.

❖

"Want another beer?" Parker asked, pushing her chair back from the table.

Reilly reached out to steady the empties on the sticky, crowded surface of the small round table. After she'd showered and changed into jeans and a T-shirt, she and Parker had opted for dinner at a neighborhood bar where they could watch a baseball game on the big screen TV. Over the course of a couple of hours, they ate chicken wings and spicy curly fries and drank beer out of the bottle. Parker had drunk most of the beer.

"Are you driving somewhere later on?" Reilly asked.

Parker squinted at the round clock behind the bar. The letters spelling out Schlitz on the dingy face were faded from decades of smoke, even though no one was smoking inside now.

"I've got a little time," Parker said. "I'm crashing a birthday party."

"Now that sounds like a hot time."

"It is when it's Candace and her friends."

Reilly sucked in a breath. "Oh. Well, if you're driving, you'd better go easy on the brew."

"Don't worry, I'm spacing 'em out."

While Parker went to get refills, Reilly watched the game. Or tried to. She wondered where the party was. She wondered if Liz would be there. If Candace was going to be there, Bren and Liz probably would be too. She told herself it wasn't a good idea to think about Liz, but she'd been telling herself that all week and it hadn't really worked.

She tried logic again. Liz had told her to stop, because she didn't want to be involved. That made sense. There was no law against pregnant women dating, except they weren't talking about dating. If Liz hadn't stopped her, Reilly had a feeling that kiss would have turned into a lot more very quickly. And that spelled complications, for both of them. No, they both made the right decision. Bad timing. Bad idea. Use your head, Reilly. Let it go.

"Whatever you're thinking, it looks pretty heavy." Parker dropped into the chair opposite Reilly and passed a mug of sweating draft beer across to her.

"Nah," Reilly said. "I was just zoning."

"Huh."

"So. A birthday party."

"Yeah. Bren's." Parker sipped her beer. "At the Blue Diamond. Ever been?"

Reilly shook her head. "After hours place?"

"Strip club."

"Girls? Stripping, I mean?"

"Yep. And lots of girls in the audience, too."

Reilly laughed. "And this is where Bren's going for her birthday?"

"Yeah, kind of sounds like Candace's idea, doesn't it? But it wasn't." Parker shook her head. "Candace says it was Bren's."

"So, um, I guess they're all going?"

"You mean all of them including Liz?"

Reilly looked away.

"You know," Parker said, rubbing her face gingerly. "Even with the shades, the lights hurt my eyes. I'm not so sure I can drive in the dark. I didn't think about that when I came in this afternoon."

"You can stay at my place tonight if you need to," Reilly said.

Parker said, "Thanks. I appreciate it."

"And," Reilly added slowly, "if you need a ride down to the Blue Diamond, I'll take you."

Parker grinned. "That would be great."

CHAPTER SIXTEEN

The minute Bren walked through the door of the Blue Diamond, she felt as if she had stepped into a scene from a William Gibson post-apocalyptic cyber-fantasy. The walls and ceiling were painted black, and blue bulbs in recessed fixtures drenched the room in a murky haze, obscuring everything except the raised platform which took up the length of one entire side of the room. Featureless, nearly formless figures of indeterminate sex occupied most of the tables. Three upright silver poles gleamed beneath tightly focused spotlights on the stage. At the moment, it was empty, but a pounding bass beat reverberated through the floor and shimmered in the air.

"I think the act is about to start. Let's grab a table," Bren urged.

"I can't see a thing," Liz muttered, stumbling into a chair.

"You're not supposed to," Candace replied, grabbing her arm. "That way you can get a hand job under the table without anyone noticing."

Bren snorted, moving a little faster as her eyes adjusted. She wasn't sure why, but she didn't want to miss any of the acts.

"I'm not sitting on these chairs then," Liz announced.

Laughing, Candace tugged Liz's hand. "Come on, I'll take care of you. I'll find you a nice safe seat."

"There's a table open right at center stage," Bren said. It was almost as if it was waiting for them, because as near as she could make out in the gloom, the other tables with good views of the stage were occupied. "I'll grab it."

Before they'd reached the square wood pedestal table, the room grew even darker and the music ratcheted up a notch. Almost by feel, Bren found an empty chair and slid into it, and Liz took the seat next to her.

"I want a drink," Candace shouted above the blaring music. "I'm not sure there's table service."

Bren thought about the note that might or might not be waiting for her, and quickly focused on the stage. If there *was* a note at the bar, it would be there later. If there wasn't, she didn't want to know right now. She liked the anticipation, the excitement, of thinking that Jae was here somewhere, possibly watching her. Of course, Jae wouldn't know what she looked like, because there were no pictures of her as her author persona. But still, she had a feeling that Jae would know her, and that she would know Jae.

"I'll have a screwdriver," Bren said.

"Be right back." Candace disappeared into the gloom.

"Okay, confess," Liz said into Bren's ear.

Bren started in surprise. "What do you mean?"

"Why did you pick this place?"

"Oh." Bren considered any number of plausible replies, but it was something about the tone of Liz's voice that caused her to say the one thing she never expected to say. "I might be meeting someone here."

"Really," Liz said with interest. "Who?"

"I don't know."

Liz shifted her chair closer. "Like a blind date?"

"Something like that."

"You let Candace set you up on a blind date after swearing you wouldn't do it ever again?"

"Oh no." Bren laughed. "Candace's blind dates were always disasters. We're not interested in the same kind of women."

"So who set it up?"

"She did. The woman I'm meeting. Maybe."

"So…you know her."

"No. We've never met," Bren said.

"You know this is very confusing, right?"

"I know."

"I've thought for a long time there was something you weren't telling us."

"I know, I'm sorry."

Liz patted Bren's thigh. "Don't apologize. It's your birthday. Have a good time and explain it all to us later."

"Yeah?"

"Yeah."

"I love you, you know," Bren said.

"That's a ditto."

"Here we go," Bren said, as a statuesque blonde sauntered onto the stage in six inch heels, a black satin G-string, and a black leather jacket that stopped just above the perfect round globes of her full, tight ass. She strutted to one of the poles as the rhythm picked up, grabbed it with both hands, and pressed her crotch against it. Then she did a perfect split as she swung slowly around in a circle, the steel shaft jutting upward between her widely spread thighs.

Candace slid in beside them and passed glasses around the table. "How does she do that?"

"Flexibility," Bren murmured, studying the woman as her generous breasts threatened to spill out of the partially unzipped jacket. The blonde was attractive, and she had a great body, but Bren felt nothing other than a vague curiosity.

After a few more impressively acrobatic and undeniably sensuous moves that looked as if she was masturbating on the pole, the blonde slinked to the near edge of the stage and went down on her knees with her thighs splayed. She stretched her torso back and let the jacket fall from her arms, leaving her breasts exposed and jutting upward into the harsh lights. Her skin shimmered with sweat and the narrow G-string did little to obscure her glistening sex.

Candace gave a low murmur of approval and Liz bumped her shoulder.

"You are such a pervert."

"I am not," Candace whispered. "I just have a healthy sense of appreciation for the female form."

"Uh-huh."

Shadowy figures from the audience approached the stage, tucking folded bills under the dancer's G-string or dropping them onto her tight stomach as she undulated to the pounding beat, her pelvis thrusting with the unmistakable rhythm of sex. As the tempo pulsed faster and the air grew heavy with heat and collective arousal, the blonde fondled her breasts and stroked her fingers between her thighs until, real or imagined, she and the music climaxed together. Then the room went dark and silence fell like a thunderclap.

"Well," Candace said a little breathlessly. "That was nice."

Liz wrapped her arm around Bren's shoulders and playfully nuzzled her ear. "Enjoying your birthday so far?"

Bren laughed. "Who wouldn't?"

"You've got a point."

Bren scanned the room as the lights came up high enough to prevent patrons who were making a mad dash to the bar between acts from stumbling. A few disappeared down a hallway she hadn't been able to see earlier. The bartender, a bald African-American man the size of a Volkswagen moved with the grace of a running back in his tight runway, mixing drinks and passing bottles of beer at lightning speed. When the blonde who had just performed emerged from the hallway in a miniscule bikini and walked to the end of the bar, he handed her what looked like a glass of champagne and nodded toward a lone man seated at a nearby table. The blonde took the drink and joined the customer.

Bren watched for a second as the blonde straddled the man's lap, then looked away as the blonde began a slow grind. A petite brunette and a painfully thin blonde with enormously enhanced breasts, both in various stages of nudity, appeared from somewhere backstage and worked their way between the tables. When the brunette slithered onto the lap of an attractive woman with shoulder length brown hair and rubbed her breasts across the woman's face, Bren decided she'd had enough of the floor show. Turning in the opposite direction, she stared, not certain at first she wasn't imagining the two women wending their way between the tables toward them. Then she heard Liz's swift intake of breath beside her, and she knew she was right.

"Hey! Parker! Reilly, over here," Bren called.

❖

Liz hadn't seen Reilly in five days, and she couldn't take her eyes off her. Her tight white T-shirt stretched over her strong shoulders and arms and clung to the swell of her breasts. Her jeans were just tight enough to show off her athletic legs. Her hair was shaggy around the edges. She looked a little disheveled, a little unpolished, and a lot sexy. Liz liked the look. What she didn't like was the fact that Reilly had her arm looped around Parker's waist. Parker leaned against her as they walked, and they looked good together. Liz hadn't noticed before just how fluidly attractive Parker was. Next to Candace's cover girl beauty, Parker seemed androgynously handsome, but when snuggled against Reilly, she projected a softer sensuality. It would have been exciting to think about that sexual flexibility if she hadn't been with Reilly at the moment.

"Well that didn't take her long," Candace muttered.

"Who?" Liz replied.

"Both of them," Candace snapped.

Liz didn't answer because Parker and Reilly grabbed chairs from a nearby table and dragged them over.

"Mind if we crash the party?" Parker said with a big grin.

"Looks like you already did," Candace grumbled.

"Great! Drinks everyone?" Parker asked, apparently oblivious to Candace's snarl.

"None for me," Reilly said, watching Liz.

"I'm good," Liz replied.

Candace and Bren gave Parker their orders and she sauntered off. After a second, Bren jumped up. "I'll give her a hand."

"I'm going to the restroom," Candace said to no one in particular as she bolted after them.

Reilly indicated the empty chair next to Liz. "Okay if I sit down?"

"Of course."

"I hope it's okay we showed up. Parker said—"

"It's fine."

"So. How are you?"

"Good," Liz replied, thinking *fat and terminally horny and really glad to see you and wishing I wasn't.*

"That's good." Reilly rubbed her hands on her thighs and looked around the room. "Is it just me, or is this place particularly sleazy?"

Liz laughed and felt herself relax a little. "Extraordinarily sleazy."

"Bren having fun?"

"We all are."

Candace dropped into the chair on the opposite side of Liz and casually draped her arm around Liz's shoulders. "So where did you find Parker, Reilly?"

"We met at the hospital and had dinner," Reilly replied, her gaze flickering to Candace's hand cupping Liz's upper arm.

Candace smiled frostily. "That's nice."

Liz shifted just enough to cause Candace to move her arm to the back of the chair, but then her thigh snugged up against Reilly's. Reilly didn't move away, and neither did she.

❖

"So Bren," Parker said expansively, "this is some place you picked for a party, honey."

"Isn't it?" Bren softly touched Parker's cheek on the uninjured side. "How are you feeling? You look like you might've started the party a little bit early."

"Feeling great. I only had a few beers." Parker frowned. "Except I did have that pain pill right before dinner."

"You be careful with the drinks from now on, okay?"

"Yes ma'am. Anything you say, ma'am."

"And Reilly's driving, right?"

"Yeah that Reilly, she's terrific."

Bren nodded. "Can you make it back to the table with the drinks?"

"Oh yeah, sure sure. I'm fine. Feeling great. Hey, where did Candace go?"

"I think she's back at the table now."

At least Bren hoped so. She hadn't missed the fact that Candace wasn't too pleased to see Parker show up with Reilly, and Candace had gotten quite a few looks as she'd sashayed to the bathroom. At least two men and one woman had said something to make her laugh in passing. Candace on the prowl was always unpredictable.

"She's really gorgeous, isn't she?" Parker said.

"Yes, she is."

Parker leaned over and kissed Bren gently. "But ya know, so are you."

Laughing, Bren pressed her palms to Parker's chest and held her at arm's length. "And you, my friend, are a sweet talker. Go sit down now."

"Oh, right. Right. That's where I'm going."

"I'll be right there."

The lights suddenly dimmed again, and for a few seconds, Bren couldn't see anything. Then the music started and the spotlights lit up center stage. This time, the dancer was a tall, curvaceous redhead wearing white cowboy boots with tassels, a brown suede vest, a two-gun and holster set, and a white thong so narrow that from where Bren was standing it looked as if her sex was bare. She twirled her guns and bent over with her very shapely ass to the crowd. Then she dropped her head low enough to smile between her spread legs at the anonymous faces. Her red hair streaked down toward the floor like flames. Licking her lips, she dragged one of the gun barrels up her thigh and rubbed it back and forth over her labia. The light glinted off the barrel as if it were wet.

For just an instant as the woman smiled up at her, Bren had an image of sliding that gleaming rod ever so slowly inside the redhead. The sudden tingling between her legs was both exciting and disturbing. She turned her back on the dancer and found the bartender a few feet away, regarding her contemplatively. She glanced the length of the bar and realized she was the only one not watching the show.

"Get you something?" he said in a deep rumble.

"I was wondering if you might have a message for me."

He regarded her impassively.

"A note…" Bren almost didn't finish the sentence, because the absurdity of the whole situation was almost more than she could discount. But he seemed to be waiting, so she went on, "for Melanie."

"Would you be Melanie?"

Bren didn't even hesitate, because it felt completely natural to say, "Yes. I am."

Wordlessly, he turned his back and walked away.

The disappointment was greater than she had anticipated. Rationally, of course, she knew any other outcome was impossible. For a stranger to recognize just from reading her books the needs she had successfully hidden from everyone, even herself, was highly unlikely. And for someone to actually find her and lead her here? Impossible. She peered into the dark recesses of the room, hoping to discover someone watching her, waiting for her. But no one was. She was alone with her fantasies just as she always was.

Shaking off the familiar melancholy, she started back to her seat.

"Don't forget this," the bartender said.

Slowly, she turned around. He held out a small envelope, the kind usually attached to floral deliveries. Bren tried to see something in his face, but it was smooth as stone and just as unreadable. She took the envelope and sat down on the bar stool, swiveling so her back was to the bar and the bartender.

On the stage, the redhead had taken off her vest and was snapping the hammers of her revolvers on her nipples. Bang. Bang. Bang.

Bren examined the sealed envelope. There was nothing written on it. Sliding a fingernail underneath the flap, she carefully opened it, trying hard not to tear the flap or the paper. The small card held a single embossed black rose in one corner and words written in bold, black script. She couldn't tell in the murky light, but it looked as if it had been written with a real pen. A fountain pen.

I want to dance for you. Jae.

Bren felt her sex pulse like a fist clenching, then springing open, and just as quickly, she was wet and fully aroused. She slipped the card back into the envelope and surveyed the room again. No one was paying any attention to her.

Who had written the note? Was it the redhead up on stage now? The blonde who'd masturbated on the pole? Or perhaps the brunette who had teased the female customer with her breasts. Bren tried to imagine one of them as her secret stranger, and she couldn't. But then, she'd never seen a woman who came close to fulfilling her fantasy, which is why she'd started writing to begin with. She had acquired not only success, she'd found the satisfaction she couldn't find anywhere else.

Why risk a perfect dream with imperfect reality?

"Is there any message?" the bartender asked from behind her.

Bren realized the music was climbing to a crescendo and the act would be over soon. Then the lights would come up and she would need to rejoin her friends. The friends she loved, and who loved her. Safety. Anonymity.

She spun around on the stool. "Tell her yes."

CHAPTER SEVENTEEN

"There's Bren," Liz said to Candace as the lights came up, pointing across the room.

"Well, at least one of us looks like she's having a good time," Candace muttered.

Liz, sandwiched between Candace on one side and Reilly on the other, watched Candace drum her fingers on the one small patch of table that wasn't covered with glasses and beer bottles. Candace had been agitated ever since Parker sat down next to Reilly, on the end of the semicircle of chairs farthest from Candace. Liz hadn't had much time to decipher Candace's reaction because during the entire previous act, all she'd been able to think about was Reilly's thigh pressed along the length of hers. She didn't find the stripper onstage attractive, but she had to admit that sitting in the dark watching a woman fondle herself was unexpectedly exciting. It was far more distracting, however, to know that Reilly was watching the same thing. Liz couldn't help but wonder if the striptease excited Reilly. Then, as soon as she thought it, she tried to discount the possibility. As ridiculous as it was, she didn't want to think about Reilly being aroused by anyone. Though she supposed she should be more concerned about Parker, who had her head on Reilly's shoulder at the moment, than about an anonymous stripper.

"Where did you disappear to?" Candace snapped, interrupting Liz's internal debate, when Bren dropped into the remaining empty chair.

"I got caught at the bar when the lights went down. Some act," Bren said.

"She had some nice moves."

"I guess you told Parker we'd be here, huh?" Bren said.

"I might have mentioned it. I didn't *invite* her."

"Oh, I don't mind. I really like her."

"She's a sweetheart," Candace muttered.

Before Bren had a chance to reply, Parker leaned across Reilly's lap and said loudly, "Hey Liz, can we switch seats? I've been talking to Reilly all night. I want to talk to Candace."

"Sure," Liz said, standing. As she squeezed between the table and Reilly, Reilly put both hands on Liz's hips to guide her. Her touch was gentle, and Liz found the simple contact both reassuring and exciting. Reilly had a way of noticing her—where she was, what she was doing, what she needed—that made her feel cared for, and special.

Parker jumped up unsteadily and tried to pass Liz before Liz had cleared the table.

"Wait a minute," Liz protested, laughing, "there's not room enough for both of us in this space."

"Oops, sorry." Parker's shoulder struck Liz's chest, throwing Liz off-balance.

"Oh," Liz exclaimed as she felt herself falling.

Reilly caught Liz around the waist and pulled her down into her lap, holding her firmly against her chest. "Okay?"

Automatically, Liz wrapped her arms around Reilly's neck. With her mouth against Reilly's cheek, she murmured, "Fine."

Reilly tilted her head back, squinting in the dim light to study Liz's face. "You sure?"

Their mouths were an inch apart and Liz wanted to kiss her. Instead, she danced her fingers through the shaggy hair at the back of Reilly's neck. "You need a haircut."

"Do I?" Reilly's voice was husky as she ran her hands up and down Liz's back, her fingers tracing the muscles on either side of her spine.

"Where'd my seat go?" Parker said, searching behind her with one hand.

"Hold on," Reilly whispered to Liz.

"What?" Liz asked.

Reilly slipped one arm under Liz's hips, tightened her hold around her middle, and shifted to the far outside seat. Settling Liz securely back down in her lap, she said, "Go ahead, Parker. The coast is clear."

Parker sat heavily, taking up most of the two seats Reilly and Liz had just vacated. Liz had nowhere to go, and she really didn't want to move, not when sitting crosswise in Reilly's lap with Reilly's arms around her waist felt so damn good. Nothing about Reilly's embrace suggested anything other than a friendly closeness, but her body was hard and hot, except where the soft swell of her breasts fit against Liz's. She felt so good, so right, Liz had to struggle not to burrow her hips tighter into Reilly's lap and bury her face in the inviting curve of Reilly's neck. Her physical response to Reilly always took her by surprise, because she wasn't used to being so easily aroused. Maybe her susceptibility was partly hormones, but she didn't care. She liked the feeling, and as long as she remembered nothing was going to come of it, she might as well enjoy the guilty pleasure.

"I guess I'm here for a while," Liz said.

"That's okay."

"Am I blocking your view?" Liz asked.

Reilly laughed. "No, but even if you were, it wouldn't matter. I'll take you in my lap over one of them any day."

A rush of heat made every inch of Liz's skin tingle. "I wasn't planning to lap dance."

"Too bad. I bet you'd be good at it."

"Maybe one of these days I'll give it a try," Liz said, enjoying the little flirtation.

"Just say the word."

The lights dimmed, and Liz relaxed in Reilly's arms, anticipating the next act. It was nice not to think about anything for a few minutes, but just to enjoy what was happening. Being around Reilly always made her feel lighthearted. She recognized the feeling as happiness, and recognized, too, how unusual it was.

❖

Parker swayed toward Candace and muttered, "Miss me?"

"Not in the least." Candace got up and pushed past Bren. "Excuse me."

"Where's she going?" Parker asked.

Bren reached across the empty chair and patted Parker's thigh. "Probably to the bathroom."

"Oh. Okay. I'll wait."

Bren half smiled, wishing she could orchestrate her friends' lives as easily as she did the characters in her books. But she should probably start with her own life first, and so far, she hadn't done so well with that.

She slipped her hand into the front pocket of her leather pants and felt the small stiff card. *I want to dance for you.*

As the room dropped into darkness, Bren wondered if the message was metaphorical or real, or if there was any difference at all.

Settling back, she watched the now familiar sharp cone of light focus on the far right-hand corner of the stage. Jae might not even be here. Just because the note was here and the email message had said she would be here, didn't mean it was true. In fact, Bren was more than half certain the entire thing was an elaborate hoax. A woman strode into the light and Bren sat up straight. She'd been wrong again. Jae *was* here.

"Looks like she wandered into the wrong joint," Parker said in what Bren supposed was intended to be a whisper. She couldn't answer because she was trying to take in every single detail, and she didn't know where to look first.

Her gaze danced from the thick mane of black hair to the deep set dark eyes to the square jaw softened by a wide sensuous mouth. Bren registered beauty, pride, sensuousness in the instant before she became captivated by the sight of bare breasts crisscrossed with leather straps. The inch-wide leather bands met in the center of a long flat abdomen where they attached to a wide silver ring. A matching pair of straps shot out from the lower portion of the ring and disappeared into skintight leather pants. Another band circled her waist. Her small, high breasts were distinctly different than the augmented ones of most of the other dancers, round and firm with small dark nipples. An elaborate tribal tattoo scrolled from her muscular right deltoid down her upper arm, wrapped around her biceps, and ended on the inside of her forearm just above her wrist. The leather pants covered the tops of black boots.

She was the woman in Bren's books. She was the woman from the softball field. She was the woman in Bren's every fantasy. She was Jae.

Jae looked out over the audience, her expression almost arrogant, before her gaze settled on Bren and she lowered her thick-lashed lids once in slow acknowledgment. Then she turned and strode to the center pole, the light following her. When she reached it, she faced the audience, stretched her arms above her head and grasped the pole behind her, thrusting her pelvis toward the onlookers. The music pounded steadily, echoing the roar of Bren's heart thudding inside her head.

From out of the inky darkness behind Jae, a woman's arms encircled

Jae's torso and long fingered hands with blood red nails resembling talons cupped her breasts. A figure pressed against Jae from behind, the pole between them, the light from the spot angled sharply so that all Bren could see were glimpses of pale naked limbs. Bren watched Jae's face as the disembodied hands twisted her nipples and tormented her breasts before slithering lower over her chest and abdomen, stroking, clawing, threatening to slash her skin open with their razor-sharp tips. Pleasure and pain fused into need as Jae's skin broke out into a shining sweat and her hips writhed.

"Jesus," Parker muttered from beside her. "That is so fucking hot."

The words floated past Bren as if uttered in another dimension. Nothing penetrated her awareness except Jae. The woman behind Jae gripped the waistband of Jae's pants in both hands and wrenched the leather sharply back and forth. The tearing sound ripped through Bren and made her jerk in her seat. The leather came away in the invisible woman's hands, and she threw it aside. The black leather straps stretched down from the silver ring in the center of Jae's abdomen to circle the insides of her thighs. Her shaved sex was framed by the leather, and nothing else.

Naked except for the leather straps slashing across her body, Jae kept a grip on the pole above her head. Her thighs trembled as one blood-tipped finger circled in the top of the cleft between her legs. Her back arched, her hips thrust, and she swallowed convulsively. Bren wondered at the control it took for her to keep her hands on the pole, to hold herself up, to offer her body to be used.

"I think she's gonna come right there," Parker exclaimed, sliding closer to Bren.

"No she's not," Bren said, watching Jae's lids flicker and her lips part on a moan that was lost in the pounding beat. The arousal was real, she could see it in the way Jae's body jerked as the hand stroked harder and faster between her legs. "She'll save her pleasure for someone who deserves it."

The music climbed wildly, Jae's pelvis thrust under the invading hand, and when the crescendo peaked, she finally released her grip on the pole and collapsed to her knees, her chest heaving. The room plunged into darkness and utter silence fell. In the blackness, Bren heard Jae sob for breath, and then there was nothing.

"I'm gonna go find Candace," Parker announced, pushing herself unsteadily to her feet.

"She'll be back in a minute when the lights come up," Bren said, reaching for Parker's arm. Her mind was still filled with images of Jae, but she had enough awareness not to let Parker wander around by herself. Plus, she had a feeling that Candace had gone off alone for a reason. When Candace was upset, her remedy was always the same. Find a woman to take her mind off her troubles.

The lights came up and Parker blinked, searching the room uncertainly. Then her expression darkened and Bren followed her gaze. Candace was at the bar in a clinch with a woman who had one hand on Candace's breast and the other on her ass. Apparently they were too far into their deep-throat kiss to notice that the act was over and they were visible to whoever cared to look. Or, typically for Candace, she just didn't care.

"Son of a bitch," Parker growled.

She tried to climb over Bren and almost fell. Bren jumped up and grabbed her. Parker was taller and heavier than Bren, and rapidly becoming dead weight.

"Reilly," Bren called. "Can you give me a hand here?"

"Go ahead," Liz said, sliding off Reilly's lap. "Why don't you walk her around a little bit. Maybe get her some air."

"I better. Sorry," Reilly said as she rose.

"No, that's okay. She needs you right now."

Liz moved across the empty seats and joined Bren as Reilly put her arm around Parker and led her away. "What happened?"

Bren pointed to Candace.

"Oh, what is she doing," Liz exclaimed.

"She's upset."

"Good, now so am I," Liz said angrily. "When is she going to grow up?"

"Well, not toni—" Bren stared at the woman coming toward her. Jae now wore a black leather vest, low cut black leather briefs, and calf-high black boots.

"Oh my," Liz said. "Isn't that—"

"Yes," Bren said quietly, shifting on her chair until her legs stretched into the narrow aisle between their table and the next.

Jae stopped next to Bren, leaned down, and whispered, "You wanted a dance."

"No," Bren corrected, "you wanted to dance for me."

"May I?"

"Yes."

Jae nodded toward the bar, and the lights went down and the music came up. Then she straddled Bren's lap, flexing her thighs and holding herself just a little bit above Bren so that her ass barely brushed Bren's legs. "You're not supposed to touch me, but you can."

"I'm not going to touch you," Bren said, aware that Liz had shifted away, leaving them alone. The room was dim enough to give them privacy but not so dark that she couldn't see Jae's face, and her body. "Not tonight, and not here."

"When?"

Bren wondered how long Jae could support herself without touching Bren for balance. With the same iron control Jae had shown on stage, she slowly circled her hips over Bren's lap.

"Open your vest," Bren ordered.

Without a second's hesitation, Jae flicked open the single button and the leather parted, revealing her breasts just inches from Bren's face. Her nipples were hard. Jae rolled her hips, her crotch a whisper away from Bren's stomach.

"Show me how you like your nipples touched," Bren said. Her own nipples tightened as she watched Jae grasp her nipples, stretch them out, and twist rapidly.

Jae grunted softly and her thigh muscles quivered. She murmured, "I want to rub myself against you. I need to feel you."

"Yes."

Immediately, Jae leaned forward, gripping Bren's shoulder with one hand. Her breasts brushed Bren's face, and the leather between her legs, supple and soft from the heat beneath, caressed Bren's bare stomach.

"Did you come when you went backstage?" Bren breathed the words against Jae's throat as Jae undulated against her body.

"No," Jae gasped.

"I'm not here to finish what someone else started." Bren wanted to draw Jae's nipple into her mouth and torture it with her teeth until

Jae cried out. She ached to press her fingers into the vee between Jae's thighs and work the smooth leather over her hard clit.

"I won't come without your permission," Jae groaned.

"You are not to come now."

"God, I ne—"

"When you go home tonight," Bren instructed, her lips caressing the hollow at the base of Jae's throat, "I want you to make yourself come. I want you to imagine you're licking me while you do."

Jae shuddered. "I'm close now."

"I don't care." Bren struggled not to grab Jae's hips and thrust into her, knowing if she did they would both probably come. And this wasn't the time or the place or the way she wanted it to happen. "How did you find me?"

"I didn't." Jae's voice was steel wire stretched to the breaking point. "You found me."

Bren couldn't help herself. She bit the thick muscle at the base of Jae's neck, once, sharply. "Behave."

"Oh God," Jae arched her back, pushing herself into Bren's body. "Please."

"Answer the question," Bren murmured, licking the spot she'd just bitten.

"I didn't…know if you would…come."

Sweat dripped from Jae's thighs and slicked the surface of Bren's leather pants.

"But I waited…every night."

The music was coming to an end, and Bren knew their time was almost up. She finally did what she'd been aching to do for so long she couldn't remember the first time she'd imagined holding her in her arms. She skimmed both hands up Jae's back, savoring her hot skin, and pulled her close. Jae dropped her head onto Bren's shoulder.

"Tell me your name," Bren whispered against Jae's ear.

"When I dance," the woman gasped, "I'm Jae."

Bren kissed the soft skin just below her earlobe. "The next time we meet, I'll tell you mine."

When the lights came up, Jae slipped away.

❖

"Who was that?" Liz asked. "I was trying not to be a voyeur, but it was kind of hard not to watch."

"One of the dancers."

"I got that part. But how did you end up with the lap dance?"

"She offered, I said yes."

Liz laughed. "You don't think you can get away with that, do you?"

"Not for a second." Bren looked around. "Candace is missing."

"Reilly and Parker didn't come back, either." Liz tried to keep her disappointment from showing. "Are you ready to go?"

"Yes. What do you think we should do about Candace?"

Liz sighed. "I guess we should stay and wait for her."

"Here comes Reilly," Bren said.

Liz turned quickly. "Hi. I thought you'd gone."

"Parker's asleep in my car. I think I should take her home." Reilly regarded Liz intently. "I just wanted to say good night."

"Good night," Liz said softly.

"Hey," Bren said, jumping up. "Reilly, maybe you could give Liz a ride home. I'll stay here and wait for Candace." She checked with Liz. "If you don't mind me driving your car."

"No way am I leaving you here alone," Liz said.

"I'll be fine."

"No," Reilly and Liz said simultaneously.

"Here she comes now," Reilly said. She hesitated, then said to Liz, "Looks like everyone is accounted for."

"Yes."

"I'll see you then. Take care."

"Thanks," Liz said. "I will. You too."

"Right," Reilly said, backing up a step. "Good night."

"'Night." Liz frowned as Candace sauntered over to them. "Are you okay?"

"Fine. I ran into an old friend. We're going out for breakfast."

"It's two in the morning," Liz pointed out.

"So we'll have breakfast...later," Candace said smugly.

"Fine." Liz grabbed Bren's hand. "Come on, birthday girl. Let's go."

"Oh, hey, Bren," Candace said. "Did you have an okay time?"

Bren smiled. "It was just exactly what I wanted."

CHAPTER EIGHTEEN

R eilly woke up a little after seven and went for a run, leaving Parker still asleep on the couch. She doubted Parker would wake up for another couple of hours, but she left a note with Parker's clothes telling her there was a pot of fresh coffee in the kitchen just in case. On her return circuit, she stopped for bagels and immediately thought of the morning she and Liz had shared an impromptu breakfast. That was the day she had come upon Liz in the hospital ladies' room being violently ill. *From the flu,* she recalled wryly. She couldn't remember if Annie had ever had morning sickness, but she probably wouldn't have recognized it in *her* either. Annie was so frequently ill with her diabetes, she probably would have blamed any sickness on that.

Liz looked good last night. They hadn't been able to talk much, what with everyone around and the noise level pretty much making conversation impossible, but she imagined Liz was almost over the worst of her morning sickness. She must be twelve or thirteen weeks now, even though she still didn't look very pregnant. She didn't feel very pregnant either. Liz's waistline had been soft and supple when Reilly had held her on her lap. Liz's whole body had felt soft and warm and tempting.

Reilly couldn't remember Liz ever being more relaxed, and she'd fit just about perfectly on Reilly's lap. In fact, holding Liz had felt more natural than anything she had done in years, except operate, and that was so much a part of her she never even thought about it. Maybe that's the way it was supposed to be with a woman too, something that came so naturally, that felt so much a part of you, it was almost like breathing.

Eight o'clock. Still pretty early. Liz did say she got up early, though, and her condo was only a few short blocks away. On impulse, Reilly bought an extra half dozen bagels.

Ten minutes later, she walked into the foyer of Liz's apartment building, telling herself that if Liz didn't answer after one short ring, she'd give it up. She hit Liz's buzzer for a few seconds, expecting no answer. When the speaker crackled to life, she jumped.

"Yes?"

"It's Reilly. I've got bagels, but if you're—"

The speaker went dead, the door lock clicked open, and Reilly pushed through. The elevator was empty and within a minute she was standing in front of Liz's door. She pressed the bell, her pulse hammering expectantly. She had to restrain herself from grinning too foolishly, but when the door swung open, her smile faded.

"Hi," a statuesque brunette said, her brows lifted in question. "I didn't order any bagels, but I'll be happy to take them off your hands."

Reilly surveyed the stranger, assuming from the wet hair and the short, black silk robe, underneath which she was obviously naked, that she'd just gotten out of the shower. Reilly pointedly did not linger on the full breasts and hint of cleavage exposed where the robe parted in the center of her chest. "Sorry. I didn't mean to disturb you."

"I'm Julia," the woman said. She folded her arms beneath her breasts and cocked one hip. "I guess you're not the delivery boy."

"Not exactly." Reilly held out one of the bags of bagels. "These are for Liz, but you're welcome to share."

Julia smiled slowly and took the offered bag. "I'm not really big on sharing."

"No, I wouldn't be either. Tell Liz I said hi."

"Oh, I will."

Reilly pivoted and headed back to the elevator. She didn't hear the door close right away and sensed Julia watching her. *Julia.* Reilly might have guessed she was Liz's lover even without hearing her name. Like Candace, Julia was voluptuous and seductive. Reilly glanced down at her T-shirt, cut off sweatpants, and running shoes. Definitely not in the same category as the woman who had just answered Liz's door. Liz's ex-lover. Or maybe Liz's lover still.

❖

"Bren," Liz called from Bren's kitchen. "Someone's at the door."

When Bren didn't answer, Liz put the coffee pot aside and headed for the living room. She could hear the shower running in Bren's second-floor bathroom, so she answered the door herself.

"Hi," Candace said, breezing in with her arms filled with packages. "I figured you'd be here. I brought breakfast. I hope you two didn't eat yet."

"We're just getting going," Liz said, taking a bag from Candace and heading back to the kitchen. She'd spent the night at Bren's since it was so late when she dropped her off, and because she didn't feel like going home to a cold and silent condo. Bren had provided her with a T-shirt and a pair of blue cotton checked boxers to sleep in, which she was still wearing. She'd spent the night on a futon in the room that had once been her old bedroom, and the familiarity had been comforting. She'd been tired, but keyed up, too. The arousal laden atmosphere of the club had stirred her up, and sitting on Reilly's lap for half an hour had pretty much stoked her libido to the boiling point. Funny, she hadn't the slightest inclination to take the edge off her desire herself. Consequently, she'd awakened in a black mood that the heavy thudding sensation in the pit of her stomach did nothing to alleviate.

"Coffee should be done," Liz said, knowing she sounded churlish and not caring. She doubted that *Candace* had awakened feeling undesirable and unsatisfied.

"Good. I could use some." Candace perched on one of the tall stools at the cook island opposite where Liz was setting out cups. "Do you believe that place last night? God, it was a turn on."

"The women weren't exactly my style."

"Not even the last one?"

Liz would have said no the day before, not ever having considered the leather scene or power play her kind of thing. However, watching a strong, powerful woman literally brought to her knees with desire *had* been arousing. "That was sexy."

"Yeah. I'll say." Candace rummaged around in one of the bags and pulled out a raspberry croissant. "Bren had fun, don't you think? Did she say she had fun?"

"I think she did," Liz said, plunging the French press coffee maker. If Bren wanted Candace to know about the lap dance, she'd tell her. Obviously, Candace had been too wrapped up in her evening's conquest to observe Bren's decidedly unusual behavior.

Candace broke off a piece of the croissant and nibbled it. "You and Reilly got pretty cozy."

Liz flushed. "I think we might be able to be friends. I'm glad about that."

"Looked like a little more than friendship to me," Candace commented, reaching for an empty coffee cup from the stand on the end of the counter. She held it out to Liz. "The way you were cuddled up in her lap."

"I was *sitting* on her lap," Liz said pointedly as she filled Candace's cup, "because Parker wanted to talk to you. Not that you cared."

"Parker spent the evening having dinner and drinks with Reilly," Candace said lightly. "That makes her Reilly's date, and in case you didn't notice, they looked very happy together when they arrived. I'm surprised you weren't more bothered."

Liz restrained herself from slamming down the coffee pot on Bren's new hand-painted tile countertop. "First of all, what Reilly does is not my business. Secondly, Parker was a little under the weather. And she spent most of the night trying to get your attention."

Candace turned sideways on the stool and crossed her legs with a careless shrug. "I don't play seconds to anyone."

"You're an ass."

"What?" Candace exclaimed indignantly, spinning back to face Liz.

"Uh-oh," Bren said as she walked in. "What have I missed so far?"

"Just Candace being a jerk."

"Just Liz being obnoxious."

Bren smiled and took the coffee mug Liz held out to her. "Oh, good. Nothing new. Mmm, are those croissants?"

"Yes. There's chocolate in there for you." Candace glared at Liz. "Do you mind explaining your remark?"

"It's Saturday morning, isn't it?" Liz said.

Candace frowned. "Yes."

"And did you not rush off in the middle of lunch on Thursday—that would be two days ago Thursday—to have sex with Parker?"

"Yes," Candace said slowly, tearing off another piece of croissant. "And your point would be?"

"Why would you think that Friday night when Parker showed up at the club—the club where you invited her, I might add—that she didn't come to see you?"

Bren sipped her coffee and savored her chocolate croissant wordlessly.

"Because," Candace replied, "Parker and I already discussed the fact that we weren't going to see each other again. And," she went on before Liz could interrupt, "if you'll recall, when she arrived, she was hanging all over Reilly."

"Parker had a few drinks on top of a pain pill and was looped." Liz grabbed the bag of croissants. "Are there any cheese in here?"

"Of course," Candace said haughtily.

"Besides that," Liz went on, "Parker is probably a little confused about your rules, considering you were rolling around with her just the day before."

"Parker gets it. And since when are you so concerned about my dates?"

"Since I happen to like this one, Candace." Liz set her croissant down on a paper towel and leaned with her elbows on the counter. "And I think you do too."

Candace looked away.

"You look all fresh and relaxed this morning, Cand," Bren said into the silence. "How was the rest of your night?"

"Fine," Candace said.

"Anybody we know?" Bren helped herself to more coffee.

"I don't think so."

"Did you get her name?" Liz asked.

"Sophie." Candace sighed, propped her elbows on the counter, and rested her chin in her hands. "And I didn't sleep with her."

"What? You didn't leave with her? How did you get home?" Liz exclaimed, her irritation warring with concern. "We would have waited for you if you'd said you weren't going home with her. That was crazy, Candace."

"I *did* go home with her. I just didn't sleep with her once I got there."

Bren gave a murmur of surprise. "Is that a first?"

Candace grinned. "I think so."

"Why not?" Liz asked.

Candace shrugged. "She'd been drinking."

"And?" Liz persisted, sensing there was more.

"And I wasn't really all that horny."

"And?" Liz and Bren said together.

"And I just didn't feel like it, okay?"

"Not okay," Bren said a second before Liz agreed.

Candace slid off the stool and walked across the kitchen to the open back door. She stood gazing out, the morning sunlight framing her blond hair like a spun-gold halo. Liz thought her face in profile looked as pure and flawless as a Madonna.

"It all seemed a little pointless," Candace said quietly. "She might have been able to make me come. I'm damn certain I could have made *her* come."

Liz smiled but said nothing.

"But when we were all done, the only thing we would have gotten out of it would have been a few seconds of pleasure. And they're gone almost as soon as they happen."

"Not always," Liz said quietly.

Candace threw her a crooked smile. "I know."

"Why was last night different?" Bren asked.

"I don't know."

Liz considered pointing out that this change in attitude might have something to do with Parker, but Candace had probably ventured as far as she could in that direction for the moment. Candace's fear of commitment, of any kind of relationship at all, was too deeply ingrained to be overcome so simply. Liz opted for a subtler approach, even though she really wanted to just shake her.

"Are you two up for another afternoon in the sun?" Liz said. "We can go to the softball game tomorrow."

"Is Reilly playing?" Candace said.

"I don't know," Liz replied, although she couldn't deny she secretly hoped so.

"I'm in," Bren said.

"I suppose," Candace added.

"And you," Liz stabbed a finger in Bren's direction, "don't think I've forgotten about your mystery date."

"What mystery date?" Candace strode back to the island and reclaimed her stool. "What mystery date?"

"It wasn't exactly a date—"

"That's not what you said last night," Liz pointed out.

"How come I don't know about this?" Candace stared from Liz to

Bren, her expression vacillating between outrage and hurt. "How come you two have a secret?"

Liz rolled her eyes.

"*We* don't have a secret," Bren said. "I have a secret. Sort of."

Now both Liz and Candace regarded her with avid curiosity.

"Just a minute," Bren said, and quickly left the room.

"What did I miss?" Candace asked immediately.

"Last night while you were…doing whatever you were doing at the bar—"

"Okay, okay. I got that you didn't approve of me getting a little action."

"If I disapproved of you getting a little action, we would have stopped speaking years ago."

"When are you going to forgive me for that?" Candace said quietly.

Liz stopped short. "I have."

"Are you sure?"

Liz hesitated. *Hadn't she?*

"Okay," Bren said, walking into the room with her hands behind her back. On the ride home from the Blue Diamond, she had realized she was going to have to explain more than just a date to her friends. Even if she never saw Jae again, Liz had seen them together, and she'd hinted earlier that she suspected Bren was hiding something. Her secret life hadn't seemed quite so important before, not when she could keep her writing tucked away in a separate corner of her world. But last night, something unexpected had happened. The boundaries had rippled, then cracked, and one reality had bled into another. She held out a book to each of them. "Here."

Both Liz and Candace looked surprised as they took the offering.

"Oh my God," Candace exclaimed. "It's the newest Melanie Richards. It's not supposed to be out until next month. How did you get this?"

"Mine's signed to me," Liz said as she flipped through the pages.

"Mine too!" Candace jumped down from her stool and threw her arms around Bren. "Thank you. Thank you! Aren't you supposed to be the one getting presents on your birthday? Did you go to a signing? Did you meet her? What was she like? Is she hot?"

"I didn't go to a signing," Bren replied, thinking that her publicist would be delighted if she finally decided to come out of the virtual closet. She pushed that thought away, not quite ready to have her life *that* integrated. "These are author's copies."

"Author's copies." Candace nodded knowingly. "That's how you got them early. Did you buy them on her website? I've never seen anything about that on there."

"Candace," Liz said quietly, turning the book over and over in her hands. "Author's copies are what they give to the author before the book comes out."

"Well I know that. I just said—" Candace stopped abruptly and frowned, her gaze dancing between Liz and Bren. "What are you trying to say?"

"I'm Melanie Richards," Bren said.

"No," Liz and Candace said.

Bren nodded.

"That's amazing," Liz said, half laughing.

"I'm going to kill you," Candace exploded. She dropped her book on the counter and made a grab for Bren, who jumped backward with both arms out in front of herself.

"No! No, I'm sorry. I'm sorry." Bren ran into the living room with Candace close behind.

"Not half as sorry as you're going to be when I catch you," Candace screamed, chasing Bren around the sofa. Bren jumped onto the seat and then over the back to escape.

"Why didn't you tell us?" Candace ran around the end of the sofa and tore after Bren.

"It just happened!" Bren raced into the kitchen and grabbed a chair, holding it up in front of her. "No tickling."

"I'm not going to tickle you. I'm going to strangle you," Candace growled, shifting from side to side and trying to reach around the chair.

"Candace," Liz called, "if you kill her, we won't know what happens to Jae."

"I'll make her tell me before I kill her," Candace swore, but she was starting to laugh.

"Please, please," Bren gasped, tiring from evading Candace and holding up the chair. "It won't do any good to torture me. I don't know what's going to happen to her!"

Candace stopped dead. "What do you mean you don't know? Are you the author or not?"

Bren put the chair down gratefully. "Yes. Yes, but I don't write that way. I don't know exactly what's going to happen until I write it."

"Well then what good does it do having a best friend who's Melanie Richards?" Candace sagged onto her stool with a pout.

"None," Bren said quickly. "So it really doesn't matter that you didn't know."

"Why didn't you tell us?" Liz asked. "Didn't you trust us?"

The room was suddenly completely quiet, and Bren struggled to find an answer that wouldn't hurt the two people she loved the most in the world.

"Even when we were all in school together, you both always seemed so clear about who you were and what you wanted," Bren said. "I was never sure. I'm still not sure."

Candace snorted. "You think I am?"

"Look at me," Liz said ruefully.

"Well, I guess it seemed to me that I was the only one who didn't understand what I felt. Not until I started writing. By the time I realized what a big part of my life my writing had become, I was just used to keeping it a secret."

"Years! You've been writing these books for years and you didn't tell us," Candace screamed.

"I know. I'm sorry."

"I love your books," Liz said, wrapping her arms around Bren. "And I love you. I'm sorry if I made you feel you couldn't tell me something."

Bren blinked back tears. "No. It wasn't you." She looked at Candace over Liz's shoulder. "Or you either. It was me. It just took me a long time to figure out that I was more me in my books than anywhere else."

"So," Candace said contemplatively. "Are you telling us that you're Jae?"

Bren smiled, feeling the pieces of her world, of herself, slide effortlessly together. "No, I'm Jae's Mistress."

CHAPTER NINETEEN

D id you find the aspirin?" Reilly asked when she walked into her apartment and saw Parker slumped in one corner of the sofa, her face pasty except for the lingering bruises. Parker's hair was wet and she was wearing the T-shirt and shorts Reilly had left on the coffee table for her, so she'd managed to find the shower.

"Yeah, thanks," Parker said, her voice raspy.

"Want to try something to eat?"

"Cyanide?"

Reilly laughed. "How about a toasted bagel and...I might have milk."

Parker groaned. "Coffee. I haven't drunk milk since I was twelve."

"I'll put something together."

"Need any help?"

"No," Reilly said as she crossed the small, spartan living room to her galley kitchen. "I don't think you're up for it just yet."

"Thanks," Parker called weakly.

The narrow kitchen was a little small for two to work in, and Reilly didn't want company at the moment, anyway. She was still trying to sort out her feelings about running into Julia at Liz's apartment. Julia seemed so confident and so much at home, and her proprietary air toward Liz rankled. Not that Reilly had any right to feel that way. And besides, maybe having Julia there was just what Liz wanted. And needed.

Sighing, she sliced bagels and put them in the toaster oven. Then she pushed the on button on the coffeemaker and pulled cups out of the cabinet above the Formica counter.

"Something I did?" Parker said from behind her.

Reilly turned. "Come again?"

"You're banging the cabinet doors hard enough to shake the building."

"Oh." Reilly ran her hands through her hair and let out a breath. "Sorry. Probably doesn't make your head feel too good."

"Can't make it any worse." Parker pulled over a wooden stool that Reilly kept tucked under the counter and sat down with her back propped against the wall. "I don't remember much of the ride home. And I have no idea how you got me up here."

Reilly grinned. "You walked."

"Did I?" Parker looked impressed. "Did I, uh, manage any other feats of physical prowess?"

"Other than grabbing my ass?"

Parker leaned her head back against the wall and groaned. "I was afraid of that. Sorry."

"No problem. I haven't been groped in quite a while."

"Please," Parker pleaded. "Tell me I didn't act like some frat boy at a pledge party."

"You were fine." Taking pity on her, Reilly poured a cup of coffee and handed it to her. "Here. You want cream?"

"This is good. I'll apologize now for everything I did. Whatever it was."

"Nothing to worry about." Reilly hoisted herself up on the counter and sipped her coffee. "When you weren't complaining about Candace, you were trying to talk me into bed. But talk was pretty much as far as it went."

"Sorry."

"You mean you were lying when you said you wanted to—"

"No," Parker moaned, holding up a hand. "Don't tell me."

"All right. I'll just cherish the thought forever."

Parker laughed and then moaned again. "Oh, that hurts."

"My fault," Reilly said. "I should've kept an eye on how much you had to drink."

"Not your responsibility."

"Maybe not, but that's what friends do, right? And besides, I know you've been taking pain pills all week. I'm not surprised the alcohol packed a double punch."

"Well, you got me home in one piece. And I appreciate it."

"No problem." Reilly jumped down when the timer on the toaster oven went off and pulled the bagels out. She buttered both and passed one over to Parker. "I know you don't want this, but you need it."

"Thanks." Parker traded her coffee cup for the bagel, and Reilly set the empty cup aside.

They ate in silence for a few minutes, then Parker said, "So if you weren't pissed off at me this morning, what had you so worked up?"

Reilly shook her head. "Just tilting at windmills."

"Ah. Something to do with a woman."

"How did you know?"

Parker shrugged, balancing her empty plate on her knee. "Are there any other kind of windmills that matter?"

Reilly chuckled. "I guess not."

"Anything you want to talk about?"

"No. Thanks." Reilly didn't want to reveal anything about Liz's personal situation, and what could she say? That she liked Liz, a lot—more than liked her—but they couldn't have met under more complicated circumstances, for either of them. That she'd followed her impulses and dropped in on Liz only to run into her lover. No, there was nowhere good to take that conversation.

"You know, as nice as your ass might be," Parker said, "I was kind of hoping to wake up in Candace's bed this morning."

"Something going on there?" Reilly asked, glad for the change in conversation. Talking with Parker kept her from imagining what Liz and Julia might be doing.

"Not really," Parker replied with studied casualness. "We've had a couple of pleasant...encounters. But she's a free agent."

"I sort of got the sense that you liked an open field, too."

"Yeah, well. When you're working eighty hours a week, it's tough to do much more than grab a few hours of fun wherever and whenever you can get it. It's simpler not to make too much out of it."

Reilly nodded. She understood the working part, and how easy it was to use that as an excuse not to reach out, not to connect to anyone. She hadn't meant to connect with Liz. It had happened so effortlessly she hadn't even noticed. She wasn't even sure when it had happened. She could see herself lying flat on her back in the hospital lobby with Liz leaning over her, amusement and concern in her warm green eyes, and she remembered feeling pulled in and never wanting to leave.

"Did you ever find yourself stopping," Reilly mused, "in the middle of a sentence, or maybe in the middle of a kiss, and realizing that it wasn't enough. The words, the kiss, whatever it was you were doing—it wasn't enough to get you as close as you wanted to get?"

Parker stared at her. "I wish you hadn't said that."

"Why?"

"Because I know exactly what you mean, and it scares the hell out of me."

"Me too," Reilly said.

❖

"Oh no," Candace said when Liz came down from the second floor, having changed into the clothes she had worn the night before. "You're not going anywhere yet. I want the details about Bren's mystery woman."

"I told you," Bren said, "I don't have any details. Nothing happened."

"That's not what Liz said."

"Me?" Liz exclaimed. "I didn't say anything." She shot Bren a sly look. "Although I did get an eyeful."

"See!" Candace put her hands on her hips. "There *is* something I don't know." She pointed her finger at Bren. "You. Tell."

"All right," Bren said, examining Liz with concern. "Are you okay? You're a little pale."

"I think last night is catching up to me," Liz said ruefully. "I can't party like I used to."

"Come on," Candace said, taking Liz's hand. "Let's sit outside on the deck. It's shady out there. Bren, bring her something to drink."

"I'm okay," Liz protested, but she allowed Candace to lead her outside. She hadn't slept well the night before, and she did feel more tired than usual, but she was beginning to accept that she wasn't going to feel like herself again for six months. She settled down into the Adirondack deck chair and put her feet on the small wooden stool that went with it. Bren handed her a glass of sparkling water. "Thanks."

Candace perched on a stool next to Liz's feet and put one hand casually on Liz's ankle. Then she fixed Bren with a stern glare. "Tell."

Bren leaned against the wood railing and studied her hands, trying to think of how to explain to her friends what she hadn't been able to explain to herself. Sometimes, when she was wordless like this, she found it hard to believe she was actually a professional writer. She sighed. "She emailed me about my books."

"So did thousands of other readers," Candace pointed out. "I know. I have your website bookmarked, you sneaky bitch. I read your blogs. I can't believe I didn't know it was you."

Bren tried not to grin.

"If you laugh, I'm pushing you over that railing," Candace threatened.

"Okay. Okay. I won't laugh," Bren said, laughing. "And I do get a lot of email—you're right."

"But something about *her* was different," Liz suggested.

"Yes. She recognized what I was doing with Jae—the direction I was taking her character. She knew it almost before I did."

"I could've told you that Jae was looking for a dominant lover," Candace said, smiling smugly. "Us take charge girls *are* kind of popular."

Bren regarded Candace with interest. "Is that how you see yourself? A femme top?"

Candace ran her fingers absently up and down Liz's lower leg, her expression contemplative. "I never thought about it quite that way, but I know I like to be in charge in bed—most of the time. So what do you think? Do I qualify?"

"There aren't any absolutes, you know," Bren said. "No clearly definable sexual types. All you have to do is look at a roomful of lesbians to tell how different we all are. But there are some similarities, some common desires, that distinguish us as well."

Liz tilted her head back and watched the deep blue sky, filled with white fluffy clouds, revolve slowly overhead. The air was hot and still. They had spent countless lazy afternoons, the three of them, just like this—sitting around debating sexual politics or philosophy or a hundred other things. It had never occurred to her that someday they might be discussing their own lives in the same way. "You always were the deep thinker."

Bren chuckled. "God, there's not much thinking that goes into what attracts us to someone, and what satisfies us in bed. Wherever those urges come from, I think they're far deeper than anything we can tease out in a discussion."

"Let's get back to the sex," Candace said. "So Jae wants a woman to control her. I already told you I knew that."

"It's more about *how* she wants to be controlled," Bren said. "She wants to be controlled in every way—physically, emotionally, sexually. She wants to give up *all* of her control."

Candace studied Bren for a long moment. "Is that in the next book?"

"Yes," Bren said.

"When?"

"As soon as I get the damn thing written," Bren exclaimed, exasperated and amused.

"Candace, honey," Liz murmured, "you're doing that avoidance thing again."

"What avoidance thing?" Candace asked archly.

"Where you talk about sex when you're nervous about something else."

"I do not," Candace stated adamantly.

"Yes you do," Bren and Liz affirmed.

Candace pursed her lips and fell silent.

"So Jae—what's her real name, by the way," Liz asked.

"I don't know," Bren replied. "She told me it's Jae, and that's how I've been thinking of her."

"Kinky," Candace interjected.

Liz swatted Candace on the shoulder. "Shut up. Okay, so Jae recognized where you're going with your character and that made her stand out in your mind. What else?"

Bren averted her gaze and immediately knew they would pick up that now *she* was avoiding the answer. Before they could both call her on it, she sighed and said, "She understood that I wanted to be the one controlling her. Jae that is."

"Oooo, Brenda Louise, you are *so* bad," Candace sighed.

"And you thought we wouldn't approve?" Liz asked. "That's why you didn't tell us?"

"No!" Bren shook her head. "No. I didn't quite get it myself until I started writing it in my books. And then I realized what I wanted and well, that's it, really."

"And…that's what she wants to give you?" Liz asked, clearly thinking out loud.

Bren smiled. "Yes, that's it exactly. That's what she wants to give me."

"What are you going to do?" Liz asked.

"I don't know," Bren said, thinking how the true balance of power was so different than the perception. "Whatever happens will be up to her."

❖

Liz drove home thinking about Bren's revelations. On one level she was surprised, because Bren had always been the one to keep Liz and Candace grounded, back in their crazy days. No matter what kind of drama they found themselves in, Bren was always the voice of reason. It wasn't that Bren was boring, she was just so safe. She was the one they counted on when the world shifted beneath their feet. But on another level, Liz admitted she had always sensed that Bren was far more complex than the placid surface she allowed the world to see. Liz wondered how it could be that a stranger had read Bren's books and discerned something far more intimate about her than her best friends. Perhaps it had something to do with artistic revelation and the inability to hide one's self in something as intimate as one's art. She didn't know. The law was more often than not a place to hide one's true feelings, rather than to expose them.

And yet, she thought of Reilly, and how easy it had been to be open with her. How she had been able to talk to her from the first moment, and had never felt the need to hide anything. In many ways, Reilly was like Bren, providing a solid sense of safety and comfort. Liz shook her head, because Reilly was not Bren. What she felt for Reilly she'd never once felt for Bren. Reilly flat out made her hot.

Liz pulled into the parking garage with a sense of melancholy. She was happy for Bren and the door that seemed to be opening in her life, even though she was a little worried that Bren might get hurt. Bren probably worried about her that way, too. After all, that's what friends did. She could be happy for her and at the same time feel a little jealous that while Bren was on the verge of an exciting new experience, she was going forward alone during a time that she had thought would be one of the happiest in her life.

"Oh, stop with the self-pity," Liz muttered as she got off the elevator on her floor. "After all, it's not the first time life turned out differently than you expected." She placed a hand on her stomach and looked down, feeling more than seeing the swelling in her lower abdomen. "You hear that in there? You might not be showing up exactly the way I planned, but we are going to make the best of it. More than that, we're going to have fun. We're going to have a great life."

Laughing inwardly and grateful that no one was around to hear her, Liz fit her key to the lock. When the door opened before she had chance to turn the key, she jumped back with a small cry.

"Sorry," Julia said, leaning her shoulder against the door as she held it partly open. "I heard you talking and thought we might have company."

Shocked, Liz had the disorienting sensation that she had been thrust back in time. Julia looked like she'd just gotten out of bed, and in fact, she was still wearing a robe. Liz's robe, she noticed, that was a little too small and a little too short for Julia, revealing way too much of her.

"Julia," Liz said, trying desperately to gather her wits, "there *is* no we."

"Well, darling," Julia smiled slowly, "that's what I'm here to talk about."

CHAPTER TWENTY

L iz edged past Julia, still trying to adjust to the shock of seeing her at all, let alone in her apartment. When Julia had first left, her absence had been a hollow ache that had echoed throughout the rooms and finally settled around Liz's heart. Now that Julia had suddenly returned, Liz was bombarded with conflicting emotions. Most of all, she was angry. Angry that Julia thought she still had the right to walk through a locked door and back into Liz's life. Angry at Julia for all the times they had talked about their future and Julia had never said that their dreams were not the same. Angry at herself for refusing to see the truth, even when she had lived with it. She was confused, too, by the instant pull of recognition, of familiar connection, that she'd experienced the moment she'd seen Julia's face. She hadn't thought she had any feelings left for her at all.

"What are you doing here?" Liz crossed the room and deposited her purse and car keys on a side table. She smelled coffee, and the sense of déjà vu strengthened. How many times had she come home from the office on Saturday morning, after having gone in before dawn, to find Julia waiting for her. Julia always slept late on the weekends and never started grumbling about Liz's absence until at least noon. In the beginning of their relationship, Julia had waited in bed and they would make love until the afternoon turned into evening. In recent months, even longer than that when Liz thought of it, Julia more often than not had met her with angry silence or complaints about her working too much.

"I thought it was time we talked face to face," Julia replied. "Every time I phone you, you're too busy and you never return my calls."

"Perhaps there's a message in that."

"I know you're angry. You have a right to be."

Liz spun around. "I'm so glad that you think so."

Julia smiled patiently. "I didn't handle things right at all, I know that. That's why I'm here."

"You don't live here anymore. I didn't change the locks because I knew that you had left some things behind, but I assumed you'd call first before coming over. It never occurred to me that you would just walk in when I wasn't here." Liz gestured to the robe. "And you've certainly made yourself at home. Did you sleep here?"

Julia's expression darkened. "Didn't *you?*"

"I stayed at Bren's. Yesterday was her birthday."

"I'll send her a card."

Liz sat down on the sofa and folded her arms across her chest. "You haven't explained what you're doing here."

"I took the redeye back from a meeting in LA. I thought about you all the way home, and I wanted to talk to you."

"That's what the phone is for."

"We've been over that. Besides, it was on my way, and I know you're always up early. When you didn't answer the buzzer, I assumed you were at the office and I thought I'd wait."

"And take a shower and make coffee?"

Julia shrugged. "Why not."

"I have the papers from your attorney about the condo. I'll look at them this week."

"I didn't come here to talk about the condo." Julia settled onto the sofa next to Liz and rested one hand on Liz's thigh. "I came to talk about us."

"You left, remember? You have a new lover. There's nothing to talk about."

"I don't think we should be hasty," Julia said calmly.

Liz laughed, beginning to suspect she'd tumbled into the Twilight Zone. "Hasty? There wasn't anything hasty about your six-month affair. And there wasn't anything hasty about the last two years of our relationship, when we'd been sharing the same space and nothing else."

"I'll admit, I made some bad choices and I'm sorry. But we have a lot of years together, and I don't think we should just throw those all away."

Liz shifted as far away as she could, but Julia leaned closer. Abruptly, Liz stood to escape Julia's touch. They *did* need to talk—there were things she needed to say. "I'm not blaming you for everything that happened between us. I didn't do anything when I realized we were drifting apart. But we *did* drift apart, and you found someone else."

"I had an affair. That's not the same thing."

"The distinction escapes me."

"Look, I'll stop seeing her."

"You mean you haven't yet?" Liz shook her head. "You come here wanting us to resume our relationship, but you haven't told your girlfriend about it?"

Julia was silent.

"I don't want a relationship with you," Liz said, recognizing the truth of her words and feeling the anger melt away. "Whatever we had between us has been gone for a long time. It's time for us to move on. Both of us."

"Maybe it *is* too late to go back," Julia said, rising. She stepped close to Liz and put her arms around Liz's neck. "But we can go forward. I promise, I've learned my lesson."

"I'm pregnant, Julia."

Julia's eyes widened and Liz felt her stiffen for just an instant. Then she relaxed and smiled.

"Why, that's wonderful darling. And all the more reason why we should be togeth—"

"No," Liz said, grasping Julia's arms and removing them from around her neck. "It's the most important reason why we shouldn't be together. You didn't want this baby, and I won't raise my child with someone who isn't going to be there for both of us with her whole heart."

"You'd rather be alone?" Julia asked incredulously.

Liz smiled and lightly touched her abdomen. "I'm not alone."

Julia's eyes grew stormy. "Now who's not being truthful. You've found someone else. That certainly didn't take long."

"Not that it's any of your business, but I haven't." Liz shook her head. "I'd really like it if you'd get dressed and leave now."

"Fine," Julia snapped. "Have you told your new girlfriend about your little bundle of joy?"

"I told you I'm not—"

"Five-eight, short black hair, a nice hard body, and hot eyes?"

Liz caught her breath. "What?"

"She was here. She brought bagels. I rang her up because I was curious about your early morning visitor."

"Please go," Liz said, turning her back and walking into the kitchen. A bag of bagels from her favorite deli sat on the counter. *Reilly. Oh Reilly.*

❖

Bren hurried upstairs to her office as soon as Candace left. She dropped into her desk chair and then halted abruptly with her fingers poised over the keyboard. What if there was no message? What if last night had been a test and she'd failed? What if Jae had only been playing an elaborate game and now that they'd met in person, the game had lost its appeal?

Perhaps it was better to leave fantasies where they belonged, in the realm of the possible but the unrealized. That way, dreams would never become disappointments. With a sigh, Bren logged on to her Melanie Richards website to update her blog. All of the messages were routine, and she answered some, trying to ignore her disappointment when she saw nothing that might have been from Jae. Then she checked her regular email and finally opened her Melanie email account. There were dozens of unread messages, but she saw only one header.

Last night...

Holding her breath, Bren opened the message.

I did what you told me to do. I wanted to come as soon as I got backstage, but I waited until I was home in bed because you told me to. You didn't say I couldn't, so I came twice, thinking about you in my mouth.

Bren's heart nearly pounded out of her chest. Jae hadn't climaxed on the stage when the faceless woman had teased her, but Bren knew what she looked like, what she smelled like, what she sounded like when she was excited. Bren remembered the barely perceptible brush of Jae's hot body against hers, and the way her breath tore in and out of her chest. Bren trembled as her body quickened, and now *she* was the one who wanted to come. Instead, she typed.

If I had wanted you to come more than once, I would have given you permission.

Then she did in the hardest thing she'd ever done in her life. She turned off her computer, got up, and walked away.

❖

Liz walked around Reilly's block for the fourth time. What if Reilly wasn't home? Worse, what if Reilly wasn't alone? What if she had read things completely wrong the night before, and Reilly *had* been with Parker just as Candace suspected. Or maybe after running into Julia, Reilly had decided that Parker was a much better choice of women to date.

"We're not dating anyway," Liz muttered.

Still, she couldn't bear the thought of Reilly thinking that she and Julia were…anything. She paused at the corner where she had picked Reilly up the morning they'd had breakfast, and the image of Reilly in jeans and a T-shirt, looking windblown and sexy, made her stomach tighten. With a sigh, she started around the block again. The sound of a car horn brought her up short, and she looked into the street. Reilly idled in her convertible, the top down and a puzzled expression on her face.

"Hi," Liz called, feeling inane and absurdly happy at the same time.

"You need a ride somewhere?"

Liz shook her head. "No, I'm not going anywhere."

Reilly grinned. "That sounds serious."

Laughing, Liz walked over to the passenger side and leaned her arms on the door. "You're blocking traffic."

"Why don't I take you on a ride to somewhere, then?"

Reilly's eyes were steady on Liz's face, dark and filled with possibilities. Liz didn't hesitate, but pulled the door open and quickly slid into the passenger seat. "Yes."

Reilly didn't speak again until they were speeding north on Interstate 95. Liz didn't mind Reilly's silence. She could sense her just a few feet away as clearly as if they were touching. Feeling better than she had all day, she relaxed with her head back, the warm sun on her face and a cool breeze streaming through her hair. She had left her apartment with the single intention of telling Reilly that Julia was not part of her life any more, but she didn't want to talk about Julia now. For just a few moments, all she wanted was to absorb the pleasure of being with Reilly.

After a few minutes she turned her head and watched Reilly as she drove, one hand draped over the gear shift, her fingers lightly caressing the round leather knob. Her arms were tanned below the sleeves of her polo shirt, and her black jeans hugged her long tight thighs. As usual, she wore running shoes. Liz had never met a woman who looked so sexy without even trying.

"Parker get home okay?" Liz asked.

"I was just coming back from driving her to the train station when I saw you," Reilly said, her eyes on the road. "She had a headache and needed to take a pain pill, and I didn't want her behind the wheel."

"She stayed overnight with you," Liz said, hoping she sounded casual.

"Yes. She was in no shape to go anywhere else last night."

"You're right. It was good of you to look after her."

Reilly glanced at her briefly. "How late did you stay?"

"Not too much longer after you left. Right after Bren got treated to a lap dance."

"No kidding. Not by the one with the six-guns, I hope."

Liz laughed. "No, the last one."

"The one in leather who was getting…ah…fondled up on stage?"

"That's the one. I think you were outside with Parker when she did her encore with Bren."

"Birthday present?"

"Maybe, but not from Candace and me. I think it was actually a date—sort of."

"Damn, I missed a lot. I did see Candace getting it on with someone at the bar."

"Yes."

"Parker's a little messed up about that," Reilly said quietly.

"So is Candace."

"Well then, I guess they'll work it out one way or the other."

"I hope so."

"Are you hungry?" Reilly asked.

Liz realized it was after five and she hadn't eaten anything since the croissant at breakfast. After Julia had finally left, she had curled up on the couch, tired from the late night and upset that Reilly might have gotten the wrong impression about Julia being at her apartment. She'd fallen into an uneasy sleep plagued by dark dreams and had awakened unrefreshed and restless. Without any clear plan, she'd showered and dressed and walked to Reilly's apartment.

"I missed lunch."

"That's not good."

"My schedule is a bit off today."

"I know a little restaurant in New Hope. I think you'll like it."

Liz turned in the seat and covered Reilly's hand where it rested on the gear shift. "Would you mind if I took a rain check on that?"

"No," Reilly said quickly. "Do you want me to take you home?"

"You know what I'd like? I'd like it if you could find an old-fashioned roadside hotdog stand. I'd really love a chocolate milkshake and a grilled cheese sandwich."

"O-kay," Reilly said, drawing out the word. She turned her hand and briefly clasped Liz's. "One case of indigestion, coming up."

❖

Twenty minutes later, Reilly carried a tray with two milkshakes, a hamburger, a grilled cheese sandwich, and an order of fries back to the car, where Liz waited with her head back and her eyes closed. Reilly hesitated before opening the door, indulging herself in the pleasure of looking at Liz. The sunlight brought out the slivers of golden flame in her hair, and she seemed so peaceful that Reilly hated to wake her.

"I can smell the food," Liz said with her eyes still closed. "If you don't get in here this second, I can't vouch for your safety."

Laughing, Reilly pulled the door open and slid into her seat. She balanced the tray in her lap and picked up Liz's chocolate milkshake.

"You sure about this?"

"Give me that," Liz ordered sternly, spreading open a napkin in her lap.

Reilly passed it over. "I didn't ask for pickles. Should I have asked for pickles?"

"I don't like pickles. But I want that sandwich."

"Here you go." Reilly munched her burger while enjoying Liz's small murmurs of contentment. "How's the morning sickness?"

Liz stiffened slightly. "Fine. No problems."

"Sorry. I didn't mean to get personal."

"Reilly, you held my head while I vomited. We're way past worrying about personal, don't you think?"

"I don't know, are we?" Reilly put her hamburger aside and passed Liz the French fries. "Want some?"

"Thanks." Liz finished her grilled cheese and started in on the fries. "I had an ultrasound this week. I really got it then that this is happening. Really happening."

"How so?"

"Well it's not like it looks like much of anything," Liz said, "but I heard its heartbeat. I heard it. It's growing inside me." She stared at Reilly. "I can't explain exactly how freaky that is. And amazing, too."

Reilly felt a swift stab of pain. She'd never seen an ultrasound of Annie's fetus. She looked at Liz and felt a million things she'd never felt for Annie. Protective, awestruck, strangely reverent, and constantly excited.

"I'm sorry. Is this hard for you? Because of Annie?"

Reilly shook her head. "Do you have it with you?"

"What?" Liz asked, confused.

"The ultrasound."

Liz blushed, then reached on the floor where she'd set her purse and rummaged around in it. "Here."

Reilly took the 4 x 5 inch Polaroid carefully and slanted it so the sunlight didn't glare off the surface. Among the shadows, she picked out a dark oval surrounding an irregular white crescent. She ran her finger over the tiny shape. "Look at that."

"I bet you've seen a million."

Liz sounded self-conscious and Reilly, still studying the image, reached between them and took Liz's hand. "Not like this." She looked up and caught Liz's eye. "Not this special. Did you send one to your sister?"

"First thing," Liz said quietly. "You remembered."

Reilly studied Liz, wondering why Liz sounded surprised. "I think about you."

"I think about you."

All the time, Reilly thought, *I think about you all the time.* And she didn't know if that was good or bad, but she knew she didn't want to stop. She realized she was still holding Liz's hand, and she didn't want to let go. She wondered about Julia, then decided she didn't care. Liz was here right now, and she was tired of pretending she didn't want her.

"We should get back," Liz said.

"Okay." Reilly gathered up the remains of their meal and returned the tray to the counter. When she got behind the wheel, Liz took her hand again.

"And I want you to invite me up to your apartment when we get there."

Reilly drew Liz's hand across the space between them and pressed it to her stomach. Then she started the car and backed out of the gravel lot, turned onto the one lane macadam road that would take them back to I-95 and the city, and covered Liz's hand where it lay against her middle.

"Okay."

"Aren't you going to ask me why?" Liz inquired.

"No," Reilly said. "It doesn't matter why. The answer is yes."

CHAPTER TWENTY-ONE

"Can I get you anything?" Reilly asked as she closed the door to her apartment behind Liz. Thankfully, she'd picked up the place before Parker left, and the living room was reasonably neat. She'd left a stack of medical journals on the coffee table and her gym bag in front of the closet, but the bookcases were dust free and none of her laundry was lying around.

"A soda would be great. Sprite?"

Reilly frowned. "Maybe. It might require some serious excavation."

Liz laughed. "I should have asked what my choices were."

"Water. Coke, I think. Everything else is alcoholic."

"Water is fine."

Reilly pointed to the couch. "Have a seat. Let me see what I can find."

"I really don't need anything."

Reilly hurried into the kitchen and squatted down to sort through the disorganized array of cans and bottles under the sink. Beer. Beer. Tuna fish. She frowned and put that up on the counter. Beer. Coke. And there at the back, two lonely cans of Sprite. Feeling as if she'd just downed a wild boar with a sharp wooden stick, she rose with a cry of triumph.

"Got it," she called. "Just needs ice."

"I don't mind it warm," Liz said from right behind her.

Reilly jumped and spun around. Liz stood three feet away in the doorway, watching her with an indecipherable smile on her face. "We're talking August in the city, Liz. The can is hot."

"You know, you're very nice."

"That's not what most people say," Reilly said.

"No?" Liz moved closer, stopping a few inches from Reilly, who had the cabinets at her back. She took the can from Reilly and set it gently on the counter. "What do they say?"

"My colleagues say I'm competitive." Reilly caught Liz's scent. Hot and sultry like the night breeze blowing in the open window a few feet away. Liz wore a sleeveless white blouse with the top two buttons open, baring a tantalizing triangle of lightly tanned skin. Her forest green cotton shorts came to mid-thigh, and a lot of leg stretched below them. Reilly itched to run her palms up and down that smooth expanse of thigh.

Liz rested both hands on Reilly's shoulders, her thumbs tracing the ridges of Reilly's collarbones. "What do your *friends* say?"

"That I'm competitive," Reilly said, her gaze fixed on Liz's mouth. Her lips were moist, parted slightly, and swollen, as if they'd already been kissed. "Liz…"

"Are you thinking about kissing me?"

Reilly looped her arms around Liz's waist and the space between them disappeared. "Yes."

"Good, because I'm thinking about being kissed."

Lightly, Reilly brushed her lips over Liz's. Once. Twice. "How's that?"

"Just like I said. Very nice." Liz shifted her hips until one thigh settled in the vee of Reilly's crotch. "What do your *girl*friends say about you?"

"I've forgotten."

Liz smiled. "Smart, too. Smart and nice."

"Nice is okay," Reilly whispered, sliding her hand up Liz's back before burying her fingers in Liz's thick, silky hair, "but do you think I could try for sexy?"

Liz tilted her head back and murmured appreciatively when Reilly kissed her throat. "You don't have to try for that."

"Self-improvement is a good thing to strive for." Reilly explored the hollow at the base of Liz's throat with the tip of her tongue, then kissed the skin exposed by Liz's open blouse. When she could kiss no lower, she turned her head slightly and rubbed her cheek gently over Liz's breast.

Liz drew in a sharp breath and her fingers tightened on Reilly's shoulders. "I'm very sensitive for some reason these days."

Reilly raised her head and kissed Liz's mouth, sweeping the tip of her tongue slowly over the surface of Liz's lower lip. "You're very beautiful."

"I can't imagine why you think that." Liz drew the thick strands of dark hair at the base of Reilly's neck through her fingers. "But I'm glad you do."

"I could try to tell you," Reilly murmured, her mouth against the soft skin below Liz's ear. "But I'd rather show you."

"Yes."

"Ordinarily I don't kiss women with girlfriends," Reilly said. "But I'm still going to kiss you. I'll worry about the rest later."

Liz tugged on Reilly's hair until Reilly leaned back again and looked at her questioningly. "I was on my way to your house this afternoon when you drove by."

Reilly raised an eyebrow. "Didn't you tell me you weren't going anywhere?"

Liz smiled. "I wasn't, until I saw you."

"Then I'm glad I came by."

"Me too." When Reilly dipped her head to kiss her again, Liz stopped her. "Julia told me you came by the apartment this morning."

Reilly's eyes swiftly darkened to almost black. "It was a spur of the moment thing. I should have called first."

Liz kissed Reilly, then threaded her arms around Reilly's waist. She didn't want Reilly to pull away. "I'd like very much for you to come by whenever you get the urge."

Reilly grew very still and remained silent.

"I'm sorry I missed you," Liz continued. "I wasn't there. I spent the night at Bren's."

"Then why did she buzz me up?" Reilly asked, confused.

"She said she was curious. She probably was." Liz cradled Reilly's cheek. "I didn't know she was coming and she isn't there anymore. I told her to go."

"Is that temporary or still undecided?"

"It's permanent. Very permanent."

"Does she know about—"

"Yes." Liz leaned into Reilly, her breasts swollen, her nipples so sensitive they ached to be stroked. "I don't have a girlfriend, and I really, really need you to kiss me."

"Am I going to be able to kiss you more than once?"

"As long as you want to," Liz breathed against Reilly's mouth.

Reilly kissed her a little deeper this time, teasing her tongue over

Liz's. When the heat flared in her belly and she was in danger of going too fast, she eased back. "We should get comfortable, because I don't want to stop any time soon."

Liz hesitated for just a few seconds. She had never been one to fall into bed quickly or easily, and despite the fact that her body was screaming for more—for everything—there were still so many things unspoken between them. Still, she craved Reilly's mouth and ached for Reilly's hands on her. "Good idea."

"Wait right here," Reilly said, before easing away.

Liz watched, curious, as Reilly flung open cabinet doors and finally pulled down an empty green bottle with a fat belly and a long thin neck. The bottom half was covered with a straw weave. She laughed when Reilly pulled a stumpy white candle from another drawer and jammed it into the mouth of the bottle.

"Is that a Chianti bottle?" When Reilly nodded, Liz laughed again. "I haven't seen one of those used as a candleholder since college."

"That's me," Reilly said. "I really know how to impress a date."

"You're doing fine so far."

Reilly regarded her intently, then held out her hand. "Let's see if I can keep it up."

With her hand in Reilly's, Liz followed her through the living room, down a narrow hall with a bathroom off to one side, and into a bedroom. Like the rest of the apartment, it was sparsely furnished, neat, and clean. The bed was made and a digital alarm clock sat beside a haphazard pile of books on the bedside table. More books rested on the floor within easy reach of the bed. An area rug covering the hardwood floor in front of a plain dresser completed the furnishings.

The bed brought Liz up short. She wanted to make love, and she wished it were that simple. She wasn't sure it ever had been for her, but she knew it wasn't now. Not when she didn't know if she would want to walk away in the morning or if Reilly would want her to, or if she wanted something else. She wasn't even certain she *should* want anything else right now. She had more than enough to deal with.

"Reilly," Liz said reluctantly.

"Just one minute."

Reilly tugged Liz further into the room, past the bed, and over to a wide window. Reilly handed Liz the Chianti bottle and a book of matches Liz had seen her take out of the drawer along with the candle. "Here, hold these."

Curious, Liz took the items as Reilly wrestled with the window. It obviously hadn't been opened in a while. When Reilly had it opened wide, she swung one leg over the window sill and held out her hands for the candle.

"I thought we could watch the sunset."

When Reilly pulled her other leg through, Liz bent down and saw a fire escape outside the window. Part of her was disappointed that she wouldn't be able to stretch out next to Reilly on the bed, because she wasn't ready to stop kissing. But she could hardly complain, since she had been about to put the brakes on just seconds before. She slid her leg over the sill, dipped her head, and stepped out onto the fire escape. Reilly balanced the Chianti bottle on top of an overturned orange plastic milk crate and put the matches beside it.

"Have a seat," Reilly said with a sweep of her arm.

Liz regarded the object that took up most of the fire escape. "That looks like the back seat of a car."

"It is. A '56 Buick, to be exact." Reilly settled down on one end of the wide, tan leather seat. "I always wanted to make out in the backseat of a '56 Buick."

Delighted, Liz curled up beside her and when Reilly put her arm around her shoulders, Liz wrapped hers around Reilly's middle and rested her head on Reilly's shoulder. The fire escape faced west toward the river and the huge city park. The sun was just beginning to set. A faint breeze stirred the sultry night air.

"Comfortable?" Reilly murmured.

"Very."

Reilly kissed the top of her head and ran her hand up and down Liz's bare arm. "Let me know if you get cold."

"It's August." Liz kissed the side of Reilly's throat.

"I know, but...I don't want you to get chilled."

Liz was touched by Reilly's protectiveness, although she wondered if part of Reilly's concern wasn't coming from some need of Reilly's to do for her what Reilly hadn't been able to do for Annie. The thought bothered her, even as she told herself it didn't matter.

"I can think of a few ways to keep warm," Liz said.

Reilly cradled Liz's chin and tilted her face up. "Me too."

The kiss was languorous, a slow exploration of slick surfaces and hot, smooth muscles. Liz shifted into Reilly's lap and put her arms around her neck in the position they'd been in the night before. She had wanted to kiss Reilly like this then. She kept her eyes open, although it was difficult, and thrilled to see Reilly's pupils widen and her eyes grow hazier with each passing minute. Reilly caressed her sides and her hip and the length of her thigh and before long, Liz was breathing hard and rotating her hips between Reilly's spread thighs. She caught Reilly's hand and pressed it to her breast.

Reilly groaned and slid her hand inside Liz's blouse. When she swept her fingertips inside the very top of Liz's bra, Liz moaned. Instantly, Reilly stilled.

"Don't stop," Liz whispered, sucking lightly on Reilly's neck. "You said you wanted to make out."

"I can't remember," Reilly gasped. "Is this first base or second?"

"Oh God, I don't know." Liz laughed, so turned on she could barely stand it and never wanting the feeling to end.

Reilly pushed her hand lower inside Liz's bra and cupped the undersurface of her breast. Then she squeezed gently.

Liz writhed in Reilly's lap, the ache in her breasts spreading lower. She needed more. She needed Reilly closer, and she kissed her harder, pulling Reilly's tongue into her mouth. She sucked on it and Reilly's hips jerked under her ass. Reilly's thumb and forefinger closed on her nipple and rolled lightly. Liz whimpered and tugged Reilly's polo shirt from her jeans. She worked her hand underneath and found Reilly's small, firm breasts. When she mimicked Reilly's motions, Reilly shuddered.

"Lie down on top of me," Reilly urged, turning sideways on the seat with her back propped against the iron railing.

"Unbutton my blouse." Liz shifted until she had one leg between Reilly's. She pressed her center against Reilly's tight thigh, knowing she was wet, not caring if she soaked through her shorts. She reached behind her and released her bra. When Reilly got her last button open, her breasts spilled out. Immediately, Reilly covered both of them with her hands. Liz pushed Reilly's shirt up and feathered her fingers over the tight pink nipples. Reilly arched into her hands.

"Oh look at you," Liz whispered. "So beautiful." She raised her gaze to Reilly's face and found Reilly staring at her, her eyes fathomless. "What?"

"Ground rules." Reilly hooked her calf behind Liz's and tightened her thighs, pressing hard against Liz's leg. "While I can still think."

Liz looked down at Reilly's hands inside her blouse and hers on Reilly's breasts. "We might be too late."

"Almost."

"Tell me." Liz looked around at the nearby buildings. The sun had gone down without her noticing it, and lights had come on in some of the apartments. They were shrouded in near darkness now. She shrugged out of her blouse and dropped it along with her bra on the grillwork landing. Then she stretched out on top of Reilly, curling one arm behind Reilly's neck. She caressed Reilly's breasts. "What rules?"

"No touching below the waist," Reilly whispered, running both hands up and down Liz's back.

"The way I feel," Liz murmured, nibbling along the edge of Reilly's jaw, "that might not matter."

"You want to stop?"

"Oh no." Liz kissed her again, slowly and deeply, until Reilly trembled beneath her. "I want to make out until curfew."

"Is someone waiting up for you?"

Liz nipped at Reilly's chin. "Not a soul."

"Good. I'm not wearing a watch."

Bren checked the time on the wall clock opposite her desk. Nine p.m. She wondered if Jae was already at the Blue Diamond. She wondered if she performed every night. She wondered if she had another job. If she had a lover. If she had many lovers.

She booted up her computer, opened Melanie's email program, and scanned the messages.

I'm sorry.

She clicked open the message.

I should have waited to come again, but I couldn't stop. Will you forgive me?

Bren scrolled down the list. A few hours later, another message. *I'm sorry. Will you let me apologize in person?*

The next read, *Please don't go. Let me show you I'm sorry.*

As she read, another message arrived. *I can still feel the heat of your body against the insides of my thighs, on my nipples. When I touch myself, I feel your breath on my neck. I taste you. I won't come again until you tell me to. Please.*

Jae's excitement was palpable. Bren's body clamored for attention, and she knew that Jae must need to come just as badly. She thought about how hard it would be for Jae not to climax on stage tonight, and the idea of her struggling not to give in made Bren even more excited. She needed to come right now, but she would deny herself as long as she denied Jae.

She typed quickly.

Tonight when you're on stage, I want you to imagine the hands touching you are mine. I'll be watching. You do not have permission to come.

As soon as she pushed send, she reached for her cell phone and pushed a number on speed dial. When Candace answered, Bren said, "I didn't expect you to be home on a Saturday night."

"Did you call just to make me cranky?" Candace replied.

"No," Bren laughed. "Is it still my birthday weekend?"

"What do you need? Chocolate cake? A bottle of wine? I'm at your service."

"I need a date."

"Age, physical description, sexual proclivities?"

"I was thinking of you."

Silence.

"I don't want you to sleep with me, Candace," Bren said, "just keep me company."

"Damn. And now I'm horny."

"I'm sorry."

"Where are we going?"

"The Blue Diamond."

"That works for me. Maybe tonight I'll find someone I feel like fucking when I get her home."

"I'll call Liz," Bren said.

"Okay. What time do you want me to pick you up?"

"Uh—twenty minutes?"

"That gives me five minutes to dress, darling."

"Skip underwear."

"I always do."

CHAPTER TWENTY-TWO

S o," Candace said as she pulled into the parking lot at the Blue Diamond, "what prompted this spur of the moment visit?"

"I want to see Jae again," Bren answered.

Candace turned off the ignition and regarded Bren intently. The club, looking more like a chop shop than a nightclub, crouched on a narrow strip of land between the I-95 bypass and the Delaware River, surrounded by convenience stores and empty factory buildings with boarded up windows. The lot was nearly filled with an odd assortment of vehicles—dusty pickup trucks with oversized wheels, shiny high-end luxury sedans, and a stretch Humvee limo. In the hazy yellow glow from the security lights hanging from the corners of the building, Candace's face looked eerily unfamiliar.

"What?" Bren asked, her voice echoing hollowly inside the car.

"Are you sure you know what you're doing?"

"What am I doing?"

"In case you haven't noticed, this is not a club where nice girls go to find dates."

"I already have a date."

"You don't know her," Candace pointed out.

Bren smiled, surprised at Candace's concern. "You don't know a lot of the women you bring home."

"That's true, but I have a lot more experience at it than you do."

"I'm not as naïve as you think."

"I'm beginning to get that you're a lot more of a lot of things than I thought."

"Thank you."

"I can still worry."

"I'm not going home with her," Bren said. "I came to see how well she follows instructions."

"She knows you're coming?"

"No, and I don't want her to see us."

"Okay," Candace said slowly. "I think I might like this game."

Bren leaned over and kissed Candace's cheek. "I bet you would."

"Is it too late for you to play it with me?"

Laughing, Bren pushed her door open. "Way too late."

"Damn. And now I'm *really* horny."

❖

Liz sighed and burrowed into the curve of Reilly's neck. Reilly stroked her hair and adjusted the blouse she had draped over Liz's bare back to keep her warm.

"Mmm," Liz murmured. "You smell good."

"Thank you." Smiling, Reilly kissed Liz's temple.

Liz responded by snugging her leg more firmly into Reilly's crotch. Reilly's breath caught at the unexpected pressure. Her body had never cooled below simmer, and it wouldn't take much to bring her back up to a boil.

"What?" Liz asked drowsily.

"Nothing. Go back to sleep."

Liz raised her head and looked around. It was completely dark except for the candle that flickered and flared a few feet away "We're still in the backseat of the car."

"Uh-huh."

"I fell asleep, didn't I?"

"Uh-huh."

Liz replayed the last few things she remembered, and sat up abruptly. "Oh my God. I can't believe I did that. I am so sorry."

Reilly shifted her legs, one of which was completely numb from the weight of Liz lying on her for the last hour. She didn't care. Even if gangrene had set in and her leg had dropped off, she wouldn't have given up a second of holding Liz in her arms. She'd had sex a few times in the last several years, usually with women she knew from work who'd asked her out, and she had finally given in after running out of polite ways to say no. Sometimes she was lonely, and she surrendered to the need to hear someone, even a stranger, cry out in pleasure. But she rarely felt less lonely after a night of false intimacy. In fact, she had rarely felt lonelier than when waking up with a woman she didn't really know in her arms.

"You don't have anything to be sorry about," Reilly said, taking Liz's hand. "I've had a great night."

Liz clasped Reilly's hand in both of hers. With her head down, her hair covered most of her face and Reilly couldn't make out her expression. "I wasn't talking about just falling asleep."

"I know what you're talking about. You're amazing."

"I've never done that before," Liz said in a low voice. "I didn't even know I could."

"Your body is changing." Reilly held up Liz's blouse, which had slid off when Liz bolted up. "You should put this on. The temperature's finally dropped a little bit. Should I get you a sweatshirt?"

"Did you know?" Liz took the blouse but didn't put it on. "That I…"

"That you came while we were kissing?"

Liz nodded mutely.

"Yes." Reilly leaned over and kissed her softly. "I don't think I've ever experienced anything sexier in my life."

Liz pressed her forehead to Reilly's shoulder. "God, I'm embarrassed."

"Please don't be. You were so beautiful."

"I couldn't help it—the way you kiss me. The way you touch my breasts." Liz traced Reilly's mouth with her thumb. "I felt you inside me. Everywhere."

Reilly shuddered. She wanted Liz again. She wanted to hear her soft, broken cries of pleasure and feel her tremble. She wanted the exquisite pleasure of Liz's fingers digging into her shoulders as she arched into her. She wanted that, all of that, and so very much more. Swiftly, she pulled away and kneeled on the iron fire escape in front of Liz. She wrapped her arms around Liz's waist and rested her cheek against Liz's stomach just above the top of her shorts. "While you were sleeping, I put my hand right here. I imagined I could feel a heartbeat beneath my fingers. Any day now, you'll feel movement."

Liz stroked Reilly's hair. "You're the first one to touch me there."

Reilly closed her eyes and pressed her face harder to Liz's warm flesh. She and Annie had never made love while Annie was pregnant. She knew that, because they hadn't made love for almost four months before Annie died. They had been fighting almost constantly, and she thought then it was because the demands of her residency left her absent, physically and emotionally, too much of the time. Now she wondered if it hadn't been because of the secret Annie was keeping. She wondered if she would have known, if she would have noticed any difference in Annie's body. She wondered now if she had really known Annie very well at all.

"I feel honored," Reilly said.

Liz laughed and caressed Reilly's cheek. "Believe me, there may be something miraculous going on inside me, but I am just an ordinary woman."

"You're shivering." Reilly stood and took Liz's hand. "Come inside."

Reilly climbed over the window sill and waited to help Liz. Then she pulled a T-shirt from her dresser drawer and held it out. "Here—this will be a little warmer than that blouse."

While Liz shrugged into the T-shirt and dropped her blouse on the dresser, Reilly walked to the bed, turned on the small reading lamp on the bedside table, and stretched out on top of the covers. When she held out her hand, Liz gripped it and lay down facing her.

"Warm enough?" Reilly asked.

"Perfect."

Reilly put her arm around Liz's waist and pulled her closer until their bodies just touched. "You're not ordinary. You're brave and strong, and so sexy I'm just about crazy from wanting you all the time."

"And I left you high and dry out there, didn't I," Liz said. "I still can't believe I did that."

"I told you, you're amazing. The way I felt when I realized what was happening—believe me, that was better than an orgasm."

Liz laughed. "Oh, you really are in a bad way."

"Maybe. But I'm not complaining."

Liz skimmed her hand under the back of Reilly's polo shirt, pressed against her, and kissed her. "I wanted to go to bed with you when we came up here tonight. All the way to bed—no clothes, no barriers, no doubts."

"But?"

"This is new territory for me." Liz took Reilly's hand and pressed it low on her belly. "This is new." She carried Reilly's hand to her breast and held it over her heart. "What's going on in here is new too. I don't know when Julia started to move out of my life, out of my heart. I didn't notice the emptiness until it was so huge nothing we could have done would have changed things."

"Not even the baby?"

"Especially not the baby."

Reilly frowned. "What did she say when you told her?"

"She said it was wonderful."

"She's right. How could she not think—"

"Reilly, Julia didn't know I was pregnant because she called me from California the day I was scheduled to be inseminated and told me she didn't want to have a baby."

"She was in California? Wasn't she going with you?"

"We'd been talking about the insemination for a few months, and we had finally decided to go ahead. Or at least, *I* had decided, and Julia had gone along with it. Everything was scheduled and then Julia had a meeting come up that she couldn't get out of." Liz shook her head. "We both decided that if the timing was right while she was away, I would do it alone. After all, it wasn't the mechanics that mattered, at least that's what we said."

Reilly grit her teeth to keep from commenting. She had no right to criticize Julia. Her lover hadn't been able to count on her, either, or at least that's what Annie must have believed. "Then she changed her mind, but you went ahead?"

"No," Liz said quietly. "She called from California that morning to tell me not to keep the appointment. She left a message on my cell. Maybe she thought I was in a meeting or something, but my appointment had been moved up from the afternoon to the first thing in the morning. By the time I got the message, it was already done."

"Jesus," Reilly muttered. She couldn't even imagine how Liz must have felt when she got the message from Julia telling her not to go ahead. "I'm sorry. You must have been shocked."

"I didn't know what to think. I was numb. I guess I didn't quite believe that she actually meant it until she got home and I confronted her. That's when she told me about her girlfriend."

"She doesn't deserve you," Reilly snarled.

Liz pushed Reilly over onto her back and climbed on top of her. She propped herself on her elbows and smiled down at Reilly. "You are very good for my ego."

Reilly tangled her hands in Liz's hair and kissed her throat. "She's an idiot."

Liz grasped Reilly's wrists and pinned her arms to the bed. Then she leaned down and nibbled on Reilly's neck. "I need to go home before we start in again. Because the next time I come, we're not going to have any clothes on and you're going to be inside me for real."

Reilly didn't struggle to break free of Liz's grip, even though what she wanted was to roll Liz under her and lose herself in her. Instead, she turned her head and kissed Liz on the mouth, sliding her tongue inside when Liz didn't pull away. They kissed until they were both breathless.

"Okay, that's it," Liz gasped. "Curfew time."

"I'll walk you home."

"Aren't you going to ask me why I'm leaving?"

"No. Whatever you want. Whatever you need. It's all right."

"What if I don't know?" Liz asked.

"Then we'll wait until you do."

Liz sat up, straddling Reilly's hips. "What do you want?"

"I want what you make me feel."

"What is that?"

"Alive."

❖

"God, she's hot," Candace moaned as Jae stalked onto the stage. This time she wore a black leather vest and chaps with a band of black satin between her legs that barely covered her clitoris.

"Isn't she," Bren said, sliding in behind Candace's stool at the far end of the bar so she could watch the stage over Candace's shoulder. The room was so dark, she doubted Jae could see her, but she wanted the privacy to watch Jae without Candace watching her.

Much like the night before, Jae posed and strutted, her attitude arrogant, her expression remote. When she strode to the very edge of the platform, unbuttoned her vest, and shrugged it from her muscular shoulders in one motion, Bren barely managed not to groan out loud. When she thrust her hips forward, daring those at the nearest tables to reach for her sex, Bren felt a wave of heat surge through her that settled between her thighs and left her wet.

"I would love to go down on that," Candace muttered.

"Forget it. Tonight, she's mine."

Candace swiveled on her barstool. "You really are Melanie Richards, aren't you?"

"I really am."

Bren kept her eyes on the stage, her pulse racing as Jae gave one last insolent pelvic thrust inches from the groping hands, then pivoted and sauntered to the spotlit silver pole. The room went completely black except for that bright cone of light. Jae reached above her head and fisted one hand above the other, the pole a gleaming phallus protruding from her clenched fingers. She tilted her head back, and through half-closed eyes stared directly at Bren.

"She knows you're here," Candace whispered.

"She can't."

"She *does.*"

Again, the blood-tipped fingers reached from out of the blackness and roamed Jae's body. Tonight, her skin glistened with sweat within seconds and the muscles in her stomach rippled convulsively. Her breasts flushed and her nipples tightened.

"Ooo, look at her. Whoever's playing with her is doing a number on her tonight. I bet you she comes."

"She won't," Bren said.

Jae's tormentor slid two fingers into the cleft between Jae's thighs, and when she slowly drew them out, they glistened wetly. The muscles in Jae's jaws bunched as she clenched her teeth, and her thighs trembled. Bren could almost feel the harsh, hot breath of Jae's arousal on her neck and sensed her body careening to the edge. Watching her, she saw the instant she began the inevitable climb to orgasm. Jae writhed, her back a taut bow, struggling to contain the uncontainable. She was beautiful in her utter need. The room was so quiet, Jae's agonized groan carried through the stillness like a desperate plea. Her suffering was palpable and Bren took pity on her.

"You may come," Bren whispered.

"No," Jae cried. She pushed the hands from her body and collapsed to her knees. She fell forward, head bowed, barely catching herself on outstretched arms. "No!"

The crowd gasped as one and the spotlight blinked out, leaving them all teetering on the razor's edge of desire.

"I have *got* to get laid tonight," Candace moaned.

Bren bit back the wild urge to laugh in triumph, certain that part of Jae's out-of-control arousal had been because Jae knew she was watching. Watching, and forbidding her the pleasure she craved. The lights came up just enough for customers to move around the murky room. The stage was empty.

Bren signaled the bartender, and surprisingly, he came over immediately.

"Get you something?"

"I want a dance."

"Fifty bucks. Grab an empty table if you can get one."

"No. A private dance."

"Way to go, Bren," Candace murmured.

The bartender regarded Bren calculatingly. "Who?"

"You know who. She left me a message last night."

He nodded, bent over, and pulled something from under the bar. He handed her a key. "Fourth room on the right."

"How much?"

He shook his head. "It's paid for."

"Thank you."

He shrugged and left to attend the swarm of men and a few women who clamored for drinks.

"Can I watch?" Candace asked.

"Not this time," Bren said.

Candace gripped her hand. "Are you saying I might be able to, sometime?"

"I don't know. It might be more fun to make her watch us."

Candace's mouth dropped open.

Laughing, Bren put two fingers beneath Candace's chin and gently closed her mouth. "You are so much fun to play with."

"You have no idea."

"Will you be okay if I leave you out here alone?" Bren asked.

"Will you be okay in there alone?"

"Absolutely." Bren jiggled the key. "After all, I'm just going to watch."

CHAPTER TWENTY-THREE

L iz and Reilly held hands as they walked from Reilly's apartment on Twenty-second and Pine to Liz's condo a few blocks away. Although after eleven, couples strolled toward Rittenhouse Square and soft jazz drifted out the open doors of a wine bar as they passed. If Liz let her mind drift, she could pretend she was on a date. She could imagine being free to go wherever her feelings took her, to embrace the joy and excitement of a new relationship. The euphoria lasted for a few seconds, and then she remembered that she was far from free. She had a commitment to something far more important than chasing a dream that might never be. In a little more than six months she'd be so busy juggling her work and the new baby, she wouldn't have time to think about her own needs, let alone those of another person and a new relationship.

"What are you thinking about?" Reilly asked.

"Oh, nothing. Why? Was I muttering to myself? I have a tendency to think out loud."

"No mumbling, but you just sighed as if something made you unhappy."

Liz couldn't believe Reilly was that sensitive to her mood. No one else, except possibly Candace or Bren, had ever been able to see beneath the surface of calm control she had perfected. She released Reilly's hand and slipped her arm round Reilly's waist. Reilly put her arm around Liz's shoulders.

"I'm not unhappy," Liz said. "I had a most amazing night. When I'm with you, I tend to forget about everything that's bothering me."

"Is that bad?"

"No. It's great."

"Good." Reilly kissed her temple. "I don't remember the last time I felt happy. I do, tonight."

"And that's enough?"

"Why not?"

Liz pondered the question. Was it all right to be happy, if being happy meant someone else might pay the price, even if they wanted to? Was that fair? And just how high a price was unacceptable?

"What if tomorrow you're unhappy because of tonight?" Liz asked.

"Are you going to come to the game tomorrow?"

"Yes."

"Then I'll be happy."

Liz grabbed the waistband of Reilly's jeans and dragged her into the shadows cast by an awning in front of a grocery store that was closed and gated for the night. Reilly let herself be pulled along, and Liz backed her up against the wall. Then Liz leaned into her and kissed her, seriously and thoroughly. She played with Reilly's tongue and sucked on her lower lip, taunting her with little nips before plunging into her mouth again. Reilly gripped Liz's ass and maneuvered Liz's thigh between her legs. Liz had started out wanting to taste her, but now she wanted to devour her. She pushed her hand between their bodies and squeezed Reilly's crotch.

Reilly's head banged back against the building, and she gripped Liz's wrist. "Don't go there. I already can't think."

"Sorry," Liz gasped, reluctantly moving her hand to the outside of Reilly's hip. She rested her forehead on Reilly's shoulder. "I'm not usually like this."

"Like what?" Reilly's chest rose and fell erratically.

"Like I can't get enough. Like I want to climb inside your skin. Like I've been cold forever and you're the only promise of heat in the universe." Liz raised her head. "I sound crazy, don't I? This can't be just me being pregnant, can it?"

"I hope that's not it, because I'm feeling a lot the same myself." Reilly rubbed her hands up and down Liz's back, then cupped her ass again, keeping their bodies fused. "And I'm pretty sure I'm not pregnant."

Liz laughed. "Oh, thank God."

"This morning when I saw Julia in your apartment—"

"God, I'm so sorry about that."

"No, it's okay. I understand."

"I just didn't want you to think—I hated that you might think I'd been with her."

Reilly kissed Liz, then held her a little more tightly. "I did think that, when it looked like she'd been there all night. Part of me thought that was a good thing. I can't imagine anyone letting you go, and I know you must have loved her."

Liz murmured in protest, but she didn't say anything, letting Reilly talk.

"The other part of me didn't want her to have a claim on you. Didn't want *anyone* to. I was having a pretty good running battle with myself all morning, arguing both sides of things."

Liz laughed a little shakily, and Reilly grinned.

"Yeah," Reilly went on, "I was pretty much losing all the way around. Anyhow, by the time I saw you on the street outside my apartment this afternoon, I was just so damn glad to see you I didn't care about Julia. Those few hours with you in the car this afternoon were the happiest I've spent in years. And tonight was beyond amazing."

"I don't know what I'm doing with my life," Liz said. "And I don't want you to get hurt."

"When I thought you might be getting back with Julia, I was still ready to take a chance. Stop trying to scare me away now."

Liz wrapped her arms around Reilly's neck and kissed her. "Maybe I'm the one that's scared."

"I'd be surprised if you weren't, a little bit." Reilly stroked Liz's cheek. "But you don't need to be afraid of me."

"I know." Liz eased away and gripped Reilly's hand. Part of her wanted to say more—part of her wanted to make promises and dream dreams. But she held back, because she cared about Reilly. More than cared. "You've got a game tomorrow, and I can't take many more of these late nights. Walk me to the door?"

"You bet."

Liz kissed Reilly good night in front of her apartment building. "See you tomorrow."

Reilly backed up slowly until Liz had punched in the security code and opened the door. Then she called, "Sleep well."

Liz waved, watching until Reilly had rounded the corner and disappeared. She wasn't afraid of Reilly, but she was terrified of what she was beginning to feel for her.

❖

The room was larger than Bren expected, perhaps ten feet square, and lit by red bulbs in four recessed lights, one in each corner. A narrow leather and chrome chair, sans arms, occupied the center of the room, facing the door. A bed, not much wider than a cot, was pushed up against the rear wall and covered with a surprisingly crisp-looking sheet. Otherwise, the space was empty. A small security camera hung down from the ceiling, angled in such a way as to provide a view of the entire room. Music, something with a fast pounding rhythm, reverberated from speakers set into the side walls. Bren ignored the bed and sat down in the chair, crossing her legs. Tonight, she'd worn a short leather skirt, black silk blouse, heels, and nothing else. She felt decidedly decadent, and she liked it.

The door opened and Jae walked in, still wearing her stage outfit of black leather vest and chaps, although the vest was unbuttoned and barely covered her breasts. Her arms and stomach were tightly muscled, and she looked altogether sexy and more than a little dangerous.

"What do you do in these rooms for women?" Bren asked as Jae stood silently waiting.

"I dance."

"And the bed?"

Jae kept her eyes on Bren's face. "I only dance."

"What if they want you to make them come?"

"Do you?"

Bren shook her head. "I'm asking the questions."

"Sorry."

"You said that earlier. Several times."

"I know. You make me forget myself."

"That's not good," Bren said. "Should I come back another time when you'll be able to pay better attention?"

"No. Please. I...if they want to come, I can make it happen when I dance."

"Do you touch them?" Bren pictured Jae teasing some faceless woman the way Jae had teased her the night before, and she felt herself grow rigid and wet.

"If they..." Jae's voice broke and she seemed to struggle for breath. Her hands opened and closed at her sides. "If they want me to."

"And then do they let you come?" Bren asked sharply, resenting the strangers who took their pleasure in Jae's body.

"Usually they don't care." Jae's voice was strained. "And I don't usually want to."

"But you want to tonight, don't you?"

"Yes. Yes."

"Take off your vest and cover that camera."

Immediately, Jae pulled off her vest and draped it over the lens.

"Will anyone investigate?"

"No."

"Good." Bren uncrossed her legs, raised her hips, and slid her skirt up until the hem just covered her crotch. "Then I'd like my dance."

Jae turned and rapidly pushed buttons on a small panel beside the door, and the music became slow and sensuous, with a heavy, rolling bass beat. Then she strode to Bren and straddled the chair.

Bren leaned back and gripped Jae's hips. "And tonight, I want you all the way in my lap."

Immediately, Jae lowered herself onto Bren, the bare skin on the insides of her legs sliding along Bren's naked thighs. Jae braced her hands on Bren's shoulders, undulating to the music, her breasts almost brushing Bren's face. Bren skimmed her hands over the leather chaps and cupped Jae's bare ass, massaging the taut muscles as they flexed and strained.

"You didn't come on stage tonight, did you?"

"No," Jae replied, her voice husky.

"But you wanted to, didn't you?"

"No."

"No?" Bren squeezed Jae's ass and pulled her against her crotch. Her leather skirt rode higher, exposing her center to the heat that radiated from between Jae's legs.

"No," Jae said, her hips pumping harder. "You said I couldn't."

Bren smiled thinly. Her clit ached, and Jae's breasts were so close. Jae's nipples were small hard stones in the center of smooth flawless flesh, and Bren wanted them in her mouth. "Play with your nipples."

Jae fondled her breasts and fingered her nipples, rolling and tugging, her chest heaving as she writhed faster. Bren watched her face contort with pleasure, and the pressure built between her legs.

"She made you wet."

"No," Jae groaned, her body curling forward as her stomach muscles clenched. "I imagined it was you. You touching me."

Bren couldn't help herself, she pumped upward, thrusting her swollen clit against Jae's wet sex. She needed to come so badly she was going to lose control of the scene soon. "Stroke yourself."

Jae pushed her hand between their bodies, cupping herself. Her knuckles pressed into Bren's clit.

"Remember," Bren groaned, "your orgasm belongs to me."

"Yes, Mistress," Jae whispered, her hand circling between her thighs, her forehead nearly touching Bren's shoulder. She clutched Bren's arm, shuddering. "Oh."

"No." Bren had only intended to watch while Jae masturbated, but she was so beautiful. She had to taste her. She sucked Jae's nipple into her mouth and pulled on it with her teeth.

Jae's back bowed, and she ground her crotch against her own hand. "Please may I come."

Bren was close to exploding against the back of Jae's fingers. She had to let her come or *she* would. She took both Jae's breasts in her hands and squeezed. "What did you say?"

"Please, Mistress," Jae moaned, "please...oh I'm going to...oh please."

"Yes," Bren urged, raking her teeth along the side of Jae's neck. "Yes, come now."

"Oh God," Jae groaned, trembling as her breath shattered from her.

Bren held her tightly, her own need for release eclipsed by the beauty of Jae's pleasure. She stroked Jae's sweat-soaked hair and caressed her back, cradling her until the last tremors of her orgasm rippled through her.

"Let me make you come," Jae whispered, starting to pull away.

"Stay still," Bren said, continuing to caress her. "What is your name?"

"Jae."

Bren tilted her head up. Jae's eyes were cloudy, her mouth soft with satisfaction. "Are you sure?"

"Yes. Very sure."

"Call me Brenda."

"Brenda." Jae skimmed her mouth over Bren's ear. "Don't you want to come?"

"I will. Later." Bren tightened her fingers in Jae's hair and pulled her head back. She kissed her, slowly, savoring the smoothness and heat of her mouth.

"Let me do it now," Jae pleaded. "I want you so much."

"Your clit's still hard, isn't it?"

"Yes."

"You need to come again," Bren stated.

"Yes." Jae rolled her hips in Bren's lap, bringing Bren to the edge again.

"You'd love to suck me, wouldn't you? And all the while you licked me and teased me until I couldn't hold back anymore and I came in your mouth, you'd be making yourself come, too."

"Please," Jae groaned.

"You need to go now." Bren gripped Jae's ass and slowly licked her way up Jae's throat. She skimmed her teeth along the edge of her jaw and kissed her one last time. "Good night, Jae."

Jae caressed Bren's cheek. "Will I see you again?"

"I don't know." Bren caught Jae's wrist and held her arm still as she kissed her palm, then bit the fleshy muscle at the base of her thumb. Jae sucked in her breath and moaned quietly. "Sometimes when a scene is perfect, you can never write it the same way again."

"May I ask you to do something?"

Surprised, Bren nodded.

"When you come, will you think of me?"

"I always do," Bren whispered.

"Well?" Candace asked eagerly as soon as Bren rejoined her at the bar. "What happened?"

"She danced."

"And?"

"And it was even better than I thought it would be."

"Did you...I mean did she..." Candace raised her hands helplessly. "God, I can't believe I'm asking you this. Did the dance have a *satisfying* ending?"

Bren gave her an enigmatic smile. She couldn't possibly explain, because to say yes would make it sound so simple, when it had not been simple at all. What had mattered to her had not been the orgasms, as wonderful as they were. Orgasms were not all that hard to achieve, with a little negotiation. What was far more difficult to find was a woman who understood what it took to unlock her secrets and free her passion.

"So far I've gotten everything I wanted for my birthday." She took Candace's hand. "Ready to go home?"

"I'm ready to get laid and I still don't have a date."

"Nobody here strikes your fancy?"

"You do."

The dead serious tone in Candace's voice made Bren regard her intently. "When you were with Liz, I was so jealous."

"You wanted Liz, too, huh?"

"No, Cand. I wanted you."

"Oh. Shit." Candace sighed and looked around the room. There were more than a few intriguing women, and a couple had been eyeing her all night. Any other time she would have had no problem playing with one. Or two. But she just didn't have the desire for a mindless fuck. "How many chances have I blown in my life, I wonder?"

"Maybe you haven't blown anything," Bren said gently. "Maybe your chance hasn't come yet."

"Well, how the hell am I supposed to tell when it does?"

Bren thought about Jae. "She'll be the one who makes you realize no one else will do."

"Oh fuck," Candace whispered "I am *so* screwed."

CHAPTER TWENTY-FOUR

Liz stopped halfway up the slope to the ball field and turned when she heard someone calling her name. Smiling, she waved to Bren. "Hey! I wasn't sure you were coming. I called, but I didn't get an answer."

"I was working," Bren said, pulling even with Liz. She had been writing since almost five a.m. when she had awakened from a sound sleep with an overwhelming need to write the next chapter in her almost finished manuscript. She had been stuck for a few days, uncertain of her direction. But now she realized exactly what her character needed, and what she had been avoiding. Jae, her female James Bond undercover agent, sex-stud extraordinaire character, couldn't afford to trust anyone. And because she couldn't trust, she couldn't give herself to anyone. That was the true challenge that faced her character, and Bren hadn't been willing to take her where she needed to go because... well, because every character was a little bit of the author. Sometimes, more than just a little bit, and she hadn't been ready to take that step, in her work or her life.

Jae, *her* Jae, had seen both the character and the author for who they were. Last night, she'd shown Bren what trust really meant in the most basic, fundamental of ways. She has exposed herself—her needs, her desires, her dreams. By doing so, Jae had opened the door to possibility for Bren, in her body, in her work, in her life.

"Sorry," Bren went on. "I took the phone off the hook. I do that sometimes when the words are really flowing."

"You were writing?" Liz asked, still getting used to the idea that her friend, the woman she had believed she knew so well, was also a stranger. A stranger for whom she had an affection, perhaps even an attraction, simply by virtue of having read what she had written. It was confusing trying to reconcile her feelings for the real woman with the image of her she had built in her mind.

"Yes. I had a mini-breakthrough this morning." As they started walking back up the hill, Bren added, "I called you last night, too. Candace and I decided to go out, but I couldn't reach you. Early night?"

Liz knew she was blushing. "No. I spent the evening with Reilly."

"Oh. How did that go?"

"It was really nice."

"Liz! Bren! Wait up," Candace called from across the field.

"I guess I better hold the rest of the story until she gets here," Liz said.

Bren laughed. "You should if you want to survive the rest of the afternoon. You know how she is about secrets."

"What secrets?" Candace asked as she drew alongside them. "Now what happened that I don't know about?"

"Liz was just telling me that she spent the night with Reilly."

Candace's face went through a rapid-fire sequence of expressions, starting with surprise and ending with something between shock and outrage. "You *slept* with her?"

"Don't shout, Candace," Liz murmured as several people nearby turned in their direction with inquisitive looks. They were close enough to the Angels' sidelines now that she didn't want Reilly's teammates to overhear their conversation. "I didn't sleep with her. We just spent the evening...talking."

Bren smothered a smile.

"Talking. I don't believe you," Candace said, planting both hands on her hips. "You know why? Because you have that 'I'm a satisfied woman' look in your eyes. Just like Bren. Just like everyone, except me."

Liz raised an eyebrow at Bren. "Something you'd like to tell me, Brenda?"

"You first."

"We talked and we made out a little bit. That's all."

Candace snorted. "Making out is something teenagers do. What really happened?"

"We necked in the back seat of a car for three hours." Laughing at her friends' expressions of disbelief, Liz explained about the fire escape.

"You know," Bren said, "that is really sexy."

"It was," Liz agreed.

"She didn't try to get you into bed?" Candace asked skeptically.

Liz glanced over to the infield where Reilly and her teammates were already warming up. Just at that moment, Reilly scanned the sidelines, waving when she saw Liz. Liz smiled and waved back. *If you come to the game tomorrow, I'll be happy.* When Reilly had said that the night before, Liz had been too busy worrying that she wasn't at a place in her life where she could offer Reilly anything beyond the here and now to think about her own feelings. Now, seeing Reilly's smile, she was aware of being happy too. Watching Reilly dive for a ball and come up to her knees with it in her glove, flushed and triumphant, made Liz happy. The memory of the way Reilly had touched her, with such gentle certainty, stirred her, and she wanted nothing more than to be back on that fire escape in Reilly's arms.

"Liz?"

Liz jumped. "I'm sorry? What?"

"You spent hours kissing and she didn't try to get you into bed?"

"No. I wanted her to, but she said no."

Candace appeared at a loss for words. Bren regarded her curiously.

"Why?"

"Why did I want her to, or why did she say no?"

Bren shot Reilly an appraising look. "I get the part where you'd want to go to bed with her. She's really really sexy."

"Agreed," Liz said, unable to hide her contented smile.

"So why do you think she said no?"

"Maybe because Liz is pregnant, and Reilly has better sense than to take advantage of her screwed up hormones," Candace muttered.

"You've never objected to me having sex before," Liz pointed out, regarding Candace sharply.

"You weren't pregnant then. Things are different now. Besides, you were never one to sleep around."

"If I slept with Reilly," Liz said gently, "it wouldn't be sleeping around. She's special, and I care about her."

Candace searched Liz's face and nodded slowly. "Okay. You really like her."

"Yes."

"I just don't want you to get hurt."

Liz smiled. "I know. But we all have to respect each other's choices, right?"

When Candace rolled her eyes, Bren poked her in the side and said, "We're not who we were when we met, and we aren't likely to stay the same forever. But we'll always be friends, right?"

"Right," Candace and Liz said immediately.

"So I vote that we trust each other to make the right choices, and if we screw up, we don't say I told you so."

"Agreed," Liz said.

"Deal," Candace added. Then she looked at Liz. "So? Why didn't Saint Reilly want to go to bed with you?"

"Because she knew I wasn't ready."

Candace frowned. "But you said you wanted to."

Liz wrapped her arm around Candace's waist. "Wanting something doesn't mean it's the right time to do it."

"I've always figured if I did what I wanted, when I wanted to, at least I wouldn't have any regrets about what I'd missed."

"That works for some people."

Candace watched Parker settle onto the bench on the opposite side of the field. A busty blonde in a sports bra and short shorts plastered herself to Parker's back and began to massage Parker's shoulders. "It hasn't been working for me lately."

Liz followed her gaze. "Why her, do you think?"

"Why her what?"

"Why can't you forget her?"

"Because, God damn it," Candace said in a low, tortured voice, "I can still hear her saying my name when she comes."

"That sounds serious."

"You have no idea."

❖

Reilly ran up to Liz at the sidelines just before the first inning was about to begin. She had to stop herself from catching Liz in her arms and kissing her hello. Instead, she made do with grasping her hand.

"Hi. I'm glad you could make it."

"I said I would, didn't I."

Reilly grinned. "You did. Sleep okay?"

Liz glanced around. Bren leaned against the corner of the backstop, a distant expression on her face as she scanned the groups of women gathered about or passing by on their way to the other fields. Candace slouched on the Angels' bench, her hands braced on either side of her body, her legs slightly parted. In her halter top and skintight shorts, blond hair tangled around her shoulders, and her body an open invitation, she looked like a young Marilyn Monroe—ripe and luscious and ready. Satisfied that no one could overhear, Liz said, "I had a little trouble getting to sleep."

"Oh?"

"I kept thinking about kissing you."

"Oh."

"How did you sleep?" Liz asked after a moment of silence.

Reilly glanced away.

"What?" Liz asked, suddenly anxious that Reilly regretted what had happened between them. She should have expected that Reilly would begin to analyze the situation and realize that a woman with a baby on the way was more than she wanted to take on, even casually. And she must be thinking about Annie. She'd said she hadn't wanted a baby with Annie, and she'd loved Annie. "Last night doesn't have to mean anything, Reilly. You're not obligated to me in any way. You—"

"Liz," Reilly said quietly. "Last night meant something to me. It meant a lot."

Liz stared. "It would probably be better if I didn't try to read your mind, wouldn't it?"

Reilly smiled. "My mind's not very complicated."

Liz touched her face. "That is so not true."

"I couldn't sleep because I missed holding you," Reilly said. "I haven't wanted to hold a woman all night long for years."

"You say the most beautiful things."

"I—"

"Hey, Reilly," Sean called. "Are you planning to play ball sometime tonight?"

Reilly glanced over her shoulder. Her team was at bat and she needed to get her head in the game. She shrugged apologetically. "I need to go."

"I know. Big game, right?"

Reilly grinned. "If we beat Parker's team tonight, they're out of the playoffs."

"Oh, this is serious then." Liz looked over Reilly's shoulder and frowned. Candace had disappeared. When she checked for Parker, she was gone too.

Reilly released Liz's hand. "Will you stay? Meet me later?"

"I wouldn't dream of leaving," Liz answered. "And yes, I want to see you later."

"There was another reason I couldn't sleep last night," Reilly said as she backed away.

"What?" Liz said, following her to the bench.

Reilly grabbed her bat. Then she kissed Liz quickly. "I wanted you so much I couldn't settle down enough to sleep."

Before Liz could catch her breath to reply, Reilly ran to join her team. Suddenly weak-kneed, she sank down onto the bench. A minute later, Bren sat beside her.

"Are you okay?"

"Yes. Fine."

"It's really hot. Do you need something to drink?"

Liz rested her hand on Bren's thigh. "I'm really fine. To tell you the truth, Reilly takes my breath away."

Bren smiled. "That's wonderful news. I like the way she looks at you."

"How do you mean?"

"Like you're precious."

Liz bit her lip, mortified to feel tears welling in her eyes. "You can't imagine how tender she is."

"Good. You deserve it."

"How about you? Are you all right?"

Bren frowned. "Of course. Why?"

"You never finished saying what you did last night."

"We went back to the Blue Diamond."

"And?"

"I had sex with Jae."

"Well. That's news." Liz leaned closer. "At the bar?"

Bren nodded. "Lap dance."

"Oh my God. Bren. You amaze me."

"What surprised me," Bren said, "is that it felt completely right."

"And is that it? One time and it's over, or will you see her again?"

"I don't know. I'm used to compartmentalizing my life. I'm not sure that I want to change that."

Liz gave that some thought. "How is it for you to be sharing all these things with Candace and me that you've kept secret for so long? Is it okay?"

"I realized that part of the reason I kept things a secret from you is because I was keeping things from myself, too. I told myself that I didn't tell you about my writing because it was a special secret, like a private place I kept my dreams and…fantasies. My secret garden."

"I understand that."

"But that wasn't the real reason," Bren confessed. "I didn't tell you because there were parts of my life I wasn't ready to examine. I kept them separate and only let them come out in my writing. Melanie Richards wrote those books and *she* had those feelings, not me. I felt safer when Melanie and everything Melanie wanted only existed in one corner of my world."

"But now, Melanie has come out?"

Bren laughed. "Exploded out, is more like it. I still don't quite understand everything that's happening, but I feel excited about my life for the first time in a long time."

Liz took Bren's hand. "It seems all three of us are headed for adventure."

❖

"You're not playing tonight are you?" Candace asked, intercepting Parker as she sauntered back to the bench from the adjoining field.

"I'm going to pitch the second half, or sooner if Reilly's team gets lucky and scores off Jill."

Candace checked the field and saw the Daisy Mae character who'd been hanging all over Parker head to the pitcher's mound. "You can't be serious. She plays softball?"

"She's a barracuda on the mound." Parker laughed. "And elsewhere."

Automatically checking Parker's neck, Candace was relieved to see no telltale signs of a passionate night. "Your eye is still so swollen you can barely keep it open. If you can't see out there, you can't protect yourself."

"Worried about me?" Parker asked.

"I don't want to spend another Sunday night in the emergency room."

Parker frowned. "Don't worry, I wouldn't expect you to."

When Parker started to turn away, Candace gripped her arm. "Look, I'm sorry, okay? I don't want you to get hurt."

Parker bent her head close to Candace's, kissing close. "Are you saying you care about me?"

Candace panicked. Part of the reason she didn't do relationships was for exactly this reason. It got complicated. Women wanted to make more out of sex than it was. Why couldn't two people just have a nice, simple, physical relationship that was exciting and satisfying? Why couldn't that be enough? Why did it have to be about feelings. She backed up a step.

"Don't get carried away," Candace said. "If you get hit in the face again, you'll be worthless in bed, and I wouldn't mind a repeat. It worked out the last time."

Parker's eyes narrowed and her jaw tightened. "So what, I'm just a good fuck?"

"Oh no," Candace said, dropping her eyes down Parker's body and back up to her face in a slow, appreciative appraisal. "You're a great fuck."

Parker kissed her lightly on the mouth. "So's Jill, and a couple dozen other girls hanging around here. Take your pick."

"What? You're suddenly going to play hard to get?" Candace was angry, and she had no idea why.

"Nope. The only game I'm playing from now on is softball." She kissed Candace again, slowly this time, and ran her fingers through Candace's hair. Then she brushed her mouth over Candace's ear. "Next time, ask me out on a date."

Candace watched her walk away and wanted to call after her that that would be the day when she chased after a woman. But she didn't, because she wasn't so sure that was true any longer.

CHAPTER TWENTY-FIVE

S trike three!" the ump shouted, and Reilly's team swarmed the pitcher's mound. Liz lost sight of Reilly in the melee and just clapped along with everyone else. She wasn't happy to see Parker's team lose, but she was delighted that Reilly's won.

"Are you going to wait around for the victorious hordes to get done celebrating?" Candace asked, scanning the field. She couldn't see Parker, and she suspected that Bimbo Barbie or one of the other blondes had already dragged her off somewhere.

"I told Reilly I'd wait for her," Liz said.

"Like a date?"

"Well, more or less, yes." Liz smiled shyly. "I wouldn't mind spending some time alone with her."

"Understatement," Bren muttered.

"What about you?" Candace inquired of Bren. "Got plans?"

"Not really. I have early meetings at the library tomorrow, and I have some writing to finish tonight."

Candace gave her the eye. "All these years I thought you were home reading, and you were *really* home writing."

"I've *really* been home doing both."

"I guess you're not going to let me read it before it's done, huh?" Candace asked hopefully.

"I'm going to post an excerpt on the website this week." Bren paused, and Candace leaned forward expectantly. "I'll email it to you the day before so you can have a sneak preview."

"I think I'm over being mad at you now," Candace said. "*Melanie.*"

"Good." Bren collected her empty soda can and waved goodbye to Liz and Candace. "I'll see you tomorrow for lunch?"

"I'll be there," Liz said.

"Hurry up and finish the book," Candace called.

"Where's Parker?" Liz asked, searching the field. Reilly was slapping Sean on the back just as a gorgeous androgynous blonde joined them and put her arm around Sean.

"Probably deep-throating the pitcher in a car somewhere."

"Who? Oh...the blonde with the, uh, breasts who pitched the first half of the game?"

"That's the one." Candace frowned. "Parker seems to have a never ending supply of them."

"You sound jealous." Liz gave Candace a quick hug. "And believe me, you have nothing to worry about. Parker's just playing with them."

"That's all she's been doing with me, too."

"I don't think so. When she showed up at the Blue Diamond the other night, the only thing she wanted was to be with you. Of course she was a little too incapacitated to make that clear."

"She seems to have gotten over that."

"Candace, sweetie, you went home with someone else that night, remember?"

Candace sighed and looked away. "All right, not one of my better decisions."

"Why don't you just tell Parker that you're interested in her?"

"I did."

"Let me guess," Liz said. "I bet you told her you wanted to go to bed with her, didn't you?"

"Well, yes. What's your point?"

Liz shook her head. "You know what the point is. When it really matters, it's about more than sex."

"Excuse me, but weren't you the one who was just talking about wanting to get it on with Reilly last night?"

"Damn right. And I still do." Liz checked on Reilly's progress. The two teams had lined up and were passing side by side, shaking hands and congratulating each other. Reilly was flushed and exuberant. Happiness looked good on her. "But I want a lot of other things too. I want to know what makes her smile, and what she dreams about, and what she likes to do on rainy afternoons. For starters."

Candace regarded her without expression. "You're falling for her."

"Maybe. Yes."

"You know I love you, right?"

"I know."

"Do you think it's smart," Candace said, "considering everything?"

"I don't know. I'm not certain that thinking about it is going to give me any answers. When I'm with her, things seem clearer."

Candace took a deep breath and tipped her chin toward the players. "Then you should go get her."

"Thanks. I think I will." Liz squeezed Candace's hand. "Are you going to be okay?"

"I'll be fine. I've got a desk full of work at home. The only thing I like as much as women is money. I think I'll go make some."

Liz knew that wasn't true, but she respected Candace's defenses. She had plenty of her own. She kissed her cheek. "See you tomorrow."

"Have fun. I mean that."

"Hey," Liz said. "Don't be so hard on yourself."

"I'll be fine. All I need is a woman to take my mind off my troubles. I'd look for one tonight, but I think I'm going to swear off softball players for the rest of the summer." Candace smiled wryly. "Night, darlin.'"

"Night." Liz watched Candace stride down the slope, lithe and graceful and effortlessly seductive. She might *wish* she'd sworn off softball players, but Liz doubted it was true.

❖

Reilly extricated herself from the throng and worked her way through the enthusiastic crowd to the sidelines were Liz waited. When she wiped her face on her sleeve, she left behind a streak of sweat and dust.

"Congratulations!" Liz called, hurrying toward her.

Reilly held out both hands to stop her. "I'd give you a hug, but I'm filthy. It was that slide into home that did it."

Liz frowned and touched Reilly's jaw with one finger. "You've got a scrape here too. That needs to be cleaned up."

"If you can wait to eat," Reilly said, "I'll go home and shower and then maybe we can have dinner?"

"Why don't you come over to my place? We'll get your face taken care of, and then you can jump in the shower while I cook us something for dinner."

"I don't think you should cook," Reilly said firmly. "It's Sunday night and you've had two late nights in a row. You should relax."

"All right," Liz said softly, surprised all over again by Reilly's care. She'd gotten used to a solitary existence, even when she and Julia had still been a couple. Their schedules were so different they rarely ate together, went to bed together, or got up at the same time. "Then come to my apartment now. I'll order Thai delivery from the car. By the time you're done with a shower, dinner will be ready."

Reilly grinned. "You've got a deal. I'll follow you."

Twenty minutes later, Liz waited in the lobby while Reilly parked. Then she buzzed her in and they rode the elevator up to her condo.

"Hopefully you won't have any unexpected visitors," Reilly commented as Liz slid her key into the lock.

"She's not going to be here," Liz said.

"Even if she is," Reilly said, "I'm not leaving."

"Good, because I don't want you to." Liz held the door for Reilly, then gestured for her to follow. "The guest bathroom is down here. I'll leave a T-shirt and sweatpants in the adjoining bedroom. When you're ready, call me and I'll put some antiseptic on those cuts."

"Thanks," Reilly said.

Liz hesitated when they reach the bathroom. They hadn't touched since they'd left the softball field, and she very much wanted to touch her. Remembering the way she'd felt last night, and how difficult it had been to stop touching her, she resisted. Awkwardly, she backed away. "Well, the food should be here any second. Call me. When you're done."

"Okay."

As soon as Reilly shut the door, Liz had the overwhelming urge to join her in the shower. To keep her mind off how good Reilly looked in gym shorts and a tight T-shirt, and how much better she'd look without them, she hurried into the living room to clear the coffee table and wait for the food delivery.

She didn't have long to wait. When one of the regular delivery guys buzzed the apartment, she told him to come up and met him at the door.

"Thanks, Kenny," she said, handing him two twenties. "Keep the change."

Juggling the bags, she pushed the door closed with her foot and turned toward the kitchen. When she saw Reilly standing at the end of the hall in nothing but a bath towel, she almost dropped the food.

"There weren't any clothes in the bedroom," Reilly said apologetically.

Reilly's hair was damp, and the towel didn't cover much of her. While her arms and legs were muscular, her upper chest appeared surprisingly pale and soft. The slight swell of breasts beneath the towel started an ache in the pit of Liz's stomach. Liz's throat was dry and she had to swallow several times before she could speak. "I forgot to put them out."

"Here," Reilly said, closing the distance between them. "Let me take those bags."

Liz backed up until her back hit the door. "I've got them."

Reilly stopped, frowning. "What's the matter?"

"You. You're the matter."

"What have I done?" Reilly asked, panic streaking across her features.

"Either you really don't know how sexy you are, or you're a terrible tease."

"Oh." Reilly looked down. The towel gaped at the bottom, revealing a lot of thigh and almost quite a bit more. "Oh. Sorry."

"Don't be sorry," Liz murmured. "I'm enjoying the view."

"Uh, clothes?"

"Let me put the food in the kitchen, and I'll meet you in the guest room."

Reilly nodded and disappeared down the hall. Liz took a shaky breath and carried the food into the kitchen. After collecting a T-shirt and sweatpants from her bedroom, she continued to the guest room.

"Here you go." Liz stepped into the room and held out the clothes.

Reilly stood by the side of the bed, still wearing the towel. She extended one arm. "Thanks."

"I'm going to put these down on the floor and leave now." Liz set the bundle down.

"What's wrong?"

"Nothing," Liz said quickly. "But if I come within two feet of you, I'm going to forget every single reason I have for not going to bed with you." She laughed unsteadily. "God, you're so gorgeous."

Reilly grinned. "Could you remind me again what the reasons are?"

"My life isn't exactly my own these days, Reilly," Liz said gently. "I wish I could be like Candace, and enjoy a woman for a few hours or a few days, and know that we both would come away satisfied."

"Is that what you want? Easy sex, no strings attached?"

Liz knew she should say yes. There was nothing wrong with it. It was the smartest course of action right now. And why not have pleasant, wild, wonderful sex with someone she enjoyed, rather than a stranger. She wanted Reilly. She knew Reilly wanted her. She could see it in her eyes. She felt it in the way Reilly had kissed her the night before. Why did it have to be anything more than that?

"Yes."

Reilly skirted around the clothes on the floor and stopped in front of Liz. She loosened the towel and let it fall. Liz backed up and her back hit a door yet again. She glanced down between them, then quickly averted her gaze. Reilly's naked body was sculpted and firm. Strong and quintessentially female.

"Easy sex, no strings. That's a place to start." Reilly braced her arms on the door on either side of Liz's shoulders and slowly leaned against her. She kissed Liz's throat, then her mouth.

Reilly's skin was cool and damp against Liz's bare thighs. Her mouth was soft, her tongue warm and silky. Liz ran her hands over Reilly's back, feeling the muscles ripple beneath her fingertips. Breathless, Liz murmured in surprise when Reilly dropped to her knees. Startled to realize her legs were shaking, Liz steadied herself with a hand on Reilly's shoulder and watched Reilly tug her blouse from her shorts. She was no stranger to sex, even though it had been awhile, but everything she felt, everything Reilly did, seemed new.

"Oh," Liz breathed when Reilly kissed her stomach. She could see now the swelling below her navel that had never been there before. Reilly framed the area with her hands and kissed her above the spot where the fetus grew. The caress was reverent and tender. Liz sensed her clitoris lengthen and throb, and she moaned quietly.

"Are you all right?" Reilly glanced up as she eased Liz's shorts and panties down.

"Yes, but my legs are a little untrustworthy."

"I've got you." Reilly smiled. "Lift your foot. Now the other."

Liz complied and Reilly guided her free of her clothing.

And just like that, she was half nude. Liz thought fleetingly that she should probably be embarrassed, but she wasn't. The way Reilly looked at her, the way she touched her, made her feel so wanted. More than that, it made her feel beautiful and desirable and right now, she wanted to give Reilly anything she needed.

"Tell me if you want me to stop," Reilly whispered.

"Oh, no. No, no." Liz drew strands of Reilly's hair through her fingers and closed her eyes slowly as Reilly's warm breath surrounded her. The first glancing caress of Reilly's tongue sent a shiver through her. The glide of Reilly's lips, gentle and hot, made the muscles on the insides of her thighs quiver and jump. When Reilly sucked, she felt the storm rise within, a gathering force too strong and swift to be denied for very long. "Reilly, stop. Stop please."

Immediately, Reilly rose and pulled Liz close. "What is it? Does something hurt?"

Liz clung to her, struggling for words. "I'm going to come. Any second, and I want you to be holding me when I do."

"Let's lie down," Reilly said, her arm around Liz's waist. She guided her to the bed and unbuttoned her blouse. She removed it, and Liz's bra, and stretched out on the bed, bringing Liz with her. Then, as they faced each other, their bodies touching, she eased her arm behind Liz's shoulders and held her. Then, she reached down to slip her fingers between Liz's thighs.

"Oh," Liz gasped, arching into Reilly's embrace. "That's... you're...wonderful."

Reilly dipped her head, catching a blood-flushed nipple in her mouth. She sucked rhythmically, in time with her long, firm strokes over Liz's heated flesh. When Liz cried out, her body trembling, Reilly held her breath to absorb every note of pleasure, to memorize every tremor of release. Her own body felt wound so tight she feared she might shatter.

Liz covered Reilly's hand, stilling her motion but keeping Reilly's fingers pressed tightly to her slowly pulsing flesh. She felt so vulnerable, so open and unprotected, that she needed Reilly's touch to ensure that she wasn't adrift, alone and unanchored in some endless star-filled sky.

"Don't go," Liz whispered.

"No," Reilly answered, kissing her forehead, and her mouth. "I won't." Reilly fumbled beside them, found the edge of the comforter, and pulled it over them. "Are you all right?"

Liz burrowed her face in the curve of Reilly's neck. "I'm not sure. I've never had an orgasm like that."

Reilly held her more tightly. She had been so afraid of hurting her, and she had tried to be gentle. She was sick with worry that she'd done something wrong. "Are you having cramps? Pain of any kind?"

"What?" Fuzzy-headed, Liz pulled away and searched Reilly's face, instantly seeing the anxiety in her eyes. "Oh no. Baby, no." She kissed Reilly, hard and deep, sliding one thigh between Reilly's legs. Reilly let herself be pushed onto her back and Liz rolled on top of her. Liz framed Reilly's face and ran her thumbs over Reilly's cheekbones, smoothing away the frown lines. "I feel incredible. Amazing. I feel like I came with my soul, not just my body."

"Are you sure?"

"God yes. I'm fine. Fabulous." Liz slid off to one side and propped her chin in her hand. Lazily, she trailed her fingers over Reilly's stomach, smiling with satisfaction at Reilly's sharp intake of breath and the tightening of her abdominal muscles. "I haven't had a lot of orgasms lately, but I remember exactly how they feel." She leaned over and kissed Reilly, inching her fingers lower, stopping just at the top of the delta between her thighs. "And this one was like nothing I've ever felt before."

"Maybe," Reilly said, her voice husky, "it's different because… you're pregnant."

"Maybe. And maybe not." Liz delicately licked Reilly's nipple and laughed as Reilly's body quivered like a bowstring. "You like that?"

"Yes."

"What else do you like?"

"I like it when you're on top of me."

"Mmm," Liz murmured. "I like that too." She circled her fingertips against the base of Reilly's clitoris. Reilly moaned. "You like this too?"

"Very much."

Liz nestled into the curve of Reilly's body and settled her cheek against Reilly's chest. "I want to listen to your heartbeat while you come."

Reilly caressed Liz's back. "You can have anything you want."

Somewhere deep in her consciousness, Liz knew this was true. Reilly would give her whatever she asked for, and take as little or as much as she offered. Reilly had given her the one thing she'd never had with Julia—complete and utter honesty. Liz didn't know if that frightened her or exhilarated her. But right at this moment, the only thing she wanted was to give Reilly the pleasure that Reilly had given her. She wanted to be as close to Reilly as she could be, with no doubts or fears or uncertain tomorrows between them. She wanted this perfect moment, and she believed that she deserved it. That Reilly deserved it. The morning would be time enough for questions and reason and rationalization. Right now, the truth existed for her only in the pure, unselfish beat of Reilly's heart.

"I want to give you what you gave me," Liz whispered, slipping inside her. "Let me please you."

Eyes closed, Reilly stroked Liz's hair and opened herself to Liz's passion. And when she could hold no more, she spilled over, crying out Liz's name.

CHAPTER TWENTY-SIX

L iz opened her eyes in the dark quiet bedroom and tried to identify the sound that had awakened her. Reilly spooned behind her, her arm around Liz's waist. Liz covered Reilly's hand where it rested against her lower abdomen, liking the possessive way Reilly held her. Then she stiffened as she heard a strange tapping again, as if someone were trying to get in the window. However, considering her apartment was quite a few stories above street level, the only possible visitor would be Spiderman.

"What's wrong? Reilly mumbled, kissing the back of Liz's shoulder.

"There's something...thumping."

"Beeper." With a sigh, Reilly rolled away and stumbled from the bed toward the bathroom. "Sorry."

"That's okay," Liz said, sitting up. "God, it's three thirty in the morning. Who would call now?"

"I'm backup." Reilly located her beeper on the shelf above the sink and checked the readout, although she didn't have to. There would be only one place trying to reach her at this hour. "Can I use your phone? I left my cell in my glove compartment."

"Of course." Liz snapped on the bedside lamp and blinked against the glare. Then she stared. Reilly was naked. And gorgeous. Liz's body went to full alert.

Reilly sat down next to her and punched in numbers. A moment later, she said, "This is Dr. Danvers. The trauma unit is looking for me."

Liz stroked Reilly's back and listened to the one-sided conversation while Reilly asked terse questions. She still couldn't quite believe that she had woken up in Reilly's arms. Or that she'd fallen asleep holding her. When she realized Reilly was about to leave, she wanted to wrap her arms around her and keep her there forever. She feared the morning.

She feared the rational light of day. She feared that Reilly would be sorry. She wondered why *she* wasn't, and worried if she should be.

Reilly hung up the phone, lifted the sheets, and slid underneath. She pulled Liz into her arms and kissed her. "When I was a brand new resident, the first night my chief resident left me alone on call he said two things to me. The first was, 'Call me if you need anything.' The second was the mantra, 'Remember, to call for help is a sign of weakness.'"

"Did you ever call for help?" Liz brushed the hair back from Reilly's forehead and fit her leg between Reilly's. Reilly's hips lifted as if to welcome her, and her pulse soared.

"Damn right I did. Pride has no place when lives are at stake." Reilly kissed Liz again. "Or love."

Liz caught her breath. Her skin was on fire and her body was melting. "Do you have to go?"

"One of my partners just informed me that patients are stacking up like cordwood. They just opened a second OR room for me."

"Are you all right? Tired?"

Reilly grinned. "I feel great." She nuzzled Liz's neck. "If I didn't have two open tibias and a shattered shoulder to deal with, I'd show you just how not tired I am." She groaned softly. "God, you feel so good."

"What I said earlier," Liz said, "about casual and no strings?"

Reilly grew still. "Yes?"

"I said what I thought I should be feeling. It wasn't really what I wanted to say."

"What did you want to say?"

"I wanted to tell you that I've never felt so safe with anyone before. I've never felt as wanted. I've never been this excited by anyone's touch."

"From the day we met," Reilly said, "I haven't been able to think of anything except you."

"I think I might already be past casual, and I'm a little afraid of what that means."

Reilly caressed Liz's cheek. "What are you afraid of?"

Liz marveled at how easy Reilly made it for her to voice her uncertainties. She trusted Reilly not only to listen, but to tell her the truth. Even if the truth would shatter the dreams she was just daring to imagine. "I'm afraid you'll change your mind about seeing me—that maybe you won't want me when I'm a lot more pregnant than I am now."

"Why do you think that?" Reilly asked gently.

"You said you didn't want children with Annie, and you were in a relationship...in love with her. We're nowhere near that stage and—"

"Liz," Reilly whispered, "you're not Annie."

"We need to talk about her," Liz said.

"I know. I—" Reilly cursed under her breath when her beeper went off again.

"It's okay. Answer it."

"That's the OR telling me they're bringing the patient up. I'll call them from the car. I have to go. I'm sorry."

"No. Go. We'll talk later."

Reilly jumped from bed and pulled on the sweatpants and T-shirt Liz had offered her earlier. "I've got a full load in the OR tomorrow, and tomorrow night is Sean's black belt test. I'll be going right to the dojang from the hospital. Then Tuesday night I'm on first call." She ran her hand through her hair in frustration. "I'll call you the minute I have a chance. We'll talk. I promise."

"I understand. I'm swamped at work too." Liz got out of bed and found her blouse in the jumble of clothes on the floor. Trying to sound casual, she said, "Don't worry if you can't call. How about Friday night? Maybe dinner?"

"That sounds great, but Friday's a long ways away." Reilly strode to Liz and pushed both hands into Liz's hair, cradling her head as she kissed her. "Too long."

Liz smoothed her hands over Reilly's shoulders, wanting to pull her back to the bed. "I don't mind if you drop by for a quickie before then."

Reilly grinned. "So it's all about the sex, huh?"

"Absolutely. Is there anything else?"

"Oh yeah," Reilly whispered, holding Liz tightly. "A whole lot more."

"Then I'll see you Friday." Liz kissed the tip of Reilly's chin. "Besides, a little anticipation is a good thing."

❖

By Thursday, Liz knew she was in trouble. Her concentration was terrible. Every fifteen or twenty minutes while pretending to work at her desk, she glanced at the clock, wondering what Reilly was doing. If the phone rang, she lunged for it only to be disappointed when it was her secretary reminding her of a meeting that she had invariably forgotten about. The two times Reilly managed to call her, their brief conversations had left her both exhilarated and frustrated. She felt slightly crazed. The sound of Reilly's voice over the phone aroused her. She kept remembering how unbelievably good Reilly's mouth felt on her.

"That's it," Liz muttered, tossing aside the case file she had been reviewing. She still had an hour before lunch with Candace and Bren, but she had to get up and walk around. If she stayed at her desk thinking about making love with Reilly, she'd be too physically uncomfortable to get any more work done anyhow. A walk from her office on Market Street across campus to the tavern would do her good.

Forty minutes later she was hungry and ready to see her friends. She still longed for a glimpse of Reilly, though, and finally admitted that even one more day was just too damn far away. She called Reilly's cell and went to voice mail.

"I know you're probably in the OR all day, but please come by the apartment tonight if you can. I miss you."

Just as she crossed the street to the restaurant, her cell rang and she snatched it off her belt, hoping Reilly had gotten her message. "Hello?"

"Good," Julia said, "I finally caught you between court and meetings. Let's have lunch."

Liz stopped on the sidewalk and closed her eyes. Taking a deep breath, she said in what she hoped was a reasonable voice, "I'm sorry. That's not possible."

"I can pick you up in half an hour. I've got reservations at Nightingale's. They're holding a private table for us so we can talk."

"We don't have anything to talk about. You should have received the signed documents on the condo and—"

"I moved out of her apartment Saturday afternoon. I've been staying in a hotel."

Liz felt nothing at the announcement. "I don't see—"

"I want to move home. I know you're angry—"

"You're not moving home. It's not our home anymore." Liz sighed and started walking again. "And I'm not angry. I'm sad. I'm sad and I'm tired and I don't have anything else to say."

"I do. I have things to say. I want to apologize, and I want you to listen to reason. You've always been reasonable."

"I'm sorry, Julia," Liz said, as she slowed outside the tavern. Candace smiled and waved to her through the window. Bren, who sat across from her in her usual place, mouthed hello. The familiarity of the moment warmed her. "I've already got lunch plans. Good-bye."

Liz closed her cell phone, pushed through the doors, and made her way to the booth. "God, it's good to see you two."

"It's only been three days," Candace pointed out. "Missed you, too."

"It feels like three years," Liz said.

"Trouble?" Bren asked. "You looked upset on the phone."

"That was Julia." Liz nodded to the waitress and gave her her order without looking at the menu.

"What did super bitch want?" Candace snarled.

"To move home. Can you believe that?" Liz noticed that Candace wore jeans and a T-shirt, and not her usual power suit. She was also drinking what looked like iced tea. Liz wondered if she was mellowing or just not awake yet.

"Actually," Bren said, "I can believe it. I'm surprised it took her this long."

"To do what?" Candace asked.

"Come to her senses." Bren took a bite of her turkey club. "I would have given her new romance about six weeks to fizzle."

"I think for the first six months it was too hot for that," Liz said, noting with satisfaction that it didn't bother her any longer to think of Julia and some young college kid rolling around in a dorm room or hotel or wherever they had been trysting. Wherever and whatever, she just didn't care. "At any rate, I told her no."

"Well," Candace huffed, "I should think so."

"Does this have anything to do with Reilly?" Bren asked.

Liz thought about it. "Yes and no. If I hadn't met Reilly, I still wouldn't want Julia to come back. It's wrong for me, it's wrong for the baby—hell, it's even wrong for Julia."

"Julia is an ungrateful bitch who never deserved you," Candace stated.

Liz reached across the table and squeezed her hand. "Thank you."

"So what about Reilly?" Candace said, examining Liz intently.

"Reilly is still something of a question mark," Liz said slowly. "We haven't talked about some really important things." She patted her stomach. "Like this, for example."

"But," Bren said, "you *have* been doing a little more than talking, haven't you?"

Liz felt her face flush. "Does it show?"

Bren laughed. "It's been showing even before you did anything about it."

"You slept with her," Candace said, making it a statement and not a question.

"I did." Liz grinned. "I most definitely did."

Candace drained her iced tea and carefully set the empty glass down. "Well, good for you."

"Ditto," Bren added.

"Thank you," Liz said, looking from one to the other. "You're not going to lecture me?"

Candace rolled her eyes. "Like it would make a difference."

"It might." Liz twirled the straw in her drink.

"No, it wouldn't," Candace and Bren said together.

"No, it wouldn't," Liz agreed.

"Well," Candace said. "Tell us. She has got to be at least as good as she looks."

"I…" A montage of images raced through Liz's mind. Kisses, touches, whispered murmurs of pleasure. Reilly's hands, her mouth, her body moving against Liz's. Waking to the heat of Reilly's skin, to the softness of Reilly's breasts against her back, to the gentle sigh of her breath. "She's beautiful."

Candace, her blue eyes wide and dark, stared at Liz. "I've never seen you look like this before."

"Like what?"

"Like you were in love."

"Oh, no, that's not it," Liz said hastily. Love was such a big word, such a life-changing emotion. She wasn't sure she could handle that and all that was in store for her with the baby, too. And what about Reilly? Was she really looking for a relationship that came with so many strings attached? Needing some distance from the swirl of conflicting feelings that just thinking about Reilly stirred, she grinned at Candace. "Besides, I was pretty gone over you."

"Uh-huh. True. But we were young and in lust and what did we know?"

"We knew plenty." Liz looked from Candace to Bren. "We knew, all of us, what we had with each other."

"Stop," Bren said, "I'm not even pregnant and I want to cry."

"Yeah, seriously," Candace said gruffly. "Just be careful with your heart, okay?

"I'll try." Liz turned to Bren. "So what about you? What's happening with your sexy mystery lover?"

"Nothing," Bren said, which was true, although not the entire story. Jae had emailed her the night before. *I imagine lying on a bed, my hands and legs bound. You're kneeling above my mouth, and I make you come.*

"Are you done with her then?" Candace asked curiously.

"I haven't decided. I only know I'm not done thinking about her."

Candace sighed. "I don't know how I ever missed how sexy you are."

Bren blushed. "I think you're talking about Melanie."

"Her too."

Candace bumped Bren's knee with hers. Liz watched the exchange with interest, wondering what she'd missed in the last few weeks.

"I think you should save your energy for Parker," Bren said, wanting to divert Candace's attention from her. Candace was the kind of woman whose first response was visceral, her affections so easily translated into attraction. It was one of the things Bren loved about her, but she knew it would take a player of equal stature to handle Candace, and she wasn't that woman. Her games were of a different nature.

"Parker. Parker is off the table." Candace briefly informed them of her last conversation with Parker. "So, Parker has suddenly decided she doesn't want to play."

Bren shook her head. "You read those signals wrong. She just wants to play another game."

"I don't play unless I make the rules."

"Uh-huh," Bren said disbelievingly. "So you'll just quit?"

"Parker's call, not mine," Candace said flatly.

"I'd say she tossed out a pitch and is waiting for you to hit it back," Liz said.

"Spare me the baseball analogy," Candace groaned.

Laughing, Liz looked at her watch. "I've got to get back. Are we getting together this weekend? Maybe dinner?"

"Absolutely," Bren said.

"Sure," Candace said absently, as if her mind were elsewhere.

Liz paid for the three of them and they walked out together.

"Where are you parked," Liz asked her friends.

"I took the subway," Candace said.

"I'm in a lot across from the hospital," Bren replied as they reached the corner.

"Good," Liz said, glancing up at the light. It was green and she started to cross. "We can walk that way together then."

"So," Candace said, "is Parker in the office to—"

"Liz!" Julia called sharply, appearing out of nowhere. She grabbed Liz's arm and tugged her to a stop in the middle of the street.

"Julia!" Liz exclaimed. "What are you doing here?"

"Well, if you won't agree to meet me, I'll just have to track you dow—"

At the screech of tires, Liz shot a startled glance at the light just as it changed from green to yellow. A red pickup truck careened around the corner into the intersection, trying to outrun the red light. Julia, whose back was to the oncoming vehicle, said something Liz couldn't hear.

"Look out," Liz shouted. She grabbed Julia's arm and yanked her around, pushing her toward the opposite curb and safety all in one motion. As she did, something struck her hip and she catapulted into Julia. She and Julia landed in a heap on the ground.

Amidst the screams, Liz tried to make sense of what had just happened. The sky overhead was brilliantly blue, and fluffy white clouds moved lazily across her view. Then the idyllic scene disappeared, and Julia's face came into focus.

"Oh my God, are you all right?" Julia looked panicked.

Liz found that odd. Julia never lost her composure, even in the midst of an argument. Next to her, Candace and Bren's faces appeared, both looking terrified. A bearded man, his eyes wild, grabbed her hand.

"Lady! Jesus, lady. Jesus. I'm sorry. Are you hurt?"

"I'm fine," Liz said, pushing herself up. Her arms were shaky but she felt all right. A little numb, maybe. "Really. I think I just tripped."

"Are you sure?" Bren asked anxiously. "Just sit for a minute. You landed awfully hard."

Liz saw Bren glance at Candace, and their obvious fear spurred her into motion. Gripping Bren's shoulder, she pushed to her feet. "Really, I'm absolutely fine."

The wave of dizziness came so quickly she didn't even have time to be frightened. As she felt herself falling, she clutched Bren's arm.

"Call Reilly," she whispered.

CHAPTER TWENTY-SEVEN

Nice case, Reilly," Clint Marcum, one of Reilly's associates, said as they headed down the hall toward the main OR desk.

"Thanks." Reilly pulled off her sweat soaked OR cap and tossed it along with her mask into a trashcan. "Maybe we'll stay caught up for a few hours."

"Yeah right."

"Hey, you never know. We could get lu—"

"Dr. Danvers," the young clerk who handled the phones in the office called. "I was just going to phone down to your room when I saw you were finishing up. The operator took a message. She said it was urgent."

"Aren't they all," Reilly muttered. She'd been in the OR since seven that morning with a 16-year-old who had been med-evaced in after he had flipped his all-terrain vehicle and crushed his pelvis. Once they'd finally gotten the hemorrhage stopped, she'd had to stabilize the major undamaged bone fragments with pins and screws and then apply an external fixater. He'd be in bed for the foreseeable future, but he'd likely walk again. She was hot, tired, and hungry. Nevertheless, she held out her hand for the pink message slip. All it said was *Call Bren. Urgent.* And a number.

"I've got to get this, Clint," Reilly said as she grabbed the wall phone, her stomach knotting. There was only one emergency she could think of, and she couldn't let her imagination go there. Nothing had happened to Liz. She wouldn't be able to handle it if anything had.

"Sure," Clint said, giving her a curious look. "Catch you later."

Reilly waved absently as she waited for the operator, gripping the receiver so tightly her hand ached. "Hi, it's Dr. Danvers. I need an outside number right away." She read the phone number off the message, feeling sick and unable to keep her mind from bombarding her with images she couldn't avoid seeing. Annie, so pale and still. Liz, warm and vibrant and so wonderfully passionate. The phone rang once, twice, three times, four—just as she expected voicemail to kick in, a breathless voice answered.

"Hello?"

"Bren, it's Reilly. What's wrong?" Reilly braced her arm against the wall and shut her eyes. *Please don't tell me she's hurt. Please don't say—*

"Oh, Reilly, sorry. I had to run outside to answer my cell phone. God, I'm glad I didn't lose you. We're down in the ER with Liz."

A sheet of ice slid through Reilly's gut. "What happened?"

"We're not sure. She either fainted or fell or maybe got hit by a car. We—"

"I'm on my way."

Reilly slammed the receiver back onto the phone, punched the automatic door opener controlling the double doors leading into the OR from the hallway, and raced through them before they were barely open wide enough to accommodate her body. She didn't even look in the direction of the elevators, but shoved through the fire door and took the stairs from the third floor down to ground level two at a time. It was a trip she had taken many times, but never filled with fear so suffocating she couldn't draw a full breath. She dodged stretchers, shouldered around groups of nurses, med students, and visitors and cut across the paths of technicians pushing equipment as she sprinted down the corridor to the emergency room. The ER waiting room was on the opposite side of the hallway from the main receiving area, but she didn't glance in that direction. Bren and Candace were most likely in there, and assuredly frantic, but she needed to see Liz. She had to get to Liz. She made a sharp left into the controlled chaos of the ER and raced up to the counter where a clerk sat surrounded by stacks of charts and paperwork.

"Liz Ramsey," Reilly said breathlessly, scanning the whiteboard behind the clerk where patients' names and status were written. She didn't see Liz's name, but she might have just arrived. "Where is she?"

The harried looking middle-aged woman in a flowered smock frowned. "I don't think we've got anybody waiting for ortho, Doc. But if you want to look at a few with colds or bellyaches, we've got plenty of—"

"She'd be an MVA or maybe an OB emergency—she's pregnant." Reilly barely resisted grabbing a pile of charts and rifling through them.

"Oh, that must be the one we just called Dr. Thompson about. Let me see." The woman sorted through a stack of intake forms with maddening slowness. "I think she's in cubicle eight—no, nine."

"Thanks," Reilly called, already in motion. She slowed when she approached the curtain, not wanting to startle Liz or interrupt an examination. Still, her heart was pounding so hard her chest hurt and her hand shook when she pulled back the curtain.

Liz wore a white hospital gown covered with faded blue stars and lay on a stretcher with an IV running into her left hand. She turned her head as Reilly stepped into the small cubicle.

"Hey," Liz said wanly, and held out her hand. "Did I drag you away from something important?"

"Not a thing." Reilly's pulse settled a little when she saw Liz awake and seemingly stable. While scanning the monitors next to the bed, she took Liz's outstretched hand. Then she reached under the edge of the stretcher, released the side rail, and leaned down. She kissed Liz lightly. "How are you doing?"

"I'm fine. I think everyone's fussing over nothing."

"Are you hurt?"

"No, I'm pretty certain I just fainted." Liz rubbed her cheek against the back of Reilly's hand. "I got scared for a second, and I wanted you. I'm sorry if I worried you."

"No. You did the right thing. This is exactly where I want to be." Reilly swallowed, refusing to think about how quickly her whole life had imploded when Annie had collapsed and died within moments. "Are you having any bleeding?"

Liz gripped Reilly's hand tighter. "Not that I can tell. They called Marta…Marta Thompson, my obstetrician."

"Good." As she spoke, Reilly double-checked the readouts. Liz's blood pressure and heart rate were normal. Some of the tension in her chest eased.

"God, Reilly, I fell. What if—"

"Hey, it's okay," Reilly soothed, feeling more in control with each passing second. She wasn't going to let anything happen to Liz. "Let's just wait and see what Dr. Thompson says."

"Someone mention my name?" Marta Thompson pulled the curtain aside, pushed in a portable ultrasound machine, and slowed only long enough to yank the curtain closed again. "Fill me in, sweetie. Your chart said something about you getting hit by a car?"

"If I did, it was just a bump." Liz quickly related the incident. "I think in all the excitement I just got a little dizzy."

As Reilly listened, the muscles in her jaw tightened until her head throbbed. Liz could so easily have been killed. She swallowed down the urge to curse.

"I'm not hurt," Liz repeated, giving Reilly's hand a shake. "Really."

Reilly forced a smile.

"Well," Marta said, "let's just be sure everything's okay." She studied Liz and Reilly's joined hands, and then met Reilly's eyes. "Are you staying?"

"Yes," Reilly said instantly. Then she glanced at Liz. "Okay?"

"Of course," Liz said softly. "Thank you."

Reilly stroked Liz's hair and drew her hand to her lips. She kissed the back of Liz's fingers. "Nothing could get me out of this room right now."

The obstetrician pulled down the sheet and lifted Liz's hospital gown, exposing Liz's abdomen. She placed the lubricated ultrasound probe below Liz's navel and turned on the machine. "Then let's have a look."

Against the whoosh of the probe gliding over skin, the rhythm of a rapid heartbeat sounded steadily. Reilly listened intently, mentally counting and trying to remember what she'd learned in medical school about normal rate for a fetus at this stage. She squinted at the monitor, trying to decipher the black and gray shapes amidst the background of snow. Then, as if a camera lens were twisted into sharp focus, the gently curved shape of the fetus jumped out in sharp contrast to the shadowy echoes around it.

"Oh, sweetheart," Reilly whispered, "will you look at that."

Liz glanced from the monitor to Reilly's face, struck by the note of wonder in Reilly's voice. Reilly's mouth was curved in a faint smile and her eyes were soft. Liz had seen that tender look before, when Reilly touched her as they made love. She recognized it now as the reason she'd fallen in love with her. *I love you,* she thought, and knew it to be true.

Reilly glanced down at her as if she had spoken the words aloud. "You're both so beautiful."

"Well," Marta Thompson said, "everything seems fine. The placenta looks nice and healthy and well attached. The fetus is growing normally." She turned off the machine and set the ultrasound probe aside. "Just to be on the safe side, I want you to rest for the next twenty-four hours. That means on your back with your feet up. Don't go to work tomorrow."

Liz relaxed, the rush of relief so profound she felt lightheaded—in a good way. "Fine. I won't take any chances."

Marta glanced from Liz to Reilly. "Do you have someone you can stay with tonight?"

Reilly grimaced. "I'm on call again, but I might be able to switch with someone."

"No, don't do that," Liz said. "I'll stay with Bren." She looked at Marta. "A friend."

"Good. If you have any cramping or bleeding, even streaking, I want to know about it," the obstetrician warned.

"I understand."

"All right then. As long as there are no problems, I'll see you for your next scheduled appointment." Marta pushed the equipment cart out into the hall and left them alone.

Reilly cupped Liz's face and kissed her. "Great news."

Suddenly feeling shy, Liz tried for a casual tone. "Well, I guess I can go home then, right?"

"Let me check with the nurses and make sure there aren't any tests pending. I'll find Bren, too." Reilly kept a grip on Liz's hand. She didn't want to leave her. She didn't want to entrust her care to anyone else. The thought of not being around if something happened to Liz made her feel sick. "It might take me a little while to find someone to cover for me tonight, but I'll see you later at Bren's."

"You don't have to."

"I do."

"I know how busy you are," Liz said, but she secretly wanted

Reilly to come. She needed her, and as scary as that idea was, it felt good too.

"I want to be with you." Reilly caressed Liz's cheek. "I need to be. Is that all right?"

"Oh, it's so much more than all right."

"If you need anything at all," Reilly found the call button and pressed it into Liz's palm, "ring for one of the nurses."

"You heard Marta, I'm fine. Stop worrying."

Reilly smiled a little unsteadily. "Sure. No problem."

"Reilly," Liz said carefully. "I have a favor to ask."

"Anything."

"They brought Julia in, too. I heard someone say she might have a broken ankle. Could you check on her? Her last name is Myers."

Reilly's eyes narrowed. "What I had in mind was something closer to strangling her."

"I know it probably sounds crazy to you, but I don't want her to be alone if she's hurt. She didn't mean for this to happen."

"I'll check on her. Don't worry."

"Thank you."

It took all Reilly's willpower to leave Liz. Even though in her rational mind she knew Liz was all right, the fear of losing her was not that easy to banish.

"Okay. I won't be long." Reilly backed away. "You're all right?"

Liz smiled. "I'm wonderful. Go."

Reilly stepped out from behind the curtain and motioned to one of the nurses who stood nearby. "This patient's ready to be discharged. Can you check if there's anything pending for her?"

"Sure. It'll take me a couple minutes."

"That's fine. Someone else came in with her. A possible extremity injury. Julia Myers."

"Twelve, I think. They just finished her x-rays."

"Thanks." Reilly strode down the hall to the wall-mounted light boxes and checked the x-rays hanging there. She found Julia's and scanned first the distal tibia and fibula, then the ankle bones. Other than a great deal of soft tissue swelling, she didn't see any fractures.

"I didn't find anything," John Burke, one of the ER attendings, said as he stopped next to Reilly.

"No, I don't either."

"Ace wrap and elevation for a few days?"

"Sounds good to me. I'm just going to say hello—unofficially."

"Sure," Burke said, heading in the opposite direction. "We'll take care of the paperwork in a few minutes."

Reilly walked to the next cubicle and stopped at the edge of the closed curtain. "Ms. Myers, I'm Dr. Danvers. Do you mind if I come in?"

"Not if you're here to tell me I can go home."

Reilly recognized the throaty voice and recalled their brief meeting at Liz's apartment. She also remembered that Julia had been happy to let her think that she and Liz had been together that morning. She slipped through the opening in the curtain and stopped at the end of Julia's stretcher. "We met last Saturday."

Julia eyed her appraisingly. "I remember. What a coincidence."

"Not really. Liz asked me to check on you. The emergency room doctor will be back in a minute to talk to you, but it doesn't look like your ankle is fractured."

"How's Liz?"

"She's fine." Reilly held Julia's gaze. "So is the baby."

"That's good then."

"Yes, that's very good."

"What kind of doctor are you?" Julia asked

"I'm an orthopedic surgeon."

"Liz didn't break something, did she?"

"No. I'm here because Liz asked me to come down."

"That's interesting. She told me she wasn't involved with you," Julia said coolly.

Reilly smiled. "Well, I suppose that might have depended upon when you talked. And what kind of involvement you were discussing."

"She led me to believe you weren't intimate."

"I'm in love with her." When Julia merely stared, obviously caught off guard, Reilly went on, "If you have unfinished business with Liz, that's between the two of you. But don't put your hands on her again."

"I didn't know Liz went for the bad girl type," Julia scoffed.

"There's a lot about Liz you don't know. Don't walk on that ankle for a few days."

Then Reilly turned and walked out.

CHAPTER TWENTY-EIGHT

W ill you two stop fussing," Liz complained after Bren asked
her for the third time if she needed anything. Opposite Bren
at her desk, Candace occupied the overstuffed chair next to the sofa
pretending to read, but Liz could tell that she was staring at her more
than her book. The windows were open, and the night was still and hot,
even at a little after seven. In another hour it would be dark. Reilly had
called an hour earlier and said she had just finished a case and would
be over soon. Every minute of waiting seemed endless. Liz turned on
her side on the old familiar sofa and curled one arm under the pillow,
gazing at her two friends. "I'm perfectly all right, except I'm bored."

"You're supposed to lie on your back," Bren said. "That's what
Reilly told us."

Liz sighed deeply. "My obstetrician said bedrest. I don't think she
meant on my back literally, but just that I couldn't run around right
away."

Bren didn't look convinced, and rather than argue, Liz dutifully
shifted onto her back. "Better?"

"Yes. You still look a little pale."

"I'm tired. That's all," Liz assured them.

"I'm going to hunt that bitch down and tear her head off," Candace
said calmly.

"I'm coming with you," Bren said.

Liz shook her head. "I love that you two are ready to do damage
for me, but it's not necessary. Julia is history."

Candace snorted. "Not if she's still walking around."

"I don't know," Bren said, "she didn't look to me like she was
ready to quit this afternoon."

"I saw her for a few seconds before I left the hospital," Liz said. "I
told her I didn't want to hear from her again. She actually agreed that it
was better we didn't see one another for a while."

"She probably knows if we see her anywhere near you, she's dead meat," Candace grumbled.

Liz laughed. "Probably. Julia's no fool."

"You're wrong about that," Bren said seriously. "She let you go."

The doorbell sounded downstairs and Candace dropped her book and jumped up. "I'll get it. I think it's time for a glass of wine. Bren, you want one?"

"I'll come with you," Bren said. "How about we order pizza? Liz?"

"Sounds good," Liz said, more to alleviate her friends' worry than because she was hungry.

Alone, she closed her eyes, as mentally weary as she was physically tired. She still found it difficult to accept how little she had understood Julia, despite their years together. And she wondered how she could have ever thought what they had together was enough to build a life on, let alone start a family together. Absently, she rubbed her abdomen. The uncertainty she usually felt when contemplating the future was gone. In its place, she felt a surge of happiness.

When Liz sensed someone else in the room, she opened her eyes. Reilly stood in the doorway, watching her. She must have come right from the hospital, because she wore jeans, a scrub shirt, and her running shoes.

"Hi," Liz said.

"Hi. I thought you were asleep."

"No, not asleep, just thinking."

Reilly crossed to her and squatted down beside the couch. She stroked Liz's hair. "What were you thinking?"

"That having a baby is sort of fun."

Reilly smiled. "Glad to hear it."

"Me too." Liz leaned forward and kissed Reilly softly. "And I was wondering how I could have mistaken what I had with Julia for being in love."

"Maybe," Reilly said, her voice husky, "being in love, all the way in love, is one of those things you don't recognize until you feel it."

"I recognize it now," Liz said. "Every time I look at you."

"Me, too." Reilly cupped Liz's cheek and kissed her, a slow, deep, possessive kiss. "I'm crazy in love with you."

"Lie down with me." Liz shifted away from the edge of the couch and patted the empty spot beside her.

"Are you sure? I don't want to crowd you."

"I'll lie on top of you."

"Uh…"

Liz grinned. "You can be good, can't you?"

"It might be a hardship." Reilly kicked off her running shoes and started to ease down onto the couch.

"Jeans too. It's hot and it will get hotter with us so close together."

"You know, I go commando in the OR. Most of us do."

"Forget it then. You can't be naked with Candace in the house," Liz said immediately.

Reilly laughed and popped the button on her jeans.

"Baby, I'm serious," Liz warned, her gaze riveted to Reilly's hands. "God I love your body."

"No touching," Reilly said as she pushed her jeans down. Underneath, she wore navy blue boxers.

"Oh good," Liz sighed. "A safety net."

Reilly stretched out on her back, and Liz curled up half on top of her, her head on Reilly's shoulder. Reilly ran her hand up and down Liz's arm. "Comfortable?"

"More than comfortable. Happy." Liz kissed Reilly's throat and slipped her hand under Reilly's scrub shirt to caress her stomach. "I'm crazy in love with you, too, you know."

"I can't tell you how good it feels when you say that." Reilly kissed the top of Liz's head. "Annie and I were together three years, but I wasn't her only lover. I didn't know that at first, because she didn't think it should make any difference to me. When I did figure it out, she said she loved me, but she didn't believe in being exclusive."

"If you're asking if it would make a difference to me, it would. Both ways." Liz smoothed her hand higher in slow circles over Reilly's chest. "I can't imagine wanting anyone else to make love to me except you. And the thought of someone touching you—God, that hurts."

"I don't want anyone except you," Reilly whispered. She covered Liz's hand and squeezed gently. "Stop before you get me really turned on."

"I'm sorry. I just love to touch you."

"I love you. I hope you never stop wanting me, because I'll never stop wanting you."

"What about the baby?" Liz asked quietly. Despite that the moment was wonderful—more special, more exciting than anything she had ever dreamed—this was a dream that came with strings. And as much as she wanted Reilly, she had to know if a real future was possible.

"I want you, and the baby." Reilly stroked Liz's belly. "I want to be part of this with you. I want to love you and this child."

"But you said—"

"Annie always did what she wanted, no matter who it hurt. Including herself. *Usually* herself." Reilly tilted Liz's face up. "Annie said she wanted to get pregnant because she was getting older and running out of time. I've always suspected that having a child was part of her dream of having a normal life."

"And you didn't want her to."

"I didn't agree, for a lot of reasons. Her health, mostly. Pregnancy would have put a tremendous strain on her. Especially if she wasn't careful." Reilly shook her head. "Annie was careless with herself—she took chances with people, and with other things."

"It must have been so hard for you. And for her."

"Harder for her," Reilly murmured. "I don't know if she was trying to get pregnant or if she just did by accident. I suspected she slept with men sometimes, but I couldn't call her on it. I guess since she knew I didn't want her to be pregnant, she didn't tell me."

"That's not your fault."

Reilly closed her eyes and pressed her cheek against Liz's hair. "I shouldn't have judged her. If she had trusted me, if she had told me, I might have paid more attention to what was happening with her. I *know* I would have. Then I might ha—"

"I doubt you would have anticipated she'd have a stroke, Reilly. And even if you had, she might not have listened to reason."

"I loved her," Reilly said, "but I didn't love her the way she needed to be loved."

Liz pushed herself up so she could look down into Reilly's face. "You love me the way I need to be loved. I want to be able to give the same thing to you."

"You do." Reilly skimmed her fingers along Liz's jaw. "You make me happy. You make me excited about the future. I want to be there for you and the baby. I want to be the one with you in the delivery room when the baby is born."

"When I let myself dream," Liz whispered, "I see us. You and me. The baby. A family."

"So do I, and it's exactly what I want."

Liz buried her face in Reilly's shoulder, unable to stop the tears.

"Are those happy tears?" Reilly whispered, her throat tight, her cheeks wet.

"Oh, more than happy," Liz answered. "Much, much more than happy."

"Do you think we should wake them to eat?" Candace whispered, standing in the doorway with Bren. At close to nine, the room was dark except for the pale glow from the desk lamp. Liz slept with her head on Reilly's chest, her hand still nestled under Reilly's shirt. Reilly held Liz protectively in the circle of one arm.

"They both look exhausted, not to mention adorable," Bren said.

"Reilly is so hot," Candace whispered.

Grinning, Reilly turned her head and opened her eyes. "Thanks."

"Stop cruising my lover," Liz muttered. "I'm pregnant and can't be blamed for my actions."

"I meant 'must be hot,' you know. Like warm."

"Uh-huh," Liz said.

Candace laughed. "You two hungry?"

Liz burrowed closer to Reilly. "Later."

Reilly kissed Liz's temple and closed her eyes again.

Candace turned and followed Bren downstairs. In the kitchen she settled on the stool at the breakfast counter and picked up a slice of pizza. "So, what are you going to do the rest of the night?"

Bren smiled. "I'm going to email a certain someone about a fantasy we have in common. How about you?"

"I'm going to call a certain woman and ask her out on a date." Candace glanced toward the stairs, and thought of Liz and Reilly asleep in the surety of one another's embrace. "Do you think this is the end of the Lonely Hearts Club?"

"Oh, no. The LHC has always been about our friendship." Bren wrapped an arm around Candace's waist. "And love will only make us stronger."

About the Author

Radcly*ffe* is a retired surgeon and full time award-winning author-publisher with over twenty-five lesbian novels and anthologies in print, including the Lambda Literary winners *Erotic Interludes 2: Stolen Moments* ed. with Stacia Seaman and *Distant Shores, Silent Thunder*. She has selections in multiple anthologies including *Wild Nights, Fantasy, Best Lesbian Erotica 2006, 2007*, and *2008, After Midnight, Caught Looking: Erotic Tales of Voyeurs and Exhibitionists, First-Timers, Ultimate Undies: Erotic Stories About Lingerie and Underwear, A is for Amour*, and *H is for Hardcore*. She is the recipient of the 2003 and 2004 Alice B. Readers' award for her body of work and is also the president of Bold Strokes Books, one of the world's largest independent LGBT publishing companies.

Her forthcoming works include *In Deep Waters: 2* written with Karin Kallmaker (May 2008), *Word of Honor* (June 2008), and *Night Call* (October 2008).

Books Available From Bold Strokes Books

Deeper by Ronica Black. Former homicide detective Erin McKenzie and her fiancée Elizabeth Adams couldn't be any happier—until the not so distant past comes knocking at the door. (978-1-60282-006-7)

The Lonely Hearts Club by Radclyffe. Take three friends, add two ex-lovers and several new ones, and the result is a recipe for explosive rivalries and incendiary romance. (978-1-60282-005-0)

Venus Besieged by Andrews & Austin. Teague Richfield heads for Sedona and the sensual arms of psychic astrologer Callie Rivers for a much needed romantic reunion. (978-1-60282-004-3)

Branded Ann by Merry Shannon. Pirate Branded Ann raids a merchant vessel to obtain a treasure map and gets more than she bargained for with the widow Violet. (978-1-60282-003-6)

American Goth by JD Glass. Trapped by an unsuspected inheritance and guided only by the guardian who holds the secret to her future, Samantha Cray fights to fulfill her destiny. (978-1-60282-002-9)

Learning Curve by Rachel Spangler. Ashton Clarke is perfectly content with her life until she meets the intriguing Professor Carrie Fletcher, who isn't looking for a relationship with anyone. (978-1-60282-001-2)

Place of Exile by Rose Beecham. Sheriff's detective Jude Devine struggles with ghosts of her past and an ex-lover who still haunts her dreams. (978-1-933110-98-1)

Fully Involved by Erin Dutton. A love that has smoldered for years ignites when two women and one little boy come together in the aftermath of tragedy. (978-1-933110-99-8)

Heart 2 Heart by Julie Cannon. Suffering from a devastating personal loss, Kyle Bain meets Lane Connor, and the chance for happiness suddenly seems possible. (978-1-60282-000-5)

Queens of Tristaine: Tristaine Book Four by Cate Culpepper. When a deadly plague stalks the Amazons of Tristaine, two warrior lovers must return to the place of their nightmares to find a cure. (978-1-933110-97-4)

The Crown of Valencia by Catherine Friend. Ex-lovers can really mess up your life…even, as Kate discovers, if they've traveled back to the 11th century! (978-1-933110-96-7)

Mine by Georgia Beers. What happens when you've already given your heart and love finds you again? Courtney McAllister is about to find out. (978-1-933110-95-0)

House of Clouds by KI Thompson. A sweeping saga of an impassioned romance between a Northern spy and a Southern sympathizer, set amidst the upheaval of a nation under siege. (978-1-933110-94-3)

Winds of Fortune by Radclyffe. Provincetown local Deo Camara agrees to rehab Dr. Nita Burgoyne's historic home, but she never said anything about mending her heart. (978-1-933110-93-6)

Focus of Desire by Kim Baldwin. Isabel Sterling is surprised when she wins a photography contest, but no more than photographer Natasha Kashnikova. Their promo tour becomes a ticket to romance. (978-1-933110-92-9)

Blind Leap by Diane and Jacob Anderson-Minshall. A Golden Gate Bridge suicide becomes suspect when a filmmaker's camera shows a different story. Yoshi Yakamota and the Blind Eye Detective Agency uncover evidence that could be worth killing for. (978-1-933110-91-2)

Wall of Silence, 2nd ed. by Gabrielle Goldsby. Life takes a dangerous turn when jaded police detective Foster Everett meets Riley Medeiros, a woman who isn't afraid to discover the truth no matter the cost. (978-1-933110-90-5)

Mistress of the Runes by Andrews & Austin. Passion ignites between two women with ties to ancient secrets, contemporary mysteries, and a shared quest for the meaning of life. (978-1-933110-89-9)

Sheridan's Fate by Gun Brooke. A dynamic, erotic romance between physical therapist Lark Mitchell and businesswoman Sheridan Ward set in the scorching hot days and humid, steamy nights of San Antonio. (978-1-933110-88-2)

Vulture's Kiss by Justine Saracen. Archeologist Valerie Foret, heir to a terrifying task, returns in a powerful desert adventure set in Egypt and Jerusalem. (978-1-933110-87-5)

Rising Storm by JLee Meyer. The sequel to First Instinct takes our heroines on a dangerous journey instead of the honeymoon they'd planned. (978-1-933110-86-8)

Not Single Enough by Grace Lennox. A funny, sexy modern romance about two lonely women who bond over the unexpected and fall in love along the way. (978-1-933110-85-1)

Such a Pretty Face by Gabrielle Goldsby. A sexy, sometimes humorous, sometimes biting contemporary romance that gently exposes the damage to heart and soul when we fail to look beneath the surface for what truly matters. (978-1-933110-84-4)

Second Season by Ali Vali. A romance set in New Orleans amidst betrayal, Hurricane Katrina, and the new beginnings hardship and heartbreak sometimes make possible. (978-1-933110-83-7)

Hearts Aflame by Ronica Black. A poignant, erotic romance between a hard-driving businesswoman and a solitary vet. Packed with adventure and set in the harsh beauty of the Arizona countryside. (978-1-933110-82-0)

Red Light by JD Glass. Tori forges her path as an EMT in the New York City 911 system while discovering what matters most to herself and the woman she loves. (978-1-933110-81-3)

Honor Under Siege by Radclyffe. Secret Service agent Cameron Roberts struggles to protect her lover while searching for a traitor who just may be another woman with a claim on her heart. (978-1-933110-80-6)

Dark Valentine by Jennifer Fulton. Danger and desire fuel a high stakes cat-and-mouse game when an attorney and an endangered witness team up to thwart a killer. (978-1-933110-79-0)

Sequestered Hearts by Erin Dutton. A popular artist suddenly goes into seclusion; a reluctant reporter wants to know why; and a heart locked away yearns to be set free. (978-1-933110-78-3)

Erotic Interludes 5: *Road Games* eds. Radclyffe and Stacia Seaman. Adventure, "sport," and sex on the road—hot stories of travel adventures and games of seduction. (978-1-933110-77-6)

The Spanish Pearl by Catherine Friend. On a trip to Spain, Kate Vincent is accidentally transported back in time...an epic saga spiced with humor, lust, and danger. (978-1-933110-76-9)

Lady Knight by L-J Baker. Loyalty and honour clash with love and ambition in a medieval world of magic when female knight Riannon meets Lady Eleanor. (978-1-933110-75-2)

Dark Dreamer by Jennifer Fulton. Best-selling horror author, Rowe Devlin falls under the spell of psychic Phoebe Temple. A Dark Vista romance. (978-1-933110-74-5)

Come and Get Me by Julie Cannon. Elliott Foster isn't used to pursuing women, but alluring attorney Lauren Collier makes her change her mind. (978-1-933110-73-8)

Blind Curves by Diane and Jacob Anderson-Minshall. Private eye Yoshi Yakamota comes to the aid of her ex-lover Velvet Erickson in the first Blind Eye mystery. (978-1-933110-72-1)

Dynasty of Rogues by Jane Fletcher. It's hate at first sight for Ranger Riki Sadiq and her new patrol corporal, Tanya Coppelli—except for their undeniable attraction. (978-1-933110-71-4)

Running With the Wind by Nell Stark. Sailing instructor Corrie Marsten has signed off on love until she meets Quinn Davies—one woman she can't ignore. (978-1-933110-70-7)

More than Paradise by Jennifer Fulton. Two women battle danger, risk all, and find in one another an unexpected ally and an unforgettable love. (978-1-933110-69-1)

Flight Risk by Kim Baldwin. For Blayne Keller, being in the wrong place at the wrong time just might turn out to be the best thing that ever happened to her. (978-1-933110-68-4)

Rebel's Quest, Supreme Constellations Book Two by Gun Brooke. On a world torn by war, two women discover a love that defies all boundaries. (978-1-933110-67-7)

Punk and Zen by JD Glass. Angst, sex, love, rock. Trace, Candace, Francesca...Samantha. Losing control—and finding the truth within. BSB Victory Editions. (1-933110-66-X)

Stellium in Scorpio by Andrews & Austin. The passionate reuniting of two powerful women on the glitzy Las Vegas Strip where everything is an illusion and love is a gamble. (1-933110-65-1)

When Dreams Tremble by Radclyffe. Two women whose lives turned out far differently than they'd once imagined discover that sometimes the shape of the future can only be found in the past. (1-933110-64-3)

The Devil Unleashed by Ali Vali. As the heat of violence rises, so does the passion. A Casey Family crime saga. (1-933110-61-9)

Burning Dreams by Susan Smith. The chronicle of the challenges faced by a young drag king and an older woman who share a love "outside the bounds." (1-933110-62-7)

Fresh Tracks by Georgia Beers. Seven women, seven days. A lot can happen when old friends, lovers, and a new girl in town get together in the mountains. (1-933110-63-5)

The Empress and the Acolyte by Jane Fletcher. Jemeryl and Tevi fight to protect the very fabric of their world: time. Lyremouth Chronicles Book Three. (1-933110-60-0)

First Instinct by JLee Meyer. When high-stakes security fraud leads to murder, one woman flees for her life while another risks her heart to protect her. (1-933110-59-7)

Erotic Interludes 4: Extreme Passions. Thirty of today's hottest erotica writers set the pages aflame with love, lust, and steamy liaisons. (1-933110-58-9)

Storms of Change by Radclyffe. In the continuing saga of the Provincetown Tales, duty and love are at odds as Reese and Tory face their greatest challenge. (1-933110-57-0)

Unexpected Ties by Gina L. Dartt. With death before dessert, Kate Shannon and Nikki Harris are swept up in another tale of danger and romance. (1-933110-56-2)

Sleep of Reason by Rose Beecham. While Detective Jude Devine searches for a lost boy, her rocky relationship with Dr. Mercy Westmoreland gets a lot harder. (1-933110-53-8)

Passion's Bright Fury by Radclyffe. Passion strikes without warning when a trauma surgeon and a filmmaker become reluctant allies. (1-933110-54-6)

Broken Wings by L-J Baker. When Rye Woods meets beautiful dryad Flora Withe, her libido, as hidden as her wings, reawakens along with her heart. (1-933110-55-4)

Combust the Sun by Andrews & Austin. A Richfield and Rivers mystery set in L.A. Murder among the stars. (1-933110-52-X)

Of Drag Kings and the Wheel of Fate by Susan Smith. A blind date in a drag club leads to an unlikely romance. (1-933110-51-1)

Tristaine Rises by Cate Culpepper. Brenna, Jesstin, and the Amazons of Tristaine face their greatest challenge for survival. (1-933110-50-3)

Too Close to Touch by Georgia Beers. Kylie O'Brien believes in true love and is willing to wait for it, even though Gretchen, her new boss, is off-limits. (1-933110-47-3)

100ᵗʰ Generation by Justine Saracen. Ancient curses, modern-day villains, and an intriguing woman lead archeologist Valerie Foret on the adventure of her life. (1-933110-48-1)

Battle for Tristaine by Cate Culpepper. While Brenna struggles to find her place in the clan, Tristaine is threatened with destruction. Second in the Tristaine series. (1-933110-49-X)

The Traitor and the Chalice by Jane Fletcher. Tevi and Jemeryl risk all in the race to uncover a traitor. The Lyremouth Chronicles Book Two. (1-933110-43-0)

Promising Hearts by Radclyffe. Dr. Vance Phelps arrives in New Hope, Montana, with no hope of happiness—until she meets Mae. (1-933110-44-9)

Carly's Sound by Ali Vali. Poppy Valente and Julia Johnson form a bond of friendship that becomes something far more. A poignant romance about love and renewal. (1-933110-45-7)

Unexpected Sparks by Gina L. Dartt. Kate Shannon's attraction to much younger Nikki Harris is complication enough without a fatal fire that Kate can't ignore. (1-933110-46-5)

Whitewater Rendezvous by Kim Baldwin. Two women on a wilderness kayak adventure discover that true love may be nothing at all like they imagined. (1-933110-38-4)

Erotic Interludes 3: Lessons in Love ed. by Radclyffe and Stacia Seaman. Sign on for a class in love...the best lesbian erotica writers take us to "school." (1-9331100-39-2)

Punk Like Me by JD Glass. Twenty-one-year-old Nina has a way with the girls, and she doesn't always play by the rules. (1-933110-40-6)

Coffee Sonata by Gun Brooke. Four women whose lives unexpectedly intersect in a small town by the sea share one thing in common—they all have secrets. (1-933110-41-4)

The Clinic: Tristaine Book One by Cate Culpepper. Brenna, a prison medic, finds herself drawn to Jesstin, a warrior reputed to be descended from ancient Amazons. (1-933110-42-2)

Forever Found by JLee Meyer. Can time, tragedy, and shattered trust destroy a love that seemed destined? Chance reunites childhood friends separated by tragedy. (1-933110-37-6)

Sword of the Guardian by Merry Shannon. Princess Shasta's bold new bodyguard has a secret that could change both of their lives: *He* is actually a *she*. (1-933110-36-8)

Wild Abandon by Ronica Black. Dr. Chandler Brogan and Officer Sarah Monroe are drawn together by their common obsessions—sex, speed, and danger. (1-933110-35-X)

Turn Back Time by Radclyffe. Pearce Rifkin and Wynter Thompson have nothing in common but a shared passion for surgery—and unexpected attraction. (1-933110-34-1)

Chance by Grace Lennox. A sexy, funny, touching story of two women who, in finding themselves, also find one another. (1-933110-31-7)

The Exile and the Sorcerer by Jane Fletcher. First in the Lyremouth Chronicles. Tevi and a shy young sorcerer face monsters, magic, and the challenge of loving. (1-933110-32-5)

A Matter of Trust by Radclyffe. When what should be just business turns into much more, two women struggle to trust the unexpected. (1-933110-33-3)

Sweet Creek by Lee Lynch. A celebration of the enduring nature of love, friendship, and community in the heart-warming lesbian community of Waterfall Falls. (1-933110-29-5)

The Devil Inside by Ali Vali. The head of a New Orleans crime organization falls for a woman who turns her world upside down. (1-933110-30-9)

Grave Silence by Rose Beecham. Detective Jude Devine's investigation of ritual murders is complicated by her torrid affair with pathologist Dr. Mercy Westmoreland. (1-933110-25-2)

Honor Reclaimed by Radclyffe. Secret Service Agent Cameron Roberts and Blair Powell close ranks to find the would-be assassins who nearly claimed Blair's life. (1-933110-18-X)

Honor Bound by Radclyffe. Secret Service Agent Cameron Roberts and Blair Powell face political intrigue, a clandestine threat to Blair's safety, and the seemingly irreconcilable differences that force them ever farther apart. (1-933110-20-1)

Innocent Hearts by Radclyffe. In a wild and unforgiving land, two women learn about love, passion, and the wonders of the heart. (1-933110-21-X)

The Temple at Landfall by Jane Fletcher. An imprinter, one of Celaeno's most revered servants of the Goddess, is also a prisoner to the faith—until a Ranger frees her by claiming her heart. The Celaeno series. (1-933110-27-9)

Protector of the Realm, Supreme Constellations Book One by Gun Brooke. A space adventure filled with suspense and a daring intergalactic romance. (1-933110-26-0)

Force of Nature by Kim Baldwin. From tornados to forest fires, the forces of nature conspire to bring Gable McCoy and Erin Richards close to danger, and closer to each other. (1-933110-23-6)

In Too Deep by Ronica Black. Undercover homicide cop Erin McKenzie tracks a femme fatale who just might be a real killer…with love and danger hot on her heels. (1-933110-17-1)

Stolen Moments: Erotic Interludes 2 by Stacia Seaman and Radclyffe, eds. Love on the run, in the office, in the shadows…Fast, furious, and almost too hot to handle. (1-933110-16-3)

Course of Action by Gun Brooke. Actress Carolyn Black desperately wants the starring role in an upcoming film produced by Annelie Peterson. Just how far will she go for the dream part of a lifetime? (1-933110-22-8)

Rangers at Roadsend by Jane Fletcher. Sergeant Chip Coppelli has learned to spot trouble coming, and that is exactly what she sees in her new recruit, Katryn Nagata. The Celaeno series. (1-933110-28-7)

Justice Served by Radclyffe. Lieutenant Rebecca Frye and her lover, Dr. Catherine Rawlings, embark on a deadly game of hide-and-seek with an underworld kingpin who traffics in human souls. (1-933110-15-5)

Distant Shores, Silent Thunder by Radclyffe. Dr. Tory King—along with the women who love her—is forced to examine the boundaries of love, friendship, and the ties that transcend time. (1-933110-08-2)

Hunter's Pursuit by Kim Baldwin. A raging blizzard, a mountain hideaway, and a killer-for-hire set a scene for disaster—or desire—when Katarzyna Demetrious rescues a beautiful stranger. (1-933110-09-0)

The Walls of Westernfort by Jane Fletcher. All Temple Guard Natasha Ionadis wants is to serve the Goddess—until she falls in love with one of the rebels she is sworn to destroy. The Celaeno series. (1-933110-24-4)

Change Of Pace: *Erotic Interludes* by Radclyffe. Twenty-five hot-wired encounters guaranteed to spark more than just your imagination. Erotica as you've always dreamed of it. (1-933110-07-4)

Honor Guards by Radclyffe. In a wild flight for their lives, the president's daughter and those who are sworn to protect her wage a desperate struggle for survival. (1-933110-01-5)

Fated Love by Radclyffe. Amidst the chaos and drama of a busy emergency room, two women must contend not only with the fragile nature of life, but also with the irresistible forces of fate. (1-933110-05-8)

Justice in the Shadows by Radclyffe. In a shadow world of secrets and lies, Detective Sergeant Rebecca Frye and her lover, Dr. Catherine Rawlings, join forces in the elusive search for justice. (1-933110-03-1)

shadowland by Radclyffe. In a world on the far edge of desire, two women are drawn together by power, passion, and dark pleasures. An erotic romance. (1-933110-11-2)

Love's Masquerade by Radclyffe. Plunged into the indistinguishable realms of fiction, fantasy, and hidden desires, Auden Frost is forced to question all she believes about the nature of love. (1-933110-14-7)

Love & Honor by Radclyffe. The president's daughter and her lover are faced with difficult choices as they battle a tangled web of Washington intrigue for...love and honor. (1-933110-10-4)

Beyond the Breakwater by Radclyffe. One Provincetown summer, three women learn the true meaning of love, friendship, and family. (1-933110-06-6)

Tomorrow's Promise by Radclyffe. One timeless summer, two very different women discover the power of passion to heal and the promise of hope that only love can bestow. (1-933110-12-0)

Love's Tender Warriors by Radclyffe. Two women who have accepted loneliness as a way of life learn that love is worth fighting for and a battle they cannot afford to lose. (1-933110-02-3)

Love's Melody Lost by Radclyffe. A secretive artist with a haunted past and a young woman escaping a life that has proved to be a lie find their destinies entwined. (1-933110-00-7)

Safe Harbor by Radclyffe. A mysterious newcomer, a reclusive doctor, and a troubled gay teenager learn about love, friendship, and trust during one tumultuous summer in Provincetown. (1-933110-13-9)

Above All, Honor by Radclyffe. Secret Service Agent Cameron Roberts fights her desire for the one woman she can't have—Blair Powell, the daughter of the president of the United States. (1-933110-04-X)